Wolf headed toward the corner where the man still conversed with the two women.

The taller woman turned around.

Wolf froze.

Auburn hair peeked out of her stylish bonnet. Dark coffee-colored eyes flashed with shocked recognition. Ruby lips parted in surprise.

It was the woman from Paris, the woman who'd stolen more than his money.

Wolf's face grew hot and his heart pounded. The last woman he ever thought to see again was here in Brighton, large as life, real as flesh and blood.

She quickly composed her features. He started toward her, but coolly she raised a finger, indicating he should wait. To Wolf's surprise, he complied, but he vowed he would not wait long. There was much to say to her. And much to demand.

D0455935

Author Note

One enjoyable part of writing *The Lady Behind the Masquerade* was revisiting Brighton—in my mind, that is. I have visited Brighton twice, and as I pictured my characters walking around Regency-era Brighton, I remember doing the same. I can picture what the rows of shops looked like and the seawall with stairs leading down to a pebbled beach. Before I'd visited Brighton, I did not know beaches could be made of pebbles, not sand.

The fanciful landmark building the Royal Pavilion was not completed at the time of my story. I wish it had been, because the rooms inside would have been fun to write about. My characters attend some entertainment at the Castle Inn, but that set of buildings is gone now, long replaced by a row of four-story houses.

There are parts of Brighton that my Regency characters know that still exist today in some form. The Old Ship Hotel is one. The Steine in the center of town. The Black Lion and the Druids Head.

If this story makes anyone yearn to visit or return to Brighton, I will be very pleased.

Because I would love to go back and walk in my characters' footsteps.

DIANE GASTON

The Lady Behind the Masquerade

Recycling programs
for this product may
not exist in your area.

ISBN-13: 978-1-335-59558-4

The Lady Behind the Masquerade

Copyright © 2023 by Diane Perkins

For questions and comments about the quality of this book,
please contact us at CustomerService@Harlequin.com.

Harlequin Enterprises ULC
22 Adelaide St. West, 41st Floor
Toronto, Ontario M5H 4E3, Canada
www.Harlequin.com

Printed in U.S.A.

Diane Gaston's dream job was always to write romance novels. One day she dared to pursue that dream and has never looked back. Her books have won romance's highest honors: the RITA® Award, the National Readers' Choice Award, the HOLT Medallion, and the Gold Quill and Golden Heart® Awards. She lives in Virginia with her husband and three very ordinary house cats. Diane loves to hear from readers and friends. Visit her website at dianegaston.com.

Books by Diane Gaston

Harlequin Historical

The Lord's Highland Temptation

A Family of Scandals

Secretly Bound to the Marquess
The Lady Behind the Masquerade

Captains of Waterloo

Her Gallant Captain at Waterloo
Lord Grantwell's Christmas Wish

The Governess Swap

A Lady Becomes a Governess
Shipwrecked with the Captain

The Society of Wicked Gentlemen

A Pregnant Courtesan for the Rake

The Scandalous Summerfields

Bound by Duty
Bound by One Scandalous Night
Bound by a Scandalous Secret
Bound by Their Secret Passion

Visit the Author Profile page
at Harlequin.com for more titles.

To my wonderful friend Julie Halperson,
who has been with me on this writing journey
from the very beginning and is still
hanging in there with me.

Chapter One

Paris—November 1818

The woman tapped the mother-of-pearl counter pieces against the green baize of the gaming table, waiting for the dealer to flip a card on to the three in front of her.

Marcus Wolfdon—Wolf to his friends—leaned against the wall watching her, admiring the concentration in her incredibly dark eyes. She was counting cards, he would wager on it, even though he rarely wagered on anything. She was calculating the probability of her hand coming in under twenty-one. Not cheating, precisely, but giving her a bit of an edge in vingt-et-un.

Wolf frowned. He did not believe any gambling establishment would long tolerate players having an edge, especially this Paris casino, filled with Englishmen like himself, enjoying Paris after Napoleon and enduring the resentment of the Frenchmen running the place.

Wolf knew all about the undercurrent of resentment throughout the city. He was an aide to Sir Charles Stuart, Britain's Ambassador to France, and was aware of every violent incident of French against English. Wolf very much preferred observing this woman, and he was quite at liberty to do so.

His friend Harris had insisted Wolf come with him to this place, then Harris sat down to a high-stakes game of whist and promptly forgot him. Unless Wolf wanted to wager his own funds—which he did not—Wolf had nothing else to amuse him but the mysterious woman playing vingt-et-un.

She was quite intriguing. Her fair skin reminded him of a Sèvres porcelain vase he'd seen in a shop earlier that day. There was a hint of vulnerability to the set of her lush pink lips, but intelligence shone in the depths of those chocolate-brown eyes, an intelligence that bespoke knowledge beyond her years. She looked younger than his twenty-five years, but it was obvious she was no green girl.

Most intriguing was the essence of mystery about her. It attracted him like iron shavings to a magnet.

Wolf fully engrossed himself in speculation about her. She appeared to have come to the casino alone, as had other gaily dressed females. The others, however, attended less to the games of chance than to the Englishmen, batting darkened eyelashes at them in frank invitation.

'*Je n'ai pas d'argent.* I have no money,' he told the few who'd sidled up to him. By no means did he intend to let them know the contents of his purse. It needed to last him until his next pay. Soon enough he was ignored by the *filles de la nuit*.

The vingt-et-un woman took no notice of the men in the room. She rarely moved her eyes from the play of the cards. Wolf, therefore, was at leisure to appreciate the décolletage exposed by a gown scandalous by London standards. Her rich auburn hair was half atop her head, half loose, flowing down to caress creamy shoulders. She was as daringly attired as the women who coveted his purse, but as single-minded in her play as the most dedicated gamester.

Her face betrayed little emotion as she waited for the dealer's hit. He snapped the next card from the deck, placing it in front of her. Wolf watched her eyes lose a bit of their strain. She nodded almost imperceptibly. The dealer glanced from the cards to her face to the cards again. She had sixteen points showing. Slowly the dealer turned up his hidden card. A queen of hearts, giving him twenty-one.

The woman glanced up at the dealer, shocked. Wolf straightened. She snapped her card over, revealing a hand of twenty points. The other players looked disappointed but undisturbed.

The deal began again, two cards to each player. The woman tossed in her two counter pieces. Her hand showed a king. The dealer went round again, but she held with her two cards. The woman's gaze did not leave the dealer's face as he dealt himself twenty points. She revealed her hidden card. A nine. Nineteen points losing to the dealer's twenty.

She stood, her colour high as she glared at the dealer. Wolf thought for certain she would speak, but she abruptly turned away and left the room. He started after her, momentarily impeded by two of the *filles de la nuit* who stumbled against him. He hurried past them, finding her in the supper room seated at a table alone. A servant brought a bottle of wine to the table and only one glass.

Wolf crossed the room.

'Pardon, madame,' he said.

She looked up, her face still flushed.

He spoke in French. 'I could not help but notice. The dealer cheated, did he not?'

'Yes.' She gave a Gallic shrug of her shoulder. She looked at him a long time, as if making a decision. She gestured for him to sit. *'Monsieur...?'*

'Wolfdon,' he responded, giving her a smile other women deemed charming. He refrained from offering more detail, such as being aide to the British Ambassador, or son and heir of an English baronetcy. One could never tell who among these French still despised nobility, even as lowly a rank as baronet. 'May I have the honour of knowing your name?'

She hesitated, averting her gaze. 'Fleur,' she finally said, the idea coming, no doubt, from the *fleur de lis* pattern on the papered walls around them.

He conveyed through his voice and by his glance at the wallpaper that he knew the name was false. 'Madame Fleur.'

She lifted her wine glass to her lips.

She had allowed the *'madame'* to go uncorrected, but, since she was inclined to disguise her identity, he could not depend upon this meaning she was married or widowed.

He signalled to the servant to bring another glass. 'You did not confront the dealer, *madame.'*

She gave a soft laugh. 'Naturally, sir. I should be foolish indeed to accuse him of playing a queen that should have been at the bottom of the deck. It would be my word against his. With no one to champion me, I would likely find a dagger in my back for alerting you Englishmen to the true nature of this place.' She fell silent as the servant returned.

Wolf took the glass and waved the man away, pouring for himself. 'What a waste that would be of such a lovely lady. I would be pleased to assist you if you wish it.'

'Be my champion?' She laughed again. 'Then the dagger would be in your back. No, I will not return to this place. That is also my advice to you and to your friend.'

'My friend?' He sipped his wine.

'The fair-haired gentleman who now plays at whist.' She'd seen that he and Harris had come together.

Wolf raised his eyebrows. 'I noticed you, of course, *madame*. What man could not? I am surprised and flattered you took note of me.'

'One must notice everything.' A distracted look crossed her face. She seemed to force it away. 'You do not gamble, *monsieur*?'

He smiled. 'I dislike losing.' His eyes caught hers, and he felt the jolt of a connection between them.

She held his gaze. 'Why are you here, then? Do you seek a woman for amusement, perhaps?'

Wolf cocked his head, unsure if this was a question or an invitation. 'Are you offering, Madame Fleur?'

She glanced away. 'I assure you, I am a gambler, nothing more.' Her gaze slid back again as she took another sip of her wine. 'I was merely curious, that is all. Men come to the casino to gamble or to find a woman.'

He found himself fascinated by her eyes, as deep a brown as mahogany and at once both expressive and guarded. He almost forgot to speak. 'I am again flattered that you are curious about me. The answer is simple, I fear. I am here for want of other entertainment. One does not wish to spend one's time in Paris idling in one's rooms.'

She tapped on the glass with her fingernail. 'Is that what you have been doing, idling in your rooms?'

'In your beautiful city? Indeed not. I have explored as much of Paris as I have been able.' He reached for his glass of wine and grazed her hand.

She glanced away, and the corners of her mouth turned down into a frown.

He touched her hand again. 'You are unhappy, Fleur?' His voice was soft.

Her fingers flexed, and she slid her hand away. 'I am merely angry at being duped. That is all.' She tapped on her glass again, then gave him a deliberate sort of smile. 'Tell me what places you have seen in the city.'

He told her of visiting the magnificent Notre Dame and the Musée Napoléon, where plundered treasures were displayed. He told of searching the shops for gifts to send home to his family.

'What did you find?' she asked, sounding not so much interested as wishing him to keep talking.

He obliged her. 'A porcelain figurine for my mother. Some lace for my sisters. A penknife for my father.'

'You have sisters?' she asked.

'Three of them,' he replied.

'Ah, three.' She sighed wistfully. 'How lucky you are. Tell me of them.'

Because he would do anything to remain in her company, he'd speak of his sisters, two of whom were barely grown when he'd left in 1811, Harris's father having secured employment with Sir Charles for them both. Sir Charles was Ambassador to Portugal in those days, exciting days during the Peninsular War.

'One is older, the other two younger,' he told her. 'They are all married now.' Aristocrats all, but he'd not mention that in case she was anti-royalist. 'They all have children, but please do not ask me how many or their ages. I cannot keep them all straight.'

'And are they all in England, all your family?' The mysterious Madame Fleur's fingernail continued to tap a tattoo against her glass.

It seemed an odd question. 'Yes. All of them.'

'You are the only tourist, then?' she asked, a hint of scorn in her voice.

'I am not a tourist, *madame*,' he replied. 'I am employed here.'

Her brows rose, but, just as quickly, she took another sip of wine and seemed to lose interest.

'And you, *madame*?' he pressed. 'What is your situation? Do you have family here in Paris?'

She waved her hand dismissively. 'None to be remarked upon.' She stood. 'If you will excuse me, I believe it is time for me to leave.'

One simple question chased her away? Wolf had no wish to let her escape. The company of a beautiful and mysterious woman was a great deal more amusing than watching Harris lose at whist. 'Allow me to escort you to your home, *madame*.'

She responded with another frank stare, and he feared refusal was on her lips.

He quickly added, 'To make certain no dagger ends up in your back.'

She gave a faint smile. 'Very well.'

He stopped by the game room to tell Harris he was leaving. His friend waved him on, barely looking up from his cards. Should he warn Harris about the casino's dishonesty? No. Doing so might endanger Madame Fleur. Besides, Harris never wagered more than he carried in his pockets.

At the door, he helped Madame Fleur into her cloak, fastening it under her chin, enjoying the moment of delicious closeness. She beguiled him. So beautiful and so full of mystery.

They stepped out into the crisp cool night. A rain shower had placed a sheen on the pavement and cleansed the air, leaving only the chill of approaching winter. The streets were nearly deserted. The noise of their footsteps on the stone pavement was the only sound in the quiet night. She held his arm and did not say much as they walked, but he found himself hoping she would issue him an invitation.

She directed him into a narrow alley, to a wooden door. 'We are here,' she said.

The alley was so dark, he sensed rather than saw her looking up at him. She turned to the door, but he caught her arm, not wanting to let her go.

He held her so close he could feel her breath on his face. She finally said, 'Would you like to come in?'

His own breath accelerated as desire surged within him. 'It would be my great pleasure.' He vowed he'd show her great pleasure as well.

The door opened to reveal a narrow wooden stairway. They groped their way up two flights in the darkness and through a narrow hallway, hearing the skittering of mice making way for them. She stopped, and her key scraped against the door, seeking out the lock. Finally, the lock turned, and she opened the door into more darkness. They stepped inside, and he heard her fumbling. Then a spark from a tinder box lit the room for an instant. She was crouched beside a tiny fireplace. After several more sparks, tinder flamed, and from it she lit a taper, then an oil lamp.

It took a moment for Wolf's eyes to adjust before he could see they were in a very small, very spartan room. It held no more than a wooden table and chair, a small trunk and a bed. There were two shelves, mere wooden boards, on one wall. He had not expected a woman dressed as finely as she to have quite such humble lodgings. Why was it? Had she experienced financial reverses? Was she in need of help?

She hung her cloak on a peg by the door. 'May I take your coat, *monsieur*?'

He removed his hat and shrugged out of his greatcoat, which she hung over her cloak. When she turned to face him again, it seemed as if the air crackled between them. He took a step forward and reached out to caress the flawless skin of her cheek, still chilled from the night air.

Chapter Two

Juliana Parsons closed her eyes at the gentleness of the Englishman's fingers, surprised at how much she savoured his touch. She'd been alone for so long.

It had been like providence for him to approach her in the casino. She'd just lost her last franc, which meant a return to theft, a prospect that did not plague her conscience overmuch, but did mean greater risk of discovery. Discovery meant prison and death on the guillotine.

Like her father.

She squeezed her eyes shut. She would not think of that, nor of how his friends had abandoned him, left him behind to be arrested.

Her father's friends had abandoned her, too. She'd been alone in Paris for so long, surrounded by danger, living by her wits alone.

What else could she expect? No man could be trusted. Men, her father included, thought first of themselves, before sparing a thought about another. Men, she'd also learned, were most loving when they wanted to slake their carnal desires—at least that was a moment a woman could exploit.

This Monsieur Wolfdon was clearly interested in slaking carnal desires. She could think of no other reason he would approach her. It was fortunate, though, because she needed him. Needed his money, that is.

She preferred to play cards for money, but more than once these last few months she'd been forced to resort to a scheme her father had taught her. Use a man's desire to bed her as a lure, but pinch his purse instead, then run like the devil to get away. It worked well most of the time, if the man was not quick enough to catch her. Getting caught meant the guillotine.

She was a little afraid she could not escape this tall, strong Englishman, however. Or perhaps she merely enjoyed his banter a bit too much. He was handsome, but so many men were handsome. He was also charming and not at all encroaching. She had the notion she could send him away with one word. Oddly enough that made her loath to escape him. With each step they'd taken in the crisp night air, she'd told herself to make her move, get her fingers inside his pocket for his purse. Instead, she'd led him straight to her room. That had been foolish of her.

In the dim light of her oil lamp, she stared up at his kind, smiling face. His smile caused dimples to crease both cheeks and to make his eyes sparkle. His eyes looked smoky now, but she knew they were the same colour green as the scrubby grass that grew near the shore on the isle of Jersey. His hair, now dark as her own in the dim lamplight, had, under the brighter lighting of the casino, been the brown of Jersey's rocky coast.

Mr Wolfdon might think Paris was her city, but, to Juliana, Jersey was home. After Napoleon's exile to Elba, Juliana's father convinced her they should travel to France. A pilgrimage to honour the memory of her dear French mother, he'd said.

Later Juliana discovered the real reason her father and his partners left Jersey. There were warrants for their arrests. She could never go back.

Tears stung her eyes.

'You look near weeping.' Wolfdon broke into her thoughts. 'Tell me what distresses you. Let me help you.'

She rapidly blinked. 'It…it is nothing. My eyes water from the cold air outside. That is all.'

He gave her a sceptical look, every bit as appealing as his smile, and let his fingers slide from her face to her arm. Then he did something even more surprising. He enfolded her in a warm hug, pressing her head against his heart, like a proper father might hold a child.

'If I am not to know what troubles you, let me at least comfort you.' He gently swayed with her.

Juliana gave in to weakness and burrowed into the warmth of his chest, savouring the regular beat of his heart. She squeezed her eyes shut. She would not weep. She would not. She'd wept at her mother's death so many years ago and at her father's. She would not weep again.

He held her with great patience, and gradually she regained her composure.

She pulled away. 'I have a bottle of wine.' Her last. 'Would you like a glass?' She wanted to share it with him in gratitude for his comfort, even though his comfort was likely as illusory as his kindness.

'If you desire some,' he responded good-naturedly.

She walked over to her water pitcher and rinsed out her one glass and her teacup. She poured the wine and gave him the glass. He stared at it, as if to ask her a question, perhaps to ask her why someone as poor as she risked her money in a casino. Instead, he kept silent and gazed around the room.

She suspected her shabby room was a sharp contrast to other rooms he may have seen, rooms where women sold themselves. She was not such a woman. She was a thief, but she was not a whore. Did he think her a whore? Did he think that was why had she invited him to her room?

Why had she invited him? Merely because he'd been kind to her and pleasant?

His arms had felt so pleasant and his kindness, as fleeting as a man's kindness might be, was very seductive. It had been a long time since she'd allowed a man to make love to her. Perhaps there would be no harm in accepting what he clearly was willing to give.

Besides, she'd suddenly felt so incredibly lonely. She craved the illusion, at least, that she was not alone.

'There is only the bed to sit on.' She kicked off her shoes and climbed on to the small bed, hitching up her skirt to sit cross-legged. 'Unless you prefer the chair.'

'The bed will do.' He sat next to her and touched his glass to her teacup. 'To better times, Fleur.'

She felt as if he peeked into her soul. 'To better times.'

This wine, added to the wine she'd consumed at the casino, made her head spin. Or perhaps it was the scent of him, wool and musk and man, that gave her this dreamy dizziness. He made no move towards her, made no demands at all. It was as if he left it up to her to decide to bed him or not. She shifted back to rest against the wall, nearly sitting behind him.

His broad shoulders were very evident from this view. Every hair seemed in its proper place, and she suddenly had an urge to muss it, to test it to see if it would stick up on end like any mortal man's or if it would magically fall back into place. She also fancied running her hand across the expanse of his back, though it would be so much nicer to do so if he shed his clothing.

Wolfdon would be a gentle and generous lover, she guessed, and suddenly she was eager to discover if this theory was true. Surely it would not hurt to experience the pleasure of loving him.

She placed her empty teacup on the floor and shuffled forward, pulling the pins from her hair and combing it out with her fingers. She leaned against his back and whispered into his ear, 'Let me unbutton your coat, *monsieur.*'

He turned to her. 'Are you certain you desire this?'

She paused, again surprised he should ask such a question. She placed her lips on the nape of his neck. 'Yes, *monsieur.* I desire you.'

He pulled off his boots and swivelled around to her, taking her face in his hands and bringing her lips to his. His lips lingered lightly, as if she would break unless he took great care with her.

As if he cherished her.

Juliana unbuttoned his fine wool coat, her fingers automatically checking the bulge of his purse as she pulled the coat off his shoulders. She could almost regret the need to steal from him. Almost, except that she had no money, and Englishmen were always rich.

His light kisses rained upon her face. She removed his shirt next and nearly gasped at the sight of his magnificent bare chest. His muscles were so firm she could see their outline beneath his skin.

He averted his gaze from her. 'How you look at me, Fleur.'

He had recognised her frank appreciation. She must

take care not to reveal too much to this man who seemed to guess her emotions even before she felt them. She turned her back to him and lifted her hair. 'Undo my laces.'

His fingers were efficient. No doubt he'd unlaced the gowns of many a lady. That thought made her jealous. She wanted to pretend he was hers alone for this one night. Lancelot to her Guinevere. Romeo to her Juliet. Tristan to her Isolde.

Of course, those lovers all endured tragic ends, but they had been foolish to hope for happy endings.

She climbed off the bed and slipped out of her one pretty dress, carefully laying it across the wooden chair.

He gestured to her. 'Come, I'll undo your corset.'

He untied her laces and another layer of clothing fell away. As she turned back around, she saw desire in his eyes. Her breath caught, and her own desire flared in response.

He did not rush her. It was for her to set the pace of this lovemaking, even though the evidence of his arousal was pressing against his trousers. Her other lovers had rushed to the climax, in a hurry for their own pleasure. Not that she'd had that many lovers—only one really, because the other two had not spent more than a night or two with her.

She knelt to undo the buttons fastening his trousers. As she worked, he sat very still, hands clenching the bed linens, a soft groan emerging from his lips. Freed, she could not help but touch him, to feel him pulse under her fingertips.

'Fleur—' he moaned, putting his hands on her hips and kneading her flesh.

She felt powerful, in control, able to give pleasure

or withhold it at her whim and hers alone. It was a delicious illusion. The muscles rippling his torso and thickening his arms proved he could take whatever he wanted from her.

But he didn't.

Juliana pushed down his trousers and drawers and he kicked them off. She stepped back to survey him, seated on the bed, as perfect as a Greek statue.

He surveyed her in return. Feeling another surge of feminine power, she slowly pulled up her shift and tossed it aside, standing before him without the armour of clothing. Still, she felt strong as his eyes caressed her as potently as a finger's touch.

Silently he extended his hand, taking her cold fingers into his warm grasp. She climbed up beside him on the bed. They both knelt as he kissed her again, his hands scraping her arms in a delicious soothing rhythm that made her curse his restraint.

She slid closer to him, wrapping her arms around his neck and burying her fingers in his soft hair. She pressed against him, rubbing herself against that male part of him, teasing him into abandoning gentleness. He growled like a hungry beast and clasped the soft flesh of her buttocks, grinding her even harder against him.

Her body was fully in flames now, threatening to combust if he did not indulge her yearning. She wanted to feel him inside her, to move with her as one, to make her feel for a few delicious moments that she belonged somewhere to someone.

She lay back on the mattress, and he was above her, holding himself up by his arms for a moment before bending down to possess her lips, to nibble the sensitive skin of her neck, to taste her nipple with his tongue.

She cried out, writhing beneath him, as he continued to trail kisses down the length of her body, as his hand sought her most private place. Even there he touched her gently, reverently, giving to her as no man had ever done before.

Perhaps this was what was meant by *faire l'amour*, 'making love'. She hugged the feeling to herself, not wanting to lose it.

When he rose above her again, she held him off for a moment, splaying her hands on his chest, unsure if she could bear the complete pleasure.

'*Monsieur,*' she rasped.

He flashed a quick grin before entering her, and, as they moved as one, all thoughts, all worries, all heartaches fled, leaving only the joy of the glorious union. She abandoned herself to the experience, letting him take her where he willed, like an ash dancing on the flames. Her need grew, her urgency accelerated. When the explosion of pleasure came it rocked her and rocked her more.

But he started to withdraw. Without reaching his own pleasure? She wanted him to feel what she'd just felt.

'No!' She held him in place. 'No need. I know how to care for myself.' An old Frenchwoman had taught her long ago.

He groaned as he pushed inside her again and began the rhythmic dance again. To her surprise her pleasure grew once more and her cry melded with his as his final thrust sent his seed spilling into her.

The connection felt complete for that long glorious moment before he collapsed on top of her and eased himself off. She snuggled against him, bereft at feeling separate again. He kissed the top of her head and she vowed they should connect again this night. She wanted this illusion of love to continue for as long as she could sustain it.

Tucked in the shelter of his arm, his chest her pillow, she savoured the soothing cadence of his breathing until a hard reality made her heart constrict.

Before the sun rose, she would be taking his purse.

This was how she would repay her kind, glorious Englishman for loving her.

Wolf, half asleep, dimly heard her moving about the room. His senses still smouldered with the memory of her lovemaking, and he savoured the prospect of making love with her once more.

Typically, morning dampened Wolf's fascination with a woman. Often, he'd contrive to quickly take his leave, but this day, as he drifted between sleep and waking, he imagined how she'd appear in daylight, how the flush of pleasure would tinge her complexion when he made love with her again.

Perhaps she would tell him her troubles then—what had happened to her to cause her to live in such a spartan room. Perhaps she would tell him her name, at least. Perhaps he could help her, and perhaps all his nights in Paris could be spent in her bed.

He smiled, drifting near to sleep again, imagining her lips on his skin, feeling the warmth of her when he joined with her. He grew hard again, the memory transformed into dream and back into anticipation.

From his deep reverie he heard the click of the door latch closing. His eyes flew open.

She was gone.

He sat up. The furniture was bare of all evidence of her. Gone was the glass he'd drunk from. Gone was her teacup, the tinder box from the fireplace, the dress she'd worn and the clothing underneath. His clothing remained, folded neatly on the table, his coat neatly hung on the back of the solitary chair. Next to his clothing stood the empty wine bottle, sole evidence that the night they'd shared had not been a dream.

With a yell, Wolf bounded out of the bed, grabbing his greatcoat, which now hung alone on the peg by the door. He pulled on the garment in the hallway and ran down the stairs to the alley, catching a glimpse of her fleeing on to the street, a portmanteau in her hand.

He shouted for her to stop, sprinting after her, but by the time he reached the street, she had vanished. Disappeared as if she'd never existed at all.

Growling in frustration, he pounded the brick of the building at the alley's corner. People on the street stared at him. He was a sight, for certain. Bare legs and feet, hatless, obviously naked under his greatcoat.

He spun around and prowled back to her room, now empty of everything that had been hers. His gaze came to rest on his coat and realisation dawned. He searched his pockets.

His purse was gone.

She'd stolen his purse, all the money he possessed until his next pay. Curse her! Curse him, for being such a dupe, such a total fool for falling for her act.

And here he was ready to help her. Ready to spend more nights in her bed.

He collapsed on the bed, and put his head in his hands. Curse her.

Chapter Three

Brighton, England—July 1819

Wolf, accompanied by his father, walked a painstakingly leisurely pace along the Marine Parade. The hour was early and the sea air brisk. Wolf longed to stretch his limbs after the long carriage ride of the day before, but that would have to wait.

'Let us pause a while.' His father seemed out of breath. 'Enjoy the sea air.'

Wolf hadn't noticed his father's fatigue, one thing more to add to his guilt. 'Very well, sir.'

They leaned against the iron railing and gazed across the Channel towards France, where Wolf longed to be, back to his duties to Sir Charles, back into the tumult of Paris, still not entirely at peace after Napoleon's ignominious defeat, although all Allied military control had ended.

It had been three months since the missive from his sister reached Wolf in Paris.

Come quickly. You are needed at home. Father is dying.

Wolf had not set foot in England in almost a decade—and he'd preferred it that way—but he'd left Paris immediately.

His father had indeed been dying of an inflammation of the lungs, but he slowly and miraculously edged away from that precipice. His physician recommended a sea cure and, of course, no other seaside town would do except Brighton, the Prince Regent's favourite. And nothing would do but to have Wolf come along. What else could Wolf do, but agree? Impose this additional responsibility on his sister? She'd carried the brunt of it all these years.

Wolf slid a worried glance towards his father. 'Are you feeling ill, sir?'

His father laughed. 'No. No. Not at all. Don't have the stamina, is all. A little rest will do me very well.' He took in a few deep breaths. 'Nothing like sea air, I always say.'

Wolf wasn't fooled. The morning walk had all but spent his father.

He waited until his father breathed normally again before pulling away from the railing. 'We should return to the hotel.'

Wolf and his parents had rooms at the Old Ship Hotel not too far from where they stood at the end of the Marine Parade and the edge of the Steine, the expanse of lawn in front of the Regent's Pavilion. Fishermen once dried their nets on that lawn, it was said. Now it was a fashionable place for a stroll.

Wolf offered his arm and, to his surprise, his father accepted it. The man must feel weaker than Wolf suspected.

As they strolled by other promenaders, his father straightened. 'I'll wager there are many members of the *ton* we might know. Surely others will be here. Perhaps even the Prince Regent.'

Wolf's parents were more than social, Wolf recalled with ill humour. Although it was unlikely a lowly baronet would receive an invitation from the Prince Regent.

Wolf frowned. 'I can check the Master of Ceremonies' book later, if you like.' See who he might hope his parents would avoid.

From the time Wolf was a small boy he could remember the loud dust-ups between his mother and father, always over *Lady This* or *Lord That*. Although his sister Elizabeth tried to shield him and their two very young sisters from the arguments, Wolf eventually figured out what infidelity meant. Later he'd attended school with the sons of *Lady This* or *Lord That* and wondered if they knew.

Before Wolf and his parents left for Brighton, Elizabeth had warned him about their parents' continued peccadillos. And their penchant for gambling. And the need for keeping them under strict control. It was then that Wolf learned that Elizabeth and her new husband, the Marquess of Hale, were basically keeping the estate afloat and saving their parents from ruin. He eventually wormed the whole sordid story out of her. Her first marriage had pulled the whole family from the doors of the poorhouse, had saved the estate, provided their sisters' dowries and even funded his university.

Wolf had had no idea. The least he could do was delay his return to Paris and take over the task of keeping his parents in line while in Brighton.

He and his father made their way to the Old Ship Hotel, stopping twice to speak to gentlemen his father knew and once to greet a lady.

After the lady passed, his father murmured, 'Lady Holback here in Brighton. How delightful.'

Not delight. Trouble, Wolf suspected.

He tossed a longing glance towards the Channel and Paris.

Later that morning while his father rested, Wolf escorted his mother to the Circulating Library, the place where visitors to Brighton gathered to talk, to examine the latest caricatures, try new sheets of music and occasionally borrow or buy books. The Circulating Library was also the place to leave one's name for the Master of Ceremonies, the man who would arrange for invitations to the Assemblies and other Brighton entertainments. His mother wished to waste no time adding their names and checking to see who else had signed.

His mother kept up a constant chatter about the sights of Brighton and the people they passed by.

'I believe that is someone I know,' his mother said of two ladies they followed at some distance. 'Her name escapes me… The other I do not recognise at all.'

She referred to the taller of the two, a woman with a particularly graceful walk. Would it not be grand if Brighton offered Wolf some pleasant diversion, while he played watchdog to his parents? Did he want such a diversion? Paris had no shortage of beautiful, willing women, but Wolf had lately avoided all romantic entanglements.

Ever since that auburn-haired French woman had wooed him with mysterious eyes then snatched his purse.

The two women entered the Circulating Library. At least, Wolf would get a better look at the tall, graceful one who'd stirred his dormant interest. When he and his mother entered the building, it was not crowded—possibly a bit too early for most of Brighton's visitors to be out and about. Wolf spied the two ladies standing in a far corner, backs still to him, but they were talking to a gentleman Wolf knew very well. Lord Ashcourt. His friend Harris's father.

The Earl and Countess of Ashcourt were the very antithesis of his own family. Loving. Attentive. Sensible—well, at least Lord Ashcourt was sensible—most of the time. Seeing him here was like finding a port in a storm. Perhaps this stay in Brighton might be pleasant after all.

Wolf took a step towards that part of the room, but his mother pulled him in another direction.

'The book, Wolf dear,' she said. 'We must sign the book.'

It was on the counter where attendants waited to assist the patrons. His mother recorded her name and his father's. Wolf signed his name.

'Let me see who is here.' His mother took the book again and looked through the entries. She jabbed her finger at one. 'Lady Holback. What is *she* doing here? Of all people.'

Wolf, impatient to find Lord Ashcourt, left his mother to the book. He headed towards the corner where the man still conversed with the two women.

The taller woman turned around.

Wolf froze.

Auburn hair peeked out of her stylish bonnet. Dark, coffee-coloured eyes flashed with shocked recognition. Ruby lips parted in surprise.

Fleur.

It was Fleur, the woman from Paris, the woman who'd stolen more than his money.

Wolf's face grew hot, and his heart pounded. The last woman he ever thought to see again was here in Brighton, large as life, real as flesh and blood.

She quickly composed her features. He started towards her, but coolly she raised a finger, indicating he should wait. To Wolf's surprise, he complied, but he vowed he would not wait long. There was much to say to her. And much to demand.

Juliana turned to Lord and Lady Ashcourt, her chest aching with anxiety. She hoped these two people she called Cousin Kitty and Cousin Felix would not notice the very angry-looking man glaring at her.

Wolfdon. Her Englishman. Still tall. Still handsome. Very enraged.

She forced her voice to sound calm. 'Kitty, I believe I will step outside for some air.'

Kitty grabbed her hand. 'Do not tell me you are feeling ill! We will return to the house, will we not, Felix?'

Kitty was only ten years older than Juliana, but younger than her husband by at least another decade. She was his second wife, stepmother to his daughter Charlotte, and his son, Harris. Felix doted on her.

'Indeed, Kitty, my love. Straight away,' he responded, concern filling his eyes.

'No!' Juliana spoke a bit too sharply. 'I am not ill.'

She was worse than ill.

She was discovered.

She made herself smile. 'I am merely a bit overheated and pining for the bracing sea air. I shall return in a trice, I assure you.' She squeezed Kitty's hand and quickly started for the door, walking directly towards Wolfdon.

She did not dare look at him. When she passed him, she whispered, 'Meet me outside.'

To her relief he did not grab her arm right then and there and announce to the world where he had met her, what she had done to him.

His boots clicked on the pavement behind her as she stepped outside and walked around to the side of the building where there was at least a modicum of privacy. She no sooner got out of sight of any nearby pedestrians than she felt his fingers close on her arm.

'You are far from your Paris casino, Madame Fleur.' He spoke in French.

She winced at his use of that name, that reminder of Paris. Of their night together. Of her theft…

'Let me explain,' she answered in English, tilting her head to his face, surprised that the scent of him seemed familiar, as did the warmth of his body only inches from hers.

His eyes shot daggers as he leaned even closer, lips so close she could feel his breath. 'You speak English? Without an accent.'

'I am English,' she replied, then amended, 'I mean, half-English. My mother was French.'

He jerked her even closer. 'I care nothing of that! I will have your name. Now.'

'Miss Juliana Walsh. I am Lady Ashcourt's cousin.' The name tripped out of her with ease, though her insides quivered like jelly. She managed to meet his heated eyes without visibly flinching.

His brows rose in surprise. 'Lady Ashcourt's cousin!' He released her with almost as much force as he had seized her and glared suspiciously. 'Lady Ashcourt's cousin was soliciting gentlemen in a Paris casino?'

'I solicited no one,' she shot back, wishing she could slap him hard across the face.

'You solicited me.' He advanced on her again, backing her against the wall. 'You stole my money, and I want it back.'

'Oh, *monsieur*.' She dared to look into his eyes and speak with complete honesty. 'I am sorry for it.'

Over these last several months, she'd thought of her glorious Englishman often, though time left her wondering how much was imagination and how much memory. It still did not seem possible a man could have been so kind to her. Of course, if any of his kindness had been real, she'd betrayed it.

He made a cage of his arms, effectively pinning her to the wall and blocking her vision of the new buildings erected behind the library.

She lifted her chin. 'I will repay you,' she said impulsively. 'I will repay all of it.' As soon as she'd spoken the words, she knew she would not keep the promise. 'I cannot do so immediately. I have nothing but pin money, really, not much more money than the night we met, but I will repay you. Somehow.' A tiny frisson of regret tickled her spine, regret that she would again betray him.

'Do you think I would let you play me for a fool a second time?' His eyes lit with fire, and his breath came fast.

She felt light-headed, but it was from his nearness, not his anger. Her senses were filled with him. Her treacherous body ached with the memory of his lovemaking. It did not matter that the morning breeze was cool. She grew hot enough to wish for a fan. 'I promise I will repay you.'

His eyes softened. 'Why did you do it, Fleur?' His

tone was so low it vibrated within her. 'Why steal my money? I would have paid you—'

To her surprise, he stroked her cheek, his leather glove almost as soft as his bare fingers had once been.

She leaned into his touch and looked into his face. His eyes were now the green of the grass rippling in the morning sea breeze. 'I did not take payment for what passed between us, sir.' That much was truth.

His voice stiffened. 'You did take my money.'

'I—I was in great need...' No. That was too much truth. She straightened and looked him in the eye. 'To be clear, I stole your money. It was not a payment.'

He pushed away with a growl. 'If there is a difference, I fail to see it. You lured me to your room and into your bed to take my money.'

Her anger rekindled, she snapped back, 'I may have lured you into the street, but sharing a bed was mutual, was it not?'

He gave a derisive snort. 'Suffice to say you took my money.' He began to pace. 'Were you merely parading as a *Parisian* thief? If you were in need, why not simply come to the British embassy and identify yourself? We could have helped you. We could have sent a message to Lady Ashcourt on your behalf.'

She stared at him steadily, though the trembling inside her continued. She'd tell him just enough truth to sound genuine, the same story she'd told Felix and Kitty when she presented herself at the family's country estate not even two months ago.

'Lord and Lady Ashcourt did not know me. I had no reason to expect them to help me. My father is—was— William Walsh, Lady Ashcourt's uncle. My father left England in disgrace long ago and, as far as I know, never had further contact with the family. They knew nothing of my existence.' She took a breath. 'When Napoleon was exiled to Elba, my father brought me to Paris, the place he'd met my mother so many years before.' Her voice broke. 'But then he died there, and I was stranded.'

Her emotion was genuine.

He listened to her with arms folded across his chest.

'It is the truth,' she protested. Well, almost the truth, truth enough for him to believe her, she hoped.

He glowered. 'Why did you not speak English to me, tell me your troubles. The British had been in control of Paris for a long time. You could have asked for help. You could have asked for *my* help. Why did you not ask me?'

The idea had never occurred to her. 'Trust you?'

Something of her surprise must have shown in her face because he looked at her with a quizzical expression.

She blinked, then raised her eyes to his. 'Do you intend to tell Lord and Lady Ashcourt about me?'

He moved away from her, averting his gaze. Turning back, he said, 'Is there some reason I should not tell them?'

She shivered in fear of the consequences of such a disclosure. How would she get on if she had to flee Brighton and Kitty and Felix? She truly had no more than pin money. She would be forced back into thieving and picking pockets and risking arrest. Hanging was no better a fate than the guillotine. 'Is it not obvious that disclosing my life in Paris would be the ruin of me?'

His green eyes probed her.

She refused to look away. 'Sir?'

He frowned. 'My name is Wolfdon, in case you forgot.'

'Wolfdon,' she repeated. 'I remembered.'

He stared at her.

She felt desperation creep in, the despair of being alone, the uncertainty of survival.

She spoke quietly, truthfully. 'I needed your money to come to England. I had nowhere else to go. I still have nowhere else to go.'

He paced again, staring down at the ground. When he stopped in front of her, he stood too close. 'Do you stay with Lady Ashcourt?'

She nodded. 'I am my cousin's guest, completely at the mercy of her hospitality. If she and Lord Ashcourt discover the life I was forced to live in Paris, I am certain I will no longer be welcome.' She gave him a frank gaze. 'I beg for your silence. In return I will repay your money.'

His eyes bore into hers, cutting so deep they seemed to impale her soul. She waited in agony for him to speak.

His gaze did not waver. 'I will think about it, Fleur.'

'Juliana. Miss Walsh,' she corrected.

He gave a sarcastic smile. 'Fleur.'

'You will keep the secret?' Her heart pounded.

He paused. 'For now.'

'Then I will pay what sum you require as soon as I am able.' She cleared her throat. 'I ought to go back inside before Kitty comes looking for me. If you are returning to the library, will you wait a moment or two before following me?'

He scraped his knuckles across her chin. 'Anything else you desire?'

Her knees felt like melted wax at his touch, but she made her voice strong. 'No, that will do.'

He stepped aside so she could pass. She hurried away but looked back at him before turning to the front of the building.

* * *

Wolf leaned against the wall, staring after her, even though she'd disappeared from view. He released a long pent-up breath.

Curse her.

She was even more beautiful in sunlight, with her pale skin tinged pink from the breeze and her brown eyes glittering with emotion.

After what she had done to him before, he dared not believe this tale of repaying him. Bah! The reparation would take a great deal of pin money. He suspected this cousin of Lady Ashcourt's was trying to fool him again. One thing was certain. He would watch her carefully.

A breeze whipped past the library building, lifting the tail of his coat and threatening to toss his hat. He leaned into the wind and re-entered the building.

His mother now stood with the Ashcourts, chatting animatedly with Lady Ashcourt, Fleur—Miss Walsh— at her side. Fleur looked alarmed at his approach. Ashcourt also glanced his way and broke into a welcoming grin. Wolf crossed the room, enjoying the expression of doom on Miss Walsh's face.

He extended his hand. 'Ashcourt, good to see you.'

'Wolfdon!' Ashcourt exclaimed. 'I am so delighted! Harris wrote and told me you were in the country. Your mother says your father is doing well.'

'Indeed. We are here for the sea air. The doctor thought it would do him good.'

His mother placed a hand on his arm. 'Wolf, dear, it was Lady Ashcourt I recognised as we were walking in.' She smiled at the lady. 'Or do you prefer to be called Baroness?'

Lady Ashcourt's father had died a few years ago and,

his brother, the erstwhile father of Juliana Walsh, had already been declared dead. Lady Ashcourt had inherited his title and fortune, becoming the Baroness of Walsingham.

Lady Ashcourt blushed and blinked rapidly. 'I prefer Lady Ashcourt, of course, my husband's title, the Earl of Ashcourt.' She sent an adoring glance his way.

Wolf leaned in to give Lady Ashcourt a peck on the cheek. 'Good to see you, my lady.'

'I must present you to my wife's cousin.' Ashcourt turned to Fleur. 'Juliana, my dear, this is Mr Wolfdon. Lady Wolfdon's son, you know, and a great friend of my son, Harris.'

'Ma'am.' Wolf bowed.

Ashcourt turned back to him. 'Juliana—Miss Walsh— is the daughter of Kitty's Uncle William.'

'Sir.' Fleur lowered her gaze as she curtsied.

Ashcourt laughed. 'No need to be formal, Juliana. Call him Wolf. He is as close as family.'

'Poor Juliana was stranded in Paris after that wretched Napoleon was exiled,' Lady Ashcourt explained, her expression full of sympathy.

'How dreadful!' his mother exclaimed.

Lady Ashcourt's ringlets bobbed as she nodded. 'I cannot imagine how she got on all alone, the poor dear. We are the only family she has left in the world.'

Wolf met Fleur's gaze. 'How fortunate you are to have found Lord and Lady Ashcourt.'

'I was indeed, sir,' Fleur responded, her eyes flashing for an instant. 'I am greatly in their debt.'

Lady Ashcourt gave her a quick squeeze, pressing her cheek against Fleur's. 'Do not be silly. You shall always be welcome with us, Juliana dear. Will she not, Felix?'

Ashcourt regarded his wife with a fond look. 'Indeed, most welcome.'

Lady Ashcourt beamed. 'You can imagine our surprise, sir, when Juliana appeared at our door. We had just returned to Ashcourt House from London. She had travelled all alone on the public coach and walked from the village, the poor dear.'

His mother gasped and took Fleur's hand in a consoling squeeze.

Wolf slanted a look to a stiff-faced Juliana. 'I dare say you must have wondered who she was.'

'Oh, indeed!' Lady Ashcourt nodded energetically. 'She could have been anybody! But Felix was wise enough to hear her out and examine the papers proving who she was. I confess, I knew with the first glimpse she was my cousin! I tell you I wept at the description of all she endured. My heart just broke for her, and I was determined then and there to make up to her for all she suffered. That is why we are in Brighton.'

Wolf wrinkled his brow. 'I do not follow. You are in Brighton at Miss Walsh's request?'

Lady Ashcourt laughed. 'Not at her request, indeed no! So she might mingle with the *ton*, you see. Take her rightful place in society.' She gazed adoringly at her husband. 'Felix, of course, indulged me in this. Juliana needed a new wardrobe, you know, so first we had to travel back to London so she could visit the best modistes and be properly attired, and, let me tell you, we spared no expense. My Felix has been all that is generous to my dear, newly discovered cousin.'

Ashcourt flushed with pleasure at his wife's compliment. 'My dear, you know very well it was your money that was spent.' He turned back to Wolf. 'You must call upon us, my son.'

It always warmed Wolf's heart when Ashcourt called him that.

'Oh, yes, you must,' his wife agreed. 'Charlotte will be delighted to see you.'

'Charlotte is here?'

Charlotte was Harris's younger sister who used to plague them unmercifully when Wolf visited during school holidays. Wolf knew her better than his own younger sisters, now married and busy with their own lives.

'And you must call upon us,' his mother interjected. 'We are staying at the Old Ship Hotel.'

Lady Ashcourt nodded in agreement.

Wolf said, 'I should bring Charlotte a gift when I call. Would she like a book, I wonder?'

Lord Ashcourt laughed. 'I dare say she would. Always has her nose in some novel or another.'

While Ashcourt spoke, Juliana edged away, but Wolf perversely moved closer to her. He addressed Lady Ashcourt. 'Do you have a book to suggest?'

'I am certain I do not know what young ladies would read.' Lady Ashcourt giggled. 'Juliana, you would be a better judge. You are closer in age.'

'How old is she now?' Wolf asked.

Fleur stepped back a little. 'Seventeen.'

'Oh, my goodness!' Wolf's mother tossed her head. 'At that age I suppose she would like something scandalous.' She fluttered her lashes. 'Would you not say so, Lord Ashcourt?'

Good god. Was his mother flirting with Ashcourt?

Ashcourt reddened. 'I would indeed, my lady.'

Lady Ashcourt seemed oblivious to all this, though. 'Juliana, you must go with Wolf and help him select a book. I am certain you will find just the thing from the Minerva Press.'

Wolf flashed a warning glance towards his mother, who ignored it. 'I would be very grateful for your assistance, Miss Walsh.'

Fleur's smile seemed fixed. 'As you wish.'

Wolf guided her by the elbow to the counter where he told the clerk what sort of book he was seeking.

The young man responded, 'I'll bring several possibilities.'

The clerk left, and the others were out of earshot. 'Are you an avid reader as well as a card player and thief, Fleur?' Wolf asked.

She scowled at him. 'I have read a book or two, *Wolf.*'

The clerk returned with one book. 'Young ladies like this one. I'll bring others.' He left again.

Fleur picked up the book and looked at the title. *'Emilie de Coulanges.* I know this one. It is about French émigrés living in England.'

He gave her a sarcastic smile. 'Ah, like you, coming from France to England.'

She glanced at him. 'That is so.'

He frowned, wanting to know more about her and hating himself for his curiosity. 'Your mother was French, you said. Where is she now, Fleur?'

Her eyes turned sad, but only very briefly. 'She died when I was eleven.'

Something resembling sympathy flashed through him. He did not want to feel sympathy any more than he wanted to be curious. He certainly did not want to feel any tender emotions towards her.

He took the book from her hand. 'Maria Edgeworth? Does she write those ghastly Gothic novels? Or is this book scandalous, as my mother recommends?'

'I would better characterise it as a moral tale.' She kept his gaze and turned hers into a challenge.

He much preferred locking horns with her. She stood fast with him, like a worthy adversary.

'I suspect Charlotte could profit from a moral tale.' He leaned closer to Juliana. 'Do you read moral tales, Fleur?'

She did not waver. 'I did at one time, sir, before I needed to worry about where I might find food to eat.'

Without realising it he put a compassionate hand on her arm. Her eyes darkened, and he felt his senses spring to life, sprouting in her presence like a spring crop in newly ploughed earth. His mind screamed that she was a thief, a liar, a stealer of hearts, plucking at tender emotions while plotting for her own gain, but the rest of him merely wanted her.

He moved closer so his breath mingled with hers. She did not move away but continued to gaze into his eyes while his heart raced faster and faster.

'Juliana?' Lady Ashcourt's tinkling voice reached their ears and parted them.

Juliana stepped away. 'I am at the counter, Kitty.'

The shorter, plumper woman skipped over to her. 'Felix says we ought to leave. We are to meet with Mr Busby.'

Wolf had heard of Busby, a Brighton designer who was in great demand for the latest in parlour, dining and drawing room decor.

Lady Ashcourt smiled at Wolf. 'Do we see you at the Assembly tonight, Wolf, dear?'

'Mother and I have only just put in a request for invitations,' he responded. 'But if they arrive in time, I am certain she will want to attend.' He glanced at Juliana. 'Perhaps we shall meet again tonight, Miss Walsh.'

She curtsied. 'Perhaps.'

As he watched her hurry away with Lady Ashcourt, Wolf rubbed his thumb over the book she'd chosen. The attendant returned with two more selections, but Wolf handed him the copy of *Emilie de Coulanges*.

'I'll purchase this one.'

The transaction complete, he found his mother, who'd been chatting with another acquaintance. By the time they stepped out the door of the Circulating Library, Lord and Lady Ashcourt and their felonious cousin could still be seen across the Steine. Juliana Walsh's alluring gait was still evident even at a distance. They soon disappeared among the buildings in the most fashionable part of Brighton.

Chapter Four

Juliana sat at the dressing table in the elegant bedchamber, her lady's maid threading a ribbon through her hair for the Assembly that night. Her image in the mirror was cast in the soft evening light from a window facing the alley behind the building. Felix and Kitty's bedchamber and that of their daughter had a view of the sea, but this was a minor matter. The rooms Felix had secured for them in Brighton were more comfortable and stylish than any other place Juliana had known, except, of course, the Ashcourt country estate and their London town house.

Her father had always promised her this sort of finery—the finery his partner, Turstin, had promised him. Her father had also taught her to never take good fortune for granted. His lesson had certainly been driven home this day by her Englishman's appearance.

Her lovely Englishman. *Wolfdon—Wolf.* How apt a name.

He was no longer the Englishman of her memory, though, idealised into perfection, a man who acted as if he were a hero in a Minerva Press novel. Her fictional Englishman had warmed lonely Parisian nights after she'd finished gambling in the casinos to build upon the stash of money she'd stolen from him. Now he had appeared again, in the flesh, as handsome and masculine as she'd remembered—but seething with anger.

She could not blame him. She had betrayed him and he was her enemy now. Surely, he would betray her in time. Like her first lover had done. And Turstin. All men were selfish. Even her father had always assumed she'd agree with whatever scheme he came up with. Flesh-and-blood men were not at all like heroes in novels.

There was a sharp rap at the door and Kitty bounded in. 'Are you ready, Juliana? No, I see you are not.' Kitty stood behind the maid, watching the girl's handiwork in the mirror. 'I declare, your hair is such a lovely colour, I am all envy for it. The green ribbon looks divine. You must have decided on the green gown?'

'I did.' Juliana slanted her eyes towards the bed where the gown was draped.

'How is that, Miss?' her maid asked, patting the curls that seemed artfully held in place by the ribbon, rather than by the dozens of hairpins hidden underneath.

'It is lovely,' Kitty answered for her. 'A vision. Now let us see you in the gown.'

'Thank you, Sally.' Juliana smiled at the young girl whose sole job was to keep Juliana in pretty hairstyles and pressed clothes.

Sally fetched the gown and lifted it carefully over Juliana's head. The silk flowed down her body like water on a creek bed, and the skirt billowed out for a moment before settling into graceful folds. It felt exquisite and expensive. It was both.

As Sally fastened the bodice, Kitty, hands on hips,

surveyed Juliana. 'You look stunning, I must say. That shade of green is your colour for certain.'

The silk was a shimmering emerald-green, unadorned except for a wide flounce of lace in matching green around the neckline. Into the lace were sewn tiny pearls, over a hundred of them, luminescent against the green.

Kitty frowned.

'What is the matter?' Juliana asked.

Kitty appeared absorbed in Juliana's attire, walking slowly around her, pursing her lips and furrowing her brow. 'It needs something…' A moment later her expression brightened and she made a dash for the door. 'Wait a moment!'

Sally finished her ministrations and went about tidying the room. Juliana walked over to the full-length mirror, nearly gasping at what she saw. The lovely gown and graceful hairstyle made her look every bit the fine English lady.

An errant thought struck. Would *he* think so? Her lovely Englishman?

Oh, what was she thinking, mooning over him, wishing for his admiration? He was her enemy now, the one person who could expose her. How was she to buy his silence? He could expose her as a thief and yet how else could she repay him except by theft? In contriving this plan to come to Kitty and Felix, she'd thought only of the chance to leave a dishonest life behind. What if she would never be anything but a common thief?

A common thief, masquerading as a lady.

Lest her thoughts expose her, Juliana turned to and fro, pretending to examine the dress in the mirror, looking over her shoulder at the back. She did look the very image of a lady, she had to admit.

Kitty had insisted upon her having many lovely gowns from the London modiste—morning dresses, walking dresses, carriage outfits and more. Felix seemed not the least concerned about the expense of all this, merely smiling indulgently at Kitty when she explained, 'We must outfit our new cousin in the latest fashion. She must cut a dash, do you not agree, dearest?'

Her dearest, had, of course, agreed.

If there were two more generous and gullible people in the world besides Felix and Kitty, Juliana had yet to meet them. Convincing them she was Kitty's cousin had been astonishingly easy.

In fact, she trusted it would be more difficult for them to believe the truth—that her father had not been Lady Ashcourt's uncle, a baron's son. No, her father was the son of an innkeeper somewhere in Surrey. Juliana did not know precisely where, or even if that tale was true. She did not even know if her father's name, Edgar Parsons, was real. They'd used many aliases over the years.

There was no use being curious about it now, was there? Besides, her father had always said appearances were what mattered. If so, this evening she certainly appeared to be the long-lost cousin of Lady Ashcourt, daughter of her family's black sheep, William *Turstin* Walsh.

Turstin, her father's partner.

It had been Turstin who'd hastily conceived the ill-planned jewel theft in Paris. As far as Juliana was concerned Turstin caused her father's arrest. His death. The least Turstin could do was lend her the family name he'd renounced. After all, he had so renounced his family he'd fabricated his own death so they'd believe their banishment of him had killed him.

Juliana had taken Turstin's signature from papers she found in her father's things and forged it on documents to convince Felix and Kitty that she was indeed William Walsh's daughter. If she had not done so, she would not be in Brighton this evening, wearing this beautiful, expensive gown, looking every bit the lady she certainly was not.

She was not only a thief masquerading as a lady, she was a fraud, as well. That was something her Englishman and no one else must ever know.

Voices sounded outside her door.

'Why not, Mama?' It was Charlotte, Kitty's step-daughter.

Charlotte's mother had died when she was just a baby, and Kitty was the only mother she'd ever known, as devoted a mother as Juliana could ever imagine.

'I am seventeen,' Charlotte went on. 'Quite old enough to attend an Assembly.'

'Not this one, Charlotte dear,' Kitty responded. 'Let your father and me see what the Assemblies here are like.'

Kitty opened the door and flew back in the room, Charlotte behind her.

'Mama,' Charlotte pleaded. 'Please let me come with you—' She broke off on seeing Juliana. 'Oh, you look beautiful, Julie!'

Juliana felt her cheeks flush. Charlotte's compliment had been so spontaneous and heartfelt. How lovely it would be to truly deserve such praise.

'And these will be just the thing to complete her ensemble.' Kitty handed Juliana a black velvet box. 'You must wear them.'

Juliana opened the box and drew in a quick breath.

In the box were a large teardrop-shaped pearl on a

delicate gold chain and matching teardrop pearls for earrings.

'Oh, the pearls!' exclaimed Charlotte. 'Yes. They will be just the thing.'

Kitty's eyes danced with excitement and begged for Juliana's approval.

If only Kitty knew she was handing over the sort of jewellery Juliana had been taught to steal. 'I have never seen anything lovelier!'

Kitty beamed.

Charlotte walked over. 'I'll help you put them on.'

'Thank you, Charlotte.' Juliana handed the box to the girl and watched in the mirror while she fastened the necklace. Juliana put the earrings on herself and turned to Kitty and Charlotte. 'What do you think?'

The maid spoke first. 'They look made for the dress, Miss.'

'I told you they were perfect!' Kitty gave Juliana a quick hug. 'Are they not perfect, Charlotte?'

'Yes, Mama!' Charlotte's eyes sparkled in appreciation, her own plight forgotten for the moment.

'Let us show your father.' Kitty squeezed her stepdaughter's hand. She turned to Juliana. 'We are ready now, are we not?'

'I could not ask for more,' Juliana said, truly meaning it.

She gathered her green Indian silk shawl and twined her arms through Kitty's and Charlotte's as they walked to the drawing room where Felix waited.

He turned at their entrance, a glass of port in his hand. 'Oh, my!' he exclaimed. He scanned all three, but his gaze settled on his wife, who wore a very flattering daffodil-yellow gown. 'You look as beautiful as a garden in spring.'

Felix and Kitty might be gullible, but they were also completely besotted with each other.

Juliana envied that.

Felix's looks were passable, the sort of even, ordinary features that defied description. His brown hair was streaked with grey, showing his age. His figure was neither corpulent nor slim. Height, average. He was a forgettable sort of creature, unless you were Kitty who adored every inch of him. Felix did not lack intelligence, but he and Kitty were so eager to be of use to someone, *anyone,* that they both had eagerly accepted Juliana's story.

Juliana's father had always taught her to put as much truth as possible into any lie to make it ring true. So she had inserted Turstin's name in her own history. Instead of her father, it became Turstin who married her French mother. Turstin who fathered her. Turstin who died, leaving her alone.

Turstin had not died though. His scheme to fake his death had worked so well that he was officially declared dead. That was why Kitty had inherited the barony that Turstin had always disdained, vowing he'd never return to British soil.

Indeed, if Turstin had died, Juliana would not have wasted a moment in mourning. But he had not died, as everyone thought. He was very much alive and had been when he left her father to his terrible fate on the guillotine. He'd abandoned Juliana, as well, running off to Naples or some other foreign place. Good riddance to him. At least Juliana had nothing to fear from him. It was one blessing in her life that she'd never have to see or hear from him again—as long as she stayed in England.

No, Wolf was Juliana's only threat. He could ruin her by merely describing her life in Paris, her theft of his purse, her gambling in casinos, her making love to him. He could ruin the most peaceful life she'd ever known, living with Kitty and Felix.

Felix strode forward, breaking into Juliana's thoughts. 'I shall be the envy of every gentleman at the Assembly.'

'I wish I could go with you.' Charlotte pouted. 'I could be ready in a trice.'

Felix put his arm around his daughter and placed a kiss on her cheek. 'Maybe the next one, sweetling. We'll see.'

Charlotte sighed but nodded.

He turned to Juliana and his wife and gallantly offered them each an arm. 'Shall we go, ladies?'

Charlotte fussed with Juliana's shawl. 'Be sure to tell me all about it.'

'I will,' Juliana promised.

Had she ever been seventeen and so eager to be considered grown? She could not remember ever feeling like a child.

They walked the short distance to the Castle Inn. The brisk air felt invigorating. As they entered the ballroom where the Assembly was held, Felix was drawn aside by a group of gentlemen. Kitty led Juliana to a place where they could see and be seen. The musicians were just taking their seats and the discordant tuning of instruments mixed with the hum of multiple conversations.

Kitty grabbed Juliana's arm, inclining her head towards a short, stout gentleman whose red-veined nose hinted at too much drink. 'There is Lord Ruskin. He is a widower and has a modest fortune. You must not even consider him, however. He is such a reprobate.'

Kitty considered it her duty—indeed her highest priority—to find Juliana a husband. When Juliana first conceived her plan to become Kitty's fictitious cousin, she'd thought only to see how long she might prevail on their hospitality before seeking some reputable profession— what sort of profession she did not know. She certainly was not fit to be a governess. Maybe a lady's companion?

But Kitty almost immediately began speaking of finding her a wealthy society gentleman to marry. The idea had taken root. Why not become some wealthy man's wife? Why not live with the comfort money and power could provide? It would be a masquerade to last a lifetime. And a wealthy husband would eventually tire of her, of course, and she would have more freedom.

All men eventually tired of a woman.

Except Felix, perhaps. He certainly had not tired of Kitty after over a decade and a half of marriage. Juliana shook her head. Felix and Kitty were an aberration. There was no other explanation for them.

Kitty nudged her, directing her gaze to a handsome, black-haired man, leaning to murmur something in a woman's ear. 'There is Baron Lymond, but he will never do. He is a notorious rake and you should never have a moment's peace married to him.' The woman giggled and slapped Lord Lymond with her fan. Juliana would have recognised that gentleman as a *roué* within a second even without Kitty's warning.

'Kitty, really, you are too kind. But you mustn't work so hard to find me a husband. If I should meet someone, it will all happen naturally.' Juliana did not really believe this foolish drivel. She did not believe in romance at all but knew Kitty would adore the idea of *true love*.

Kitty gave her a scolding look. 'Of course I must help you, Juliana dearest. Whatever are cousins for but to help each other?' She patted Juliana's arm. 'Besides, I know these gentlemen and you do not. I shall be able to save you so much trouble. One must fall in love with the right gentleman.'

Juliana gave her a teasing smile. 'And who helped you fall in love with Felix?'

A dreamy look came over Kitty's pale blue eyes. 'The moment I spied him across a room just like this one, it was as if time ceased moving. His eyes met mine and I knew we were destined for each other.'

Rubbish! Certainly, he took into account her dowry and her parents saw to the proper widow's settlement and other pecuniary matters that constituted a *ton* marriage. Still, Juliana could not help but find Kitty's notions endearing.

'Oh, there is Wolf!' Kitty cried.

Juliana glanced towards the door of the Assembly room to watch Wolf walk in behind his mother and a distinguished older gentleman who must be his father. Wolf looked in her direction, and their gazes caught. He looked resplendent in his formal attire—ivory waistcoat, white neckcloth, perfectly tailored black coat, black thigh-clinging breeches and knee stockings. She sucked in a breath.

Kitty lowered her voice. 'He is charming, isn't he? So handsome. You know, his family was one step from debtors' prison a while ago. Without the help of his sister—she's married to the Marquess of Hale now, but then it had been Viscount Varden—they'd be penniless, poor things. There is an estate, of course, but not much money there. Besides, Wolf earns his money as a diplomat.' She sighed. 'Wolf insists he will remain a diplomat. He and Harris. It is their passion, they say.'

It turned out Harris, Felix's son by his first marriage,

was Wolf's lifelong friend. Just Juliana's luck that Wolf-don would be so connected to the Ashcourts.

Kitty went on. 'But Harris will do his duty when the time comes—' Her voice cracked and tears formed in her eyes at the thought of her husband dying and Harris assuming his title.

Juliana touched her hand comfortingly but suffered a pang of guilt. Had Wolf needed the purse she'd pinched from him that night in Paris?

Kitty glanced back at Wolf. 'On the other hand, perhaps it would be just thē thing to lure Wolf and Harris back to us...'

What would be just the thing? Kitty had better not set her sights on matchmaking between her and Wolf!

Wolf smiled and nodded to Kitty and headed directly towards them. Juliana's pulse quickened and she was unable to breathe—because of the risk he posed to her.

Nothing else.

He first bowed to Kitty. 'Lady Ashcourt, good evening. May I be permitted to say you look lovely this evening?'

Kitty blushed and tittered, 'Well, Felix did say so.'

Wolf turned to Juliana. 'Miss Walsh.'

Kitty, showing no signs of noticing his more caustic tone towards Juliana, chattered, 'I see you did receive your invitations in time, because you are here, of course. And your parents. So, you will also be at the other entertainments, I expect. We will be seeing you often, will we not? Will that not be nice?'

'Very nice, indeed, ma'am. It will be my pleasure.' He slanted a glance at Juliana.

'Oh, yes.' Kitty favoured him with her dimpled grin, but still scanned the room. 'I see your mother, of course.

And your father. He is feeling well enough to attend? That is good.'

Wolfdon's expression sobered. 'I hope he is well enough.'

The Master of Ceremonies chose that moment to step up on the orchestra's raised platform. The discordant tuning of instruments ceased.

'Ladies and gentlemen,' the man announced, 'the dancing will commence. The first dance will be a gavotte. Take your places, if you please.'

Felix appeared at his wife's side. 'I am here, Kitty, to claim the first dance.' He spoke as if he were a lovestruck suitor instead of a long-married man.

Kitty returned an equally enraptured smile but managed to speak before he swept her away. 'Wolf, dear, Juliana has not yet been engaged for the first dance.'

Juliana's cheeks burned. What was she trying to do?

Wolf turned to her, a sardonic look in his eye. 'I suppose that means I must ask for this dance, Fleur.'

'Do not feel obligated, sir,' she responded, her heart pounding again.

He extended his hand. 'I would not disappoint Lady Ashcourt for the world.'

Juliana met his eye defiantly. 'In that case, I would be delighted.'

He offered his arm, and they stepped on to the dance floor, where other couples were forming a circle for the old-fashioned dance that would open the Assembly.

The music began, and they joined hands, beginning the intricate sliding steps that turned the wheel of dancers in a decorous pattern. Juliana tensed at the pressure of Wolfdon's fingers on her own, remembering the feel of his bare hands on her skin. His gaze burned into her, too much like that passion-filled night they'd shared. She didn't want to be so affected by him, by the reminder of their night together. He posed the biggest threat to her, and he rightfully despised her for what she'd done to him.

It did not make it any easier that Wolf effortlessly executed the steps of the dance, as if he'd not had to give them a thought. Or that she noticed other ladies smiling admiringly at him from across the circle, although why that should bother her, she did not know.

At the end of the set, Wolf did not immediately release her hand.

And she did not pull away.

He returned her to Kitty who stood with her husband. 'How nice the two of you shared the first dance.' Kitty gave Wolf a charming smile almost as dazzling as the smiles reserved for her beloved Felix.

'Indeed,' responded Wolf, with less enthusiasm. He bowed to her. 'Lady Ashcourt.' And to Juliana. 'Miss Walsh.'

'I am certain we will see more of you, Wolf,' Felix said warmly.

Juliana could breathe again after Wolf walked away.

Kitty wasted no time in leaning towards her conspiratorially. 'That went well, by the looks of it, but we cannot put all our eggs in one basket, can we?'

Juliana was certain Kitty had never had to gather eggs in any kind of basket—or steal them in pre-dawn hours before the farmer woke.

'I have found another gentleman for you,' Kitty went on. 'He will be here in a moment.'

'Kitty—' she said, but the approach of a tall, elegant gentleman with greying temples stopped her.

'Juliana, allow me to present Lord Seabane to you.'
Kitty's voice was eager. 'My lord, this is my cousin, Miss
Walsh.'

'A pleasure to meet you, Miss Walsh.' He bowed.
'Would you do me the honour of the next dance?'

Kitty nodded vigorously behind him.

'Thank you, sir.' He seemed pleasant enough with his
elegant manners and the glint of a diamond stickpin on
the lapel of his coat.

They joined the line of the country dance. To Juliana's
dismay, Wolf also joined the set, standing a mere two
couples away, escorting a lovely blonde. Juliana could
barely heed her partner's conversation. Wolfdon's prox-
imity was too distracting.

Lord Seabane was not nearly the dancer that Wolf had
been. More than once Seabane took a misstep. When
he turned the wrong way and bumped into her, Juliana
felt the unmistakable bulge of a small purse in his coat
pocket.

It would be so easy to lift. Too easy. One quick motion and she would have money, money she might well
need if Wolf exposed her.

The next time he bumped into her, Juliana made herself fall against him. In one fast and fluid motion, she
pulled the purse from his pocket and shoved it down her
dress, trusting her corset to hold it in place.

At the end of the set, oblivious to his loss, Lord Seabane walked her back to Kitty.

'May I bring you ladies a glass of wine?' he asked in
a gallant tone.

'That would be so kind,' she replied.

Kitty nodded in approval.

When he went off on his errand, Kitty whispered, 'Lord Seabane has a tidy fortune. He's a widower and in search of a wife. He would do, Juliana, if Wolf doesn't come up to snuff.'

At least Juliana was assured Seabane would not need his purse.

Could she seriously consider Kitty's marriage scheme? Marry some eligible man and be secure for life? A tiny part of her protested.

But she responded, 'He seems quite nice.'

Wolf approached a tall, stately-looking young woman, Juliana noticed. He smiled and both dimples creased his cheeks. The lady seemed to sparkle under his attention.

This elegant lady looked every bit the heiress she most assuredly was, with her fine ivory silk gown and stately tilt of her chin. Juliana could not help but dislike her on sight. She looked the sort of young woman who took a life of ease for granted and always received whatever she desired.

Would she desire Wolf?

Why would Juliana care if she did? Wolf was her enemy, she reminded herself.

Chapter Five

Wolf watched Lord Seabane leave Fleur's side. Had he seen what he thought he'd seen? Had Fleur nicked Seabane's purse? The action had been so swift he was not certain. He'd just asked Seabane's daughter, Lady Allyse, for the next set. Lady Allyse was an old friend who'd once held a *tendre* for his friend Harris. He couldn't allow Fleur to steal from Lady Allyse's father.

Her father was an eligible widower. It stood to reason he would be attracted to this exotic newcomer, Lady Ashcourt's long-lost cousin. But if Fleur truly was on the marriage mart, with Kitty playing matchmaker, why steal from the man?

Was that her intent? To steal from as many gentlemen as possible? He must watch her, difficult when talking to another lady.

On the other hand, it was difficult to take his eyes off her. Fleur looked magnificent in that rich green gown that brought out the red tones in her hair and made her coffee-brown eyes look meltingly enticing. When he'd approached her before he'd meant merely to taunt her with his presence. Instead, it was her presence that taunted him. He could hardly take a step without being acutely aware of where she stood and who kept her company.

And of what she was about.

It had been perverse of him to ask her for the first dance, although, to be truthful, it would have been ungentlemanly to walk away from her, leaving her alone. She cast her spell upon him again with how gracefully she performed the steps, how she outshone every woman in the circle.

He mentally chastised himself. Mooning over the Parisian thief was not going to do him any good. He'd do better to protect the other men from her.

He escorted Lady Allyse to the dance floor.

Juliana danced with another eligible and wealthy fellow. Wolf tried to keep her in view, but not only did he have to attend to the dance and his partner, but his father's distinctive cough reminded him he must watch out for him. He spied his father sitting next to a lady around his age, engrossed in her conversation.

Lady Holback.

How could he forget Lady Holback? When he'd been a child her name had often been bandied about in loud rows between his parents. His sisters had warned him that she was still out and about.

Then he caught a glimpse of his mother, glaring at his father while being escorted to the dance floor by Lord Lymond, of all people. Did not his sisters say Lymond had recently jilted Lord Crafton's daughter? And that she and her father had fled London for a hasty trip to the Continent. Now Lymond was dallying with his mother?

Damnation. Wolf thought he'd escaped this sort of drama when he left England. You'd think his father's brush with death would have made some impact on the both of them.

He'd lost sight of Fleur, but quickly found her again among the dancers. She could have taken advantage of his distraction and nicked that gentleman's purse in that time.

He needed to pay closer attention.

At the end of the set, Wolf returned Lady Allyse to her companions and noticed his mother had gathered several admirers around her. It was his father's turn to glare at her, his interest in Lady Holback faltering for the moment.

Wolf rolled his eyes.

The Master of Ceremonies then announced the supper dance. What better way to ensure Fleur behaved herself? Wolf strode across the room to where Fleur stood. Lady Ashcourt whispered in her ear.

Lady Ashcourt took Juliana's arm and glanced his way. He heard her say, 'Never mind Lord Plackstone. Wolf is coming.'

Juliana's eyes widened when Wolf bowed to her.

He minced no words. 'Are you engaged for this dance?'

She cleared her throat. 'I am not engaged.'

'May I have the honour?' He said the word *honour* with some sarcasm.

Her eyes narrowed, but she responded, 'As you wish.'

He offered his arm, as he had once offered it to her on that damp Paris street. How fitting that this dance should be a French waltz.

As she joined her hands to his for the march, he had every intention of accusing her of stealing from the hapless gentlemen who had partnered her. But the touch of her hand brought a memory of how his bare hands had felt against her naked flesh. He could not make himself speak as they faced each other.

She curtsied. He put his arms around her, and she rested her hands on his shoulders as the dance required. She looked up into his face, and her eyes seemed to glow with the passion they'd briefly shared. He could not look away.

The violin carried the melody of the music, sounding dreamlike as Wolf led her into the gentle turns of the waltz. They seemed to float on the sweet music, like a bird's feather he'd seen that morning dancing on the sea breeze. He drew her closer, forcing himself not to exceed a respectable distance. It was tempting to press her against his chest, to again feel the softness of her breasts.

'Fleur,' he murmured, insides aching with desire for her.

Her gaze seemed to fill with the same acute pain.

He ought to be confronting her about stealing from Seabane, reminding her of her falsehoods and her betrayal, how she'd made love with him, then stole his purse, how he suspected she might be stealing even now, but it was as if they danced in a cloud, no others around them. No other thoughts were possible except the pleasure of holding her in his arms again.

He hoped the dance would end quickly.

Or that it would never end.

When the music eventually stopped, he did not immediately release her. She slid her hands off his arms and stepped out of his embrace.

'I will escort you into supper,' he said, his voice low.

This was expected of the gentleman who secured the supper dance. Wolf had counted on the chance to spend more time with her.

He noticed Lady Ashcourt give an approving look as they walked towards her. Surely Lady Ashcourt was not including him in her stash of eligible gentlemen?

In the supper room the food was set out on a large buffet—cold meats, cheeses, sweetmeats, jellies, cakes, delicacies of all kinds. Tables covered with white linen and chairs with brocade seats dotted the rest of the space. Guests seated themselves. Wolf chose a table in the corner but scanned the crowd looking for his parents. They were not together.

A servant appeared, bringing Wolf and Juliana glasses of wine.

'Shall I fix a plate for you?' he asked her.

'Thank you,' she replied in a voice so quiet, he only read the words on her lips.

He hurried to the buffet and quickly selected a sample of delicacies for them both, filling two plates. When he returned, he set the plates on the table and lowered himself into the chair next to hers.

Stepping away from her had broken the spell. 'I saw you take Seabane's purse, Fleur.'

She flinched but quickly responded, 'You could not have seen it when I did no such thing.'

'I did see you,' he insisted, although he was not at all certain. It had been so fast.

She met his eye. 'I stole nothing. How dare you think so!'

He raised his brows, but her unwavering gaze made him doubt himself. He changed the subject. 'Are you seeking a wealthy husband, then, Fleur?'

Her eyes narrowed. 'Why do you ask?'

He frowned. 'Because of the eligible men of fortune who partnered you.'

She lifted her chin. 'You danced with me. Do you believe I am seeking *you* as a wealthy husband?'

A muscle in his cheek twitched. 'Marriage to me would mean returning to Paris with me, and I doubt you want that.'

She averted her face, but he could see the mention of Paris disturbed her. She turned back to him. 'Are you feeling some obligation to inform these poor, helpless gentlemen of my desperate history in that city? You accuse me of repeating my sins even now.'

'I do accuse you,' he countered, but suddenly he was not sure of anything. Except he'd really reacted viscerally to her question of him as a potential suitor. 'But I'll say nothing. For now.'

Her eyes revealed a hint of vulnerability. 'I had no choice in the life I led,' she murmured.

That took the wind from his sails. She played on his sympathies much too successfully.

He managed to recover. 'I'll be watching, though.'

She sighed, sounding resigned, and they lapsed into silence as the chatter of other guests and clatter of silverware against china filled his ears.

Wolf noticed his father at a table with other gentlemen, all talking animatedly. He could not see his mother from where he sat but could hear her laugh. No one else came to fill the other chairs at the table.

Finally, the Master of Ceremonies announced that the dancing was about to start again, and Wolf escorted Juliana into the ballroom, back to Lady Ashcourt. To his surprise he felt regret at leaving her. He told himself it was because he could not watch her closely if he was not by her side.

He glanced around the room but could not find his

parents at the moment. Lady Allyse stood by herself, so he ambled over to her and asked for a second dance.

The dance was pleasant, even though he could not keep his eyes from Juliana, partnered by that lush Ruskin. When the dance was over Juliana did not wait for Ruskin to escort her off the dance floor but walked hurriedly away. Instead of joining Lady Ashcourt, however, she headed in the opposite direction.

Ruskin glanced around the room, then made his way to same door Juliana used to leave the ballroom.

A planned assignation, perhaps? No. Not with that miscreant. Wolf trailed him to the veranda door and watched Ruskin glance from side to side before stepping through the doorway.

The night was too cool for most couples to be standing on the veranda or strolling the garden. The veranda would be even more private than usual, Wolf suspected.

He reached the door and heard voices. One was Ruskin, the other, a lady. Wolf quietly moved through the doorway, waiting a moment for his eyes to adjust to the darkness.

On the other end of the veranda, Ruskin's hands were on Juliana.

She shoved him away and her voice rose. 'Leave me, sir!'

Ruskin laughed, advancing on her again. 'You came to this private place, did you not, Miss Walsh? You wanted my company.'

'I did not.' She pushed against his chest and brought her foot down hard on his.

'Ow!' Ruskin released her and stumbled backwards.

'Go. Now!' she ordered.

'You little witch.' He spun around to leave, and Wolf

quickly stepped into the shadows. Ruskin whooshed past him, limping towards the veranda door.

Wolf stepped out into the open. 'Fleur?'

She gave a cry and sprang back, raising her hand as if to strike.

He caught her wrist. 'I did not mean to frighten you.'

Her breath came fast, her chest rising and falling, making it difficult for him to look away.

'You did frighten me,' she managed to say. 'Was that your intention or were you merely spying on me?'

He still held her. 'I was spying on you.'

Her brow furrowed. 'Why? Did you think I was stealing his purse?'

He loosened his grip, rubbing her arm. 'Or arranging an assignation.'

She grimaced. 'Do you think me a fool? He is unpleasant in the extreme.'

He gave a half-smile. 'I might think you many things, Fleur, but a fool is not among them. Why did you come out here?'

Her eyes flashed. 'I needed air.'

His brows rose. 'It is cold out here.'

She held his gaze. 'It was close inside.'

He remembered stepping out into the Paris night with her. This felt too much the same. The cool air invigorating his senses. The illusion they were alone. The connection between them that he could not quite dispel.

He took a bracing breath. 'Did you steal his purse?'

She did not look away. 'I did not steal his purse.'

'Good.'

He leaned closer, inhaling her scent, something like roses in a summer garden. She looked much like she had in Paris. Alluring. Mysterious.

'Fleur,' he murmured.

Her voice turned to a rasp. 'Not Fleur. Juliana.'

'Fleur,' he repeated, leaning closer still.

Wolf felt his power over her. He could so easily blackmail her into kissing him. Would she not do anything to keep him from revealing the truth about her? Yes, he wanted her kiss, burned for her kiss. He wanted, for one moment at least, to feel as he briefly felt in Paris.

That they were lovers.

'Do I risk you stomping on my foot?' he whispered, ceding his power to her.

She stared at him, her eyes liquid. Slowly she reached up and cupped her soft gloved hand against his cheek. 'No.'

Wolf crushed his lips against hers. She wrapped her arms around his neck and returned the kiss with an ardency that was all he could desire. As their tongues melded intimately, his loins ached with the memory of slaking his desire for her.

The sound of laughter wafted from the doorway, and reason returned. He released her and stepped away.

'I should not have done that, Fleur.'

She nodded, breathing as hard as when he'd startled her. 'I must return to the Assembly room,' she said.

He reached for her again but withdrew his hand. 'I will wait a moment, so no one knows we have been out here.' He backed away and let the darkness cover him.

On the walk back from the Assembly, Kitty twined her arm through Juliana's.

'I think that went very well, Juliana.' She leaned towards her husband. 'Did you not think Juliana a great success, Felix?'

'I did indeed.' Felix walked shoulder to shoulder with his wife. 'There were several gentlemen who asked me about her.'

'Truly?' Kitty dropped Juliana's arm to grasp her husband's. 'Tell us who.'

'Seabane, of course. He seems most interested. And Plackstone in his reserved way. I do not countenance Ruskin or Lymond. They are not suitable at all.'

Juliana agreed with Felix's assessment, especially concerning Ruskin. How dare he touch her! Well, she'd dealt with him. Not only had she stomped on his foot, but she'd nicked his watch fob as well. So Wolfdon was not entirely wrong about that encounter. She'd not lied, though. She'd not stolen Ruskin's purse.

Of course, she had lied about stealing Seabane's purse, but, really, what other choice was there? Wolf was the cause of her needing the money. If he revealed her past, she needed money to run. In any event, he could not have seen her steal it, not clearly, at least. She was too well practised for that.

What did it matter if he had seen her or not? Wolf could still ruin her at any moment he chose.

Kitty sighed. 'I still hold out hope for Wolf,' she said to Felix. 'They look so perfect together.'

Juliana touched her gloved finger to her lips, still tingling from his kiss. She'd not minded Wolf's hands upon her, not minded at all, but that was because of the memory of Paris, surely.

'You are so silent, Juliana.' Kitty frowned at her. 'Did you prefer Lord Seabane or Lord Plackstone to Wolf?'

Juliana tried not to betray herself. 'I cannot think so seriously of anyone after such a brief encounter.'

Or another brief encounter. One kiss. It did not mean

he would ever kiss her again or repeat that glorious night of lovemaking they'd shared in Paris. It did not mean he was any less furious at her, or less inclined to expose her as a harlot, a gambler and a thief.

She pressed her hand to her abdomen and felt Lord Seabane's bag of coin safely inside her corset, next to Ruskin's watch fob.

'Just think. If Wolf married Juliana and decided to settle here, then Harris would certainly come home as well,' Kitty mused.

Felix laughed. 'That is a great deal of speculation.'

And would never happen, Juliana thought. Far more likely she would have to run.

Kitty sighed. 'But Wolf is so handsome and did he not ask Juliana for more than one dance?'

'And sat with her at supper,' Felix added.

Juliana bit her lip. Before his kiss she might have said Wolf was merely watching her closely, looking for an excuse to expose her.

Her step faltered and she lagged behind.

'What is it, Juliana?' Kitty turned back to her with a worried look. 'Are you feeling ill?'

She hurried to re-join them. 'No, I merely tripped on a stone.'

Felix offered his arm. 'I think perhaps I should hold on to both of my ladies. I would not wish any mishap to befall either one of you.'

Kitty pressed her cheek against his coat. 'You are too good, Felix.'

Both of them were too good, Juliana thought. While she'd been thinking of the fob and coin she'd stolen and the man she'd bedded, they, completely devoid of selfishness, were plotting good fortune and a secure future for her. It was a wonder. Absurd, even.

She laughed.

Kitty asked, 'What is the jest, Juliana?'

'You are,' she responded truthfully. 'Both of you. Because you both are so good to me.'

Kitty and Felix beamed and exchanged another of their adoring glances towards each other.

With a look a mischief, Felix grabbed hold of their hands and, with the energy of a much younger man, pulled them into a run, their skirts flying, their shawls waving like flags behind them. By the time they reached the door to their residence, all three of them were laughing.

Chapter Six

The next morning Wolf woke later than usual, after a fitful night's sleep, disturbed by thoughts of Juliana—Fleur. He was entirely to blame for that kiss. She'd done nothing to entice him. It was he who'd been unable to resist the desire burning inside him. That she'd felt the desire, as well, kept it smouldering even now.

He rose and dressed and left his bedchamber.

His room at the Old Ship Hotel had a private entrance, but his sitting room was also connected to his parents' sitting room and the dining room that was for their exclusive use. Wolf entered the dining room where breakfast had already been laid out on the buffet.

His father, seated at the table, his nose in the *Brighton Herald*, looked up at Wolf's entrance. 'Good morning, my son.'

Wolf mumbled a good morning back and fixed himself a plate. He lowered himself into a chair directly across from his father. After pouring his tea, Wolf roused himself enough to peruse his father closely. His father's colour was good. Probably better than Wolf's own.

'Anything of consequence in the paper?' he asked.

His father placed it on the table. 'The Assembly was a success, it reports. But we knew that, did we not?'

A success? Was it a success for Wolf or a complication? 'I suppose it was.'

His father grinned. 'Of course, it was! Very desirable set of guests, would you not say?'

Wolf had certainly desired one.

His father did not wait for an answer. 'I came upon the most amazing information.' His father brought his head close to his son's. 'An investment proposition. A once-in-a-lifetime opportunity. Whispered to me by—I must not say who. Guaranteed to triple any amount, he said. More, perhaps.'

Too good to be true, Wolf thought. 'You don't say.'

His father folded his arms across his chest. 'It is also highly confidential. Only a select few will be privy to it, so say nothing to anyone.'

As if Wolf would mention any investment that interested his father.

In his childhood, when his parents were not railing at each other for their infidelities, they spent money with abandon, his mother on her wardrobe and the newest decor, his father on gambling and bad investments, which this one undoubtedly would be. Now, at least, his sister and her husband controlled the finances with iron fists, so his father could talk about tripling his money all he wished.

'I must write to Hale about it.' Hale was the Marquess of Hale, his sister's husband.

His father started to say more, but the servant entered to remove the dishes and replenish the sideboard. His father quickly put a finger to his lips.

As soon as the servant left, his father leaned forward and whispered, 'Treasure.'

'Treasure?' This was beginning to sound even more ridiculous than Wolf had imagined.

His father looked around as if eavesdroppers might appear at any moment. 'Napoleon's treasure. Ships meant for Egypt lost at sea, their holds filled with gold and treasure.'

'At the bottom of the sea.' Wolf kept his voice neutral.

'Aha.' His father raised his arms triumphantly. 'But that is the thing. The treasure is salvageable.'

'At the bottom of the Mediterranean, it is salvageable.' Wolf restrained his sarcasm.

'It is indeed.' His father gave a smug smile. 'By submarine.'

'Submarine?'

His father fashioned an example with his hands. 'A tiny boat that can carry a man underwater.'

'I have heard of a submarine, Father,' Wolf replied. 'Our navy looked at its use years ago.'

'Well, these fellows have their hands on the submarine made by that American—Fulton, you know. He first made the vessel for the French and that is the vessel they have procured. They also know the precise location of the treasure and have a solid plan for its recovery.'

Wolf averted his gaze, fearful his father would perceive the scepticism he could not disguise. He reached for the teapot and poured another cup.

His father held up one finger. 'They need to outfit the submarine with a retrieval mechanism.' He held up another finger. 'They must purchase a ship to go to Egypt.' Another finger. 'Hire a trusted crew both for the ship and the submarine.' A fourth finger. 'And arms to secure the treasure from theft.' He waved his hand. 'The gentlemen who have devised the plan need money to fund all this. They have thought of everything.'

Wolf nodded slowly, at a loss for words. Had his father not learned? He'd lost huge sums in other sea-faring investments. Did he not remember that any investments involving the sea were only one storm away from total loss? Besides, this scheme did not even sound real. Napoleon's treasure, indeed.

But Wolf was reluctant to burst his father's bubble with any talk of reality. The excitement of it seemed to rejuvenate his father. That seemed a good thing.

'Do you expect Hale to invest in this…proposition?' Hale would never agree, so no harm done.

His father's eyes gleamed. 'I intend to urge him to release some of *my* funds. He *must* agree. But I will not be hasty.' He puffed out his chest. 'I told the fellow I am not so easily convinced.'

Perhaps his father had a modicum of sense left.

'The gentleman is in Brighton and will demonstrate the submarine,' his father went on. 'He will need a few more investors, but not too many. This must be kept very confidential. You see, the treasure will be split. The fewer who invest the more each will receive. You must meet him, of course. As my heir, you will share in this fortune.'

Wolf doubted it. A submarine. A ship. A crew. An armed guard. Paid for by a few investors. Hale would undoubtedly be wise enough to avoid the foolhardy scheme. Wolf's family's finances would be safe.

'We'll see,' he said.

That was enough to please his father apparently.

His father returned to perusing the newspaper but lowered it again. 'Oh. Did you hear? Lord Ruskin's watch fob went missing. He's told everyone it was stolen at the Assembly.'

Wolf's anxiety flared. 'Stolen?'

His father laughed. 'Likely he dropped it somewhere. Or pawned it. Can't trust a word that man says.'

This time Ruskin was likely telling the truth, though.

Wolf took another sip of tea. His anger flared. But he did not know if he was angry at Fleur for stealing or at Ruskin. What if Ruskin accused her?

Did Wolf want Fleur ruined or safe?

That evening the Master of Ceremonies hosted a card party and most of those who had attended the Assembly the night before now gathered at tables to play cards. The ballroom of the Castle Inn was now set up with tables covered in green baize, like one huge casino. Juliana stood with Kitty a short distance from the doorway.

Kitty was determined Juliana should be Wolfdon's partner in whist, the card game for two couples that most would be playing this night.

'Think of it,' she'd said to Juliana. 'He is young and handsome. And, although he is not impressively rich, he does stand to inherit a nice property and a title, even if it is only a baronetcy.'

Juliana certainly did not share Kitty's illusion that Wolf would ever court her. She could think no further than how it would be to sit across from him after the previous night's kiss. And his very accurate suspicions. Better to have any other partner.

As she took in the green baize-covered tables, the hum of the players' conversation, the shuffle of the cards, her heart beat faster. She would so welcome an exhilarating game of cards. The life of a *ton* lady, the life she'd been leading for more than a month, could be unceasingly boring, with its bracing walks, morning calls and visits to the Circulating Library.

She pressed a hand to her chest. The previous evening had not been boring, though. Wolf had accused her of theft. Then he'd kissed her.

What was she to do about him? In this game he certainly held all the cards. She'd spent her life buffeted by the whims of men in her life. Her father, certainly. His partner Turstin, obviously. She had no intention of ever allowing any man to do so again, but here she was.

Was his kiss of the night before merely that of a man taking advantage of a woman alone, like Lord Ruskin had attempted? Was Wolf just more charming about it than Ruskin? Or would this be his means of blackmail, making love to her, seeking his pleasure from her?

No. No. If so, why did he allow her to decide whether or not to kiss him? Was he simply being more clever than she was, playing upon *her* attraction to him?

She must not allow him to win this hand, no matter what.

'Oh, here they are!' Kitty whispered, nearly as loudly as if she'd shouted.

'Sir John Wolfdon. Lady Wolfdon. Mr Marcus Wolfdon,' the doorman announced.

Wolf walked in, accompanied by his parents.

Juliana's eyes riveted on Wolf, entering the room with such masculine self-assurance that he cast other men in the shade. As the night before, his dress was impeccable, though formal wear was not required this night. He wore gleaming black boots and thigh-hugging pantaloons instead of thigh-hugging breeches. Other men wore much the same attire, but none wore them quite like Wolf.

He spoke to his parents, looking stern, before they parted from him, each going their separate ways.

Kitty manoeuvred Juliana into position, so Wolf could not help but encounter them first.

'Good evening, Lady Ashcourt. You look lovely as always.' Wolf bowed. 'Miss Walsh.'

Juliana curtsied, her cheeks flaming in his presence.

'It is pleasant to see you again, Wolf dear,' said Kitty. 'Is it not, Juliana?'

Juliana darted a glance to him. 'Pleasant.'

Kitty soldiered on. 'Do you play tonight, Wolf?' She laughed at herself. 'Of course you do. It is a card party. Juliana needs a partner, do you not, Juliana? She is quite partnerless at the moment. Is partnerless a word? I may have invented it.'

Wolf did not look pleased. Juliana remembered he did not play cards at the Paris casino. 'I am not at liberty to play.' He did not explain further.

Kitty's face fell.

'If you will excuse me?' He bowed and walked away.

But Lord Seabane approached. 'Would you care to partner me, Miss Walsh?'

Kitty rallied.

'I would be delighted,' Juliana replied, although she still felt the sting of Wolf's rejection. What was that about?

'We can make up a table. I'll get Felix.' Kitty ran off.

Lord Seabane made polite conversation, but Juliana only half listened until Kitty returned on Ashcourt's arm. Seabane led them through the maze of tables until they found an empty one. He pulled out the chair for Juliana. When he sat across from her, she forced herself to lift her gaze and smile politely at him as he shuffled the cards and continued to converse pleasantly. He seemed like such a gentle and gentlemanly man Juliana felt a pang of guilt for stealing from him.

He was terribly wealthy, of course, and could not possibly miss the money in his purse. How much had that theft hurt him, then?

Still, Juliana felt ashamed.

It was all Wolf's fault. If he'd not threatened her, she would not have had to steal again. Or lie.

Seabane dealt and play commenced. Surprisingly the man was also a good card partner, skilled, daring and possessing a good memory for cards. Felix and Kitty, however, were no challenge at all. They cared more for conversation than for who won the next trick.

As Felix dealt the next hand Juliana caught Wolf staring at her from across the room, a frown on his face.

Was he watching to see if she would somehow pick Seabane's pocket again while playing cards? Or did he think she would be depraved enough to cheat at this society card game? Her fingers shook. He was so dangerous to her. How could she convince him that she deserved his protection, not his contempt?

Even though she *did* deserve his contempt. She stole. She lied. She masqueraded as someone she was not.

And yet he had kissed her.

Or *she* had kissed *him*. Why had she done such a thing?

By the time the supper break came, she and Seabane had ceded only one game to Kitty and Ashcourt and only because Ashcourt and Kitty were dealt hands with which any fool could win. Seabane insisted Juliana keep all their winnings, a generosity that did not help ease her guilt for stealing from him.

On the other hand, she could add the trifling sum to the funds she might need to flee should Wolf betray her.

Seabane dutifully escorted her into supper and engaged in more of Felix's and Kitty's conversation while Juliana continued to feel Wolf's eyes on her.

A few moments later, though, Seabane excused himself. 'I must see to my daughter.'

After he left, Kitty leaned over to her. 'Be cheered, Juliana,' she said. 'Seabane seems smitten and Wolf is still a possibility. Wolf had to keep his father from incurring more gambling debts. I'm certain that is why he did not agree to be your partner.'

Juliana was certain Wolf did not partner her because he thought he might better catch her in another theft by watching from some distance.

Kitty went on. 'But if Wolf does not come up to snuff, Lord Seabane seems interested. Now he is wealthy, if not young. He is well looking enough for a man his age, though, do you not think?'

'He seems a nice man,' Juliana responded, but her gaze followed Wolf.

He walked out of the room.

Soon after, the Master of Ceremonies announced the card play would continue. Kitty looked around. 'Where is Wolf? Perhaps he will partner you now.'

'I saw him leave,' Juliana said.

Kitty's face fell with disappointment. 'Oh, dear. And Seabane has seated himself with his daughter already, I saw. What shall we do?'

Juliana smiled. 'You must play cards with your husband. Do find other partners. I need to refresh myself, but I will find a table to join, I assure you.'

Kitty looked at Ashcourt before turning back to Juliana. 'Are you certain?'

Juliana smiled. 'Very certain. I shall not need you. I promise.'

Juliana made her way to the retiring room, the room set up with ladies' chamber pots and mirrors and maids waiting with pins, needle and thread to repair torn gowns. She pretended to fuss with her hair, feeling too unsettled and restless to hurry back to the card play even if she missed her chance to join a table.

What was she doing? Hiding from Wolfdon, she realised. Avoiding his eyes watching her. But she needed every penny she could win at cards. To escape.

Juliana straightened her spine, gave the girl a penny and strode out the door.

Let him watch her all he liked, she would not make another misstep. He'd see only the once downtrodden cousin of Lady Ashcourt. She'd somehow convince him she deserved to join her rightful place in society.

Even if that was her biggest masquerade.

If only she could pay Wolf back. That would ensure her safety from him, would it not? But it would take countless card games at these stakes to earn enough and she had no other way to earn money.

No other honest way.

Maybe a partial payment would secure his silence.

How much time would the amount in Seabane's purse buy her? Perhaps she'd offer it to Wolf.

She shook her head. Better she saved that money in case she must flee. One must plan for escape, her father always said, although he'd not escaped the guillotine.

She would play cards and win what she could.

But she paused by the veranda, letting the sea breeze cool her for a moment, the same veranda where Wolf had kissed her.

Wolf stepped in, nearly colliding with her.

'You gave me such a start,' she murmured, placing a hand on her neck. Her body flared in response to his closeness.

'Forgive me.' He took her hand and pulled her out on to the veranda. His voice was soft and as seductive as that night in Paris. 'I needed air.'

She recognised her words from the night before. Was he mocking her? Or had he felt the flames ignite as she had?

'In this cold?' She smiled, repeating what he had said back to her.

He smiled in return. 'It was close inside.'

Perhaps he was jesting with her. It made her giddy with happiness.

'Has the card playing already commenced?' She'd needed to speak lest she do something even more insane, like fling herself into his arms.

He glanced away for a moment, pausing before responding, 'I believe so.'

She ought to be disappointed. She ought to be playing. Winning. But she felt only awareness of him. No danger. No threat.

He placed his hand on her arm. 'Come walk with me.' His eyes turned dark and intense. 'We will fetch your shawl.'

She hesitated only a moment before nodding, wondering if Ashcourt or Kitty or anyone else would notice her absence. Wondering why he did not feel like her enemy right now.

A few minutes later they were heading towards the sea wall. The clock had long struck eleven p.m. Clear skies and a bright full moon gave light enough for a stroll. It would be lovely to gaze upon the sea at this time of day, to listen to its waves beat rhythmically against the shore, to watch the waning light flicker in the water.

She used to listen to the waves from her little childhood cot when her mother had been alive, and they'd lived in a tiny house on the isle of Jersey. Her father had bitterly lamented to her mother that the house was not fine enough for them, but he'd managed to find enough money for Juliana to be sent to school and for her mother to have a housemaid and a cook. It was the best she'd ever lived.

Until Kitty and Felix took her in, believing her ruse.

'Shall we go down to the water?' Wolf asked when they reached the wall.

'Oh, yes.'

Wolf held Juliana's hand as they carefully descended the stone stairway, damp in the evening air.

Why the devil had he brought her here? He'd meant only to catch her alone, to confront her again, which he could have easily done on the veranda. After hearing about Ruskin's missing fob, Wolf was convinced that she'd stolen it and had stolen Seabane's purse as he'd thought.

Seeing her, though, being close to her, made him think only of their kiss—and of their night in Paris. She was ethereal in a pale blue gown that seemed to float around her like a cloud. Before he spied her, he'd planned to play cards with her so he could watch her, but, near her, he feared he'd only succumb to her allure. He'd withdrawn to a safe distance.

His idea the night air would cool his ardour and keep his head clear was mistaken. Walking to the water's edge, side by side with her like they'd done in Paris, was enough to undo him. He wanted so desperately to believe her, to trust her, to see her as good.

He glanced at her. The expression of wonder on her face made his spirits rise. The sky was a velvet black dotted with diamonds. The sea was black and grey and silver where the moonlight shone down. Occasional whitecaps looked like tiny heads peeking up as gentle waves licked the shore. Wolf was glad he shared the sight with her.

He closed his eyes and forced himself to speak before all rational thought escaped his mind.

'I must ask you something, Fleur.' His voice seemed to rumble in his chest. He wasn't certain he'd spoken loud enough to be heard over the waves.

She turned to him, the expression of wonder still on her face. 'Ask me what?'

He knew he would break this spell. 'Are you planning another theft of Seabane or are you intending to trap him?'

Her eyes flashed. 'Trap him?'

'Into matrimony.' He turned and glared at her. 'You never answered me last night, Fleur. Is that your plan? Is Seabane the target?'

She pulled away. 'You brought me out here to ask me about Lord Seabane?'

Without another word, she spun away and hurried towards the stairs.

'Wait!' Wolf ran after her, easily catching up to her. He grabbed her arm and twisted her around to face him.

'Unhand me!' She tried to wrench herself from his grasp, but he tightened his grip. Her eyes glistened with

tears of rage. 'What do you threaten, Wolf? To tell Seabane about me? And any other man who dares show an
interest in me? That will stop me, will it not?' She took a
breath. 'Well, do it, Wolf. Do it. Take away any chance I
might have to live respectably. I have been betrayed before and I survived. I will survive you.'

He released her, angry at himself for doing what he
intended to do. Confront her. What did it matter to him
if she stole from Seabane or married him?

Though the prospect of her marrying him did somehow matter a great deal.

She dashed to the steps, and he took pursuit.

He reached the bottom of the stairs as she scrambled
up them. To his horror, she skidded on the slick surface
and lost her balance, crying out in alarm.

Thank God he caught her as she fell. He put his arms
around her and broke her fall with his body, saving her
from pitching down to the hard surface below.

Still holding her, he staggered to the bottom of the
stairs and leaned against the sea wall. He felt her chest
heaving against his.

He turned her around and cupped her face, making her
look into his eyes. 'I did not bring you here to threaten
you.'

No. He'd brought her here because he'd wanted to be
alone with her, to hold her as he was holding her now.
He knew that now.

Her breath came fast as he looked into her eyes and
his desire for her grew into intense need.

'Fleur,' he whispered.

He could take her now, willing or not. He had the power
to physically overpower her, but, more so, the power over
her reputation, her life. But he could never use his power

that way. What sort of man would he be if he forced her to pleasure him? She resorted to crime to survive. He'd be resorting to force simply for physical release.

Wolf loosened the pressure of his fingers so that his touch was as light as a butterfly's.

He waited, as he had waited the night before, as he had waited in Paris, waited to see if she wanted this, too.

Her gaze caught his, and, after a moment, she wrapped her arms around his neck and pulled him down to her lips.

'Fleur,' he breathed as his lips moved hungrily over hers.

He felt aflame, wanting his hands on her bare flesh, wanting more, wanting to feel himself inside her. With the stone wall at his back, he stroked her arms, her neck, her breasts. She pressed herself against his loins. He ached with need.

They were in the shelter of the wall. No one could see them. No one else walked the beach. Darkness covered them like a blanket.

'Make love to me, Wolf,' she murmured. 'Here. Now.'

He held her shoulders, still unsure if she thought she must do this to please him.

'I do not require this, Fleur,' he managed to say. 'You are free to refuse.'

'No. No,' she cried, unfastening the fall of his pantaloons and running her hand against his erection. 'I want this too, Wolf.'

He moved to crush his lips against hers, but again stopped himself. 'Do you have what you need to prevent—prevent—?'

'Yes!' She closed the distance between them and he tasted her lips at last. Wolf lost himself in her, as he had done in Paris. Nothing existed but her and the pleasure he knew was to come.

She pulled up her skirts.

This was madness, but a madness Wolf had no wish to control.

He lifted her off the ground and entered her with one thrust. Because she had no way to move, he set the rhythm between them. It was up to him to create the delight.

Their lovemaking was frantic and furtive, a desperate excitement, like a tidal wave they'd unleashed and could not hold back. Wolf felt as wild as a storm at sea. He heard her moan as his strong arms held her, moved her, brought her closer to her release.

And his.

He drove them faster, harder, until he thought he could hold back no longer, but he wanted her release, wanted her to feel the ecstasy the lovemaking promised.

With one final thrust he could hold back no longer, but her cry of pleasure joined his as he spilled his seed, pulsing inside her. They writhed together, rocked together joined as one, as eternal as the sea.

When the sensation ceased, it was like being spilled on to the shore, listless as seaweed.

'Ah, Fleur,' he groaned as he slowly slipped out of her, slowly set her down on solid earth again.

Still trembling, Juliana felt the hard pebbles beneath her feet. The sound of the waves filled her ears. The scent of brine reached her nostrils. She stared at the black stone of the sea wall, suddenly unable to look at him.

Realisation of precisely how madly, how wantonly she'd behaved struck her along with the return of sight, sound and smell.

She'd wanted this, wanted him, wanted that moment in Paris to return. Why? Why not spurn him as she had so many other men? He could so easily destroy her, try to force her to make love to him in return for his silence. She'd have spurned him then, for sure, if he had tried that.

But he gave her the choice. That was what undid her. He gave *her* the choice. What man did that?

'Madness…' he murmured, echoing her thoughts.

She squeezed her eyes shut until feeling his fingers lifting her chin. 'Have I hurt you?' he asked her.

She shook her head.

'I cannot believe—' He broke off this thought and blew out a breath. 'We must put ourselves to rights. I need to return you.'

She stepped away from him to straighten her skirt. He fastened his pantaloons.

'I am wrinkled,' she said in dismay.

She knew how to prevent the most difficult consequences of this act, but she had no idea how to smooth her wrinkled skirt so she could return to the card party looking like a respectable lady.

He stared down at her skirt, hands on his hips, forehead creased in thought. 'I'll walk you to your lodgings,' he finally said. 'Then I'll convey word to Lord and Lady Ashcourt that you had the headache and I escorted you home.' He lifted his head to look into her eyes. 'Will that do?'

She nodded.

'Then we'd best return.'

Before he made a move to walk her to her door, he took her in his arms again, seizing one more kiss, his mouth demanding and tender all at once.

The tenderness brought tears to her eyes.

What was she to think? The man who was her enemy was so very kind to her.

Was that illusion?

At the moment, she was happy to believe in him, the idea of him. At the moment she felt joy.

Chapter Seven

The next morning Wolf felt the need to ride, to be out of doors, to feel his horse beneath him and the wind in his face. He felt the need so urgently he passed up breakfast. No food could relieve the hunger that making love to Juliana the night before had aroused.

Or the distress.

As he rode along the sea road, he thought about how wrong it was of him to compromise her so. Of course, she had eagerly agreed, but he ought to have at least pretended she had virtue to protect.

He risked her reputation. And her desire to find some wealthy aristocrat to marry. Why did that bother him so? A respectable marriage would save her from ever needing to return to the life she'd led in Paris. He was intent on returning to that city as soon as possible. He would be leaving her behind.

Wolf gave the horse his head, driving that thought away, all thought away. The run satisfied both him and the horse, both breathing hard when he slowed the pace. He felt almost calm by the time he re-entered the town, sedately passing the Regent's Marine Pavilion, which was being transformed into something resembling an Eastern palace.

* * *

The sun was high in the sky when he returned to his rooms. His parents were both out, separately, he suspected. Where would they go together? He brushed the dust and dirt from his clothes, changed his shirt, polished his boots and had a quick bite to eat.

He ventured out again, returning to the Steine. Perhaps he would wander over to the library. Perhaps he would find Juliana there again.

Juliana. He must think of her as Juliana, not Fleur, although both aroused a passion he seemed powerless to resist.

She was more than the woman who'd betrayed his trust. After all, she'd been alone in Paris, penniless, friendless. He could almost forgive her theft of his money.

Almost. Because she ought to have confided in him then. He would have helped her get to England, to her cousin, to a place she could feel secure and cared for.

Still, it had taken courage to survive alone in Paris. It was that courage and vulnerability that attracted him in Paris and attracted him still.

As long as they were discreet, was there any reason for them not to indulge in this passion they shared? They might never find such again, especially since they must part. He, to return to Paris, she, to—to marry. What harm could it do to enjoy what existed between them while they were at liberty to do so?

Wolf entered the Circulating Library, although it was not Juliana he encountered, but Lord Ashcourt standing in a corner with a man Wolf did not know.

Ashcourt waved him over and clapped him on the shoulder. 'Wolf, I am delighted to see you. Let me present this gentleman to you.'

The gentleman standing with Ashcourt was perhaps a few years older than Wolf, a dark-haired man with the kind of polished good looks that Wolf instantly found suspicious.

'May I present Monsieur Gravier?' Ashcourt turned to the man. 'This is Mr Wolfdon, a great friend of my son's and very dear to our whole family.'

Gravier registered surprise. 'Sir John's son? Ah, yes, you must be. The resemblance.' He twirled his hand in front of his face.

Ashcourt gave Wolf a significant look. 'Your father introduced us. Gravier had spoken to him about an *investment*.' Ashcourt wiggled his eyebrows at the word.

This was the man with the sunken treasure? His father had neglected to mention the man was French.

'Gravier.' Wolf offered his hand.

The Frenchman looked him in the eye, his smile revealing even, white teeth. 'Monsieur Wolfdon, I am honoured.' His handshake was firm, his accent mild.

Ashcourt broke in. 'Gravier has filled me in on this scheme of his. Very intriguing.'

Not Ashcourt as well? Surely Ashcourt would see the folly in this unbelievable enterprise.

At that moment Lady Ashcourt approached.

Gravier took her hand and kissed the air above it. 'Lady Ashcourt, you look *magnifique*.'

Lady Ashcourt turned red and tittered in response. Turning away, she noticed Wolf. 'Wolf! What a surprise to see you, dear.'

'I hope a good surprise, my lady,' he said.

She touched his arm. 'I must thank you for seeing my cousin home last night. It was so good of you.'

He hoped his face did not flush like hers had done,

remembering why he'd escorted her. 'Nonsense. I was honoured to be of service. I hope she is recovered?'

Lady Ashcourt's brows knitted. 'She is resting today but assures me she is merely fatigued.'

Fatigued or disturbed? Because of him?

'Charlotte is with us here,' Lady Ashcourt went on. 'She will wish to see you, I am certain.'

'Charlotte?' interjected Gravier, who had not been a part of the conversation.

'Our daughter,' Lady Ashcourt explained.

With the attention back on him Gravier engaged Lord and Lady Ashcourt in charming conversation. Wolf observed him carefully. His manners were elegant but not encroaching. He seemed at ease but at the same time gave deference to Ashcourt. He flattered Lady Ashcourt but not enough to spark her husband's jealousy. There was no mention of the investment. Crafty of him not to be pushy.

Charlotte approached, unnoticed by the others.

She broke into a smile when seeing Wolf and skipped towards him. 'Wolf! Mama and Papa told me you were in Brighton!'

He took both her hands in his and smiled down at her. 'Good God, Lottie!' He and Harris always called her Lottie. 'Is this really you? When did you grow up?'

He remembered a skinny girl, all arms and legs, insisting on following her brother and Wolf wherever they wanted to go. This young woman was breathtaking.

And he was not the only one who noticed. Wolf watched Gravier take in Charlotte's flawless pale complexion, her glossy dark curls, her slightly tinted lips, her now womanly figure. Gravier's colour rose. The man straightened his spine and breathed more rapidly. His eyes glowed, and Wolf wanted to plant him a facer.

'Ah, Gravier,' Ashcourt said. 'Let me present you to my daughter Charlotte.'

Gravier found his tongue. 'Lady Charlotte, I am charmed.' He took Charlotte's hand in his and blew a kiss over it, holding it a second too long. Neither Lord nor Lady Ashcourt seemed to notice.

Charlotte's cheeks turned pink and her long dark eye-lashes fluttered.

Lady Ashcourt smiled. 'Forgive us, gentlemen, but my daughter and I must be off to the modiste.' She turned to the girl—now young woman. 'Come, Charlotte.'

Good, Wolf thought. Keep your daughter away from this Frenchman.

Charlotte took Wolf's hands again. 'You must call upon us, Wolf.'

He must. He had a book to give her. 'I will soon, I promise. Perhaps later today.'

She turned to Gravier. 'A pleasure to meet you, *monsieur.*'

Seemingly struck dumb again, Gravier merely bowed. But he watched her depart until she was out of sight.

He then seemed to collect himself and again turned his charm on Ashcourt and Wolf. 'If you gentlemen have a moment and we can find somewhere to be private, I will let you know what progress we have made on our preparations.'

Ashcourt turned to Wolf. 'Is there not a public room at the Old Ship Hotel? Let us go there.'

They left the Circulating Library and Gravier kept up pleasant conversation, mostly about Brighton, as they walked down Ship Street.

'I hear the Old Ship Hotel is a very fine place, Monsieur Wolfdon,' Gravier said.

Obviously Wolf's father had told the man they had rooms there. 'It is quite comfortable,' he agreed.

'Where are you staying, Gravier?' Ashcourt asked.

The man laughed in a self-effacing manner. 'Somewhere much more humble, I assure you. The Black Lion Inn.'

Wolf knew the place.

When they neared the hotel's door, Wolf's father emerged, saying a rather fond goodbye to Lady Holback and raising Wolf's ire. Did his father have to flaunt his affairs so publicly? And was he not forbidden to exert himself?

His father beamed with puffed-up pleasure at seeing them approach.

'Join us,' Gravier said. 'I am about to tell Lord Ashcourt and your son what progress we've made.'

'Come to our rooms,' his father said. 'We will be very private there.' He turned to Wolf. 'You mother is out. With one of her admirers, no doubt.'

Which liaison had been arranged first? Wolf wondered. His mother's or his father's? This sort of tit-for-tat had been customary in his childhood.

Gravier exuded admiration for the fineness of the hotel's hall, its staircases and his father's rooms.

'Pour us some port, Wolf,' his father ordered as he invited Ashcourt and Gravier to sit.

Wolf opened the cabinet and took out the decanter of port and four glasses. He served Gravier last.

Before Wolf had even seated himself, his father turned to Gravier. 'Now, tell us what progress you have made.'

Gravier cleared his throat and leaned forward in a gesture of barely contained excitement. 'The submarine is being fitted in France. It should soon be on its way here, transported by ship, along with a crew to operate it. I hope to make the demonstration very soon, very soon, indeed.'

Wolf took a sip of port. 'I am familiar with submarines. How do you expect to retrieve cargo with one?'

Without missing a beat, Gravier faced him. 'An ingenious set of tools work from within the vessel. This is the adaptation being devised right now. We have Fulton's original ship, restored into the excellent operating condition.' He leaned towards Wolf. 'I cannot stress how important it is to keep this secret. Very secret. I have trusted your father and Ashcourt and a very few other investors. If word escapes, especially about the location of the treasure, there will be countless expeditions searching for the sunken ships, and we will lose our singular chance.'

Gravier sounded passionate, intense, totally genuine, belying the fact that the whole idea was preposterous.

'I already told my son it was Egypt,' Wolf's father piped up.

'N'ai pas peur.' Gravier smiled. 'I will welcome your son's investment.'

'Too big a risk for me,' Wolf said.

Gravier's eyes crinkled at the corners. 'Ah, you are not the gambler, I see. *C'est vrai,* I am no gambler myself, but I am persuaded that this cannot fail.'

Wolf watched his father's eyes grow brighter and brighter as Gravier talked about coins of gold, silver and copper known to have been carried on the ships. He listed the items of Maltese treasure rumoured to be on board when the ships sank off the coast of Egypt, as well. To his dismay, Ashcourt seemed equally enthralled.

Wolf tried to keep his voice casual. 'What evidence

have you to prove that the ships you've found are Napoleon's ships?'

Gravier smiled and pulled coins from his pockets, placing them on the table in front of Wolf. Gold coins, French and Austrian, dating from the reign of Louis XVI, and Maltese coins as well.

'These were retrieved by divers—' Gravier said.

Or gathered from more typical land sources, Wolf thought.

'But the divers, they could not swim long enough under the water to reach the rest. They reported caskets littering the sea floor.' Gravier swept his arm in a huge arc. 'Our submarine will pick them up and carry them to the surface.'

Wolf's father was nearly giddy. He picked up the coins and ran them through his fingers. 'See? This is what I have told you, Wolf. I wrote to Hale this morning.'

Wolf did indeed see. His father was daft. Thank goodness Hale would not be.

'Impressive!' Ashcourt agreed.

It was Ashcourt Wolf most worried about. How much money could his friend's father afford to lose?

The clock struck the hour and Ashcourt rose. 'Goodness. I must get back. Kitty will be wondering where I am.'

The others rose as well.

'May I accompany you a while, Lord Ashcourt?' Gravier asked.

'Indeed!' Ashcourt responded.

'Do you attend the card party tomorrow night?' Wolf's father's question included both men. 'It will be held in this hotel.'

Another card party, Wolf thought. Not a good temptation for his father.

'Assuredly,' Ashcourt responded. 'My daughter would be desolated if we did not. Her mother and I promised her she could attend.'

Wolf watched Gravier's eyes widen with interest for a moment. 'I would be so gratified to be there. I must await the approval, you know, from the Master of Ceremonies.'

'You do not have approval?' Ashcourt's brows rose.

Wolf thought that a good thing.

Ashcourt patted Gravier's arm. 'Do not fear. We will see what we might do about that.'

Wolf inwardly shook his head in dismay. He would attend the card party, of course. Now to keep an eye on Gravier and his friend's little sister. And his father. And mother.

And Juliana.

Juliana… 'Lord Ashcourt, would it be convenient for me to accompany you and make a brief call? I would like to give Charlotte the book I purchased for her.' And to see if Juliana was still…fatigued. And if it was his fault.

Ashcourt grinned. 'Oh, I am certain Kitty and Charlotte would love to have you call. They should be back from the shops by now.'

'Give me a moment and I will fetch the book.' It was in his bedchamber.

He retrieved the book and could hardly moderate his pace as he, Ashcourt and Gravier walked out of the hotel. Gravier left them almost immediately, but Wolf was dismayed as Ashcourt effused about Gravier's scheme.

One thing Sir Charles had taught Wolf about diplomacy was to assume the other party was lying until you could prove they were telling the truth. Wolf was certain Gravier was lying, even though he seemed to have ready answers to any question.

The Ashcourts had leased a town house right off the Marine Parade accommodating even their servants, a much more expensive option than the Old Ship Hotel. The butler opened the door and took their hats and gloves.

'Are my wife and daughter at home?' Ashcourt asked.

'In my lady's bedchamber, I believe,' the butler responded.

'Excellent!' Ashcourt grinned as if he'd had the most wonderful news. 'Will you show Mr Wolfdon to the drawing room, my good man? And order tea? I will let Lady Ashcourt and Lady Charlotte know Wolfdon is here.'

'Very good, sir,' the butler responded.

Wolf followed the butler whom he remembered from his many visits to the Ashcourt's houses. 'How are you, Holmes?'

The butler almost smiled. 'Very well, sir. It is good to see you, sir.'

'And yourself,' Wolf added.

The butler opened the door to the drawing room and the first thing Wolf saw was Juliana, seated on a sofa, the doorway framing her as if she were a painting.

Juliana's heart leapt at the unexpected sight of him.

'Mr Wolfdon,' the butler announced.

She stood, holding the book she'd been reading.

'We are acquainted,' Wolf told him.

The butler bowed and left the room, closing the door behind him.

Juliana placed the book on the table beside her. 'Wolf,' she murmured.

She'd tossed and turned most of the night trying to convince herself that she must not confuse the illusion of Wolf with the more likely possibility that he would ultimately expose her masquerade and destroy her chances for a respectable life.

She was not successful. Her mind kept returning to the Wolf who gave her the choice of making love or not, the Wolf whose lovemaking was both generous and sublime. She could only see *that* Wolf standing in front of her in the drawing room.

He crossed the room to her, coming close enough to touch her. 'Are—are you unwell? Lady Ashcourt said—'

'No. No. I am in health,' she assured him. 'I simply wished for time alone.' Time to think of him, to wonder how to see him again.

But he was here!

He lifted his hand to touch her cheek. 'I missed you…'

The memory flashed of their quick, exciting, dangerous and rapturous lovemaking on the beach. Juliana fancied she saw the same reflected in his eyes.

He leaned closer, his lips almost touching hers, but she stepped back. 'Someone might see us.'

What they shared must be kept secret. Who would understand? Kitty and Felix would never understand any but the kind of devotion that was bound in marriage, not this wild, forbidden passion. Juliana did not understand it herself, but she did not wish to give it up.

Wolf stepped back, putting needed distance between them. It was a good thing because she could not think when he was so near. Still, she longed to be private with him.

His gaze caught hers. 'If only we could—'

He did not need to finish his sentence. It was as if they shared the same thought.

She closed the distance between them again, standing on tiptoe, her lips close to his ear. 'Come to me tonight,' she whispered into his ear. 'My bedchamber is in the back. You can easily climb to my window. I'll leave a candle to show you which it is. I'll place it in the window when it is safe.'

This had been her fantasy the night before when she longed to be held by him again. Could she make it real? Would he come to her?

She stepped back. 'Tell me you will come.'

His eyes reached hers again and she fancied his were filled with a like desire.

'I will come,' he said.

Chapter Eight

That night Wolf dined at the hotel with his father while his mother dined out. Throughout the meal his father threatened to go searching for his wife or to seek some entertainment for himself. Wolf held him back.

Luck had it she returned at a decent hour and after the typical row between them, his parents each finally retired to bed.

Wolf waited until he was certain they were both asleep before he quietly left his room and made his way down the stairs and out the hotel door into the crisp night air.

There were still people on the streets as Wolf walked to the Ashcourt town house. He found the alley to the back of their building and entered it, keeping track of which was the Ashcourts' house. The gate to its small yard was not secured and he slipped in. Moonlight illuminated crates and barrels stacked against the building's wall. Juliana had been correct. He could easily climb to an upper window. He merely had to wait for a candle to appear.

He'd left his topcoat at the hotel and now wrapped his arms around himself to keep the chill away. Each minute that passed ought to have convinced him to abandon this wanton plan, but time merely fuelled his desire.

Finally, he spied a light, first a soft glow, then a growing brightness with a figure behind it. A hand appeared, placing a candle on the windowsill. A moment later, Juliana's face appeared, soft in the candlelight, peering out with an expression of hopeful yearning on her lovely face.

The sight of her was as arousing as her touch. Wolf edged forward. She caught sight of him and moved the candle aside to raise the window. The climb was effortless. He quickly reached the sill, ready to hoist himself inside. Juliana, there waiting, laughed softly and kissed him, long and hard, before helping him inside.

'I feared you would not come,' she whispered.

She wore a nightdress of soft white linen, and her hair was loose, falling about her shoulders in a wealth of curls. She smiled and took his hand, pulling him towards the bed as soon as his feet hit the floor. The knowledge that she was as eager for this as he, that she had invited him, fanned his already desperate need for her.

'Are you certain we will not be discovered?' His attempt to whisper came out like a low rumble.

She put a finger to her lips. 'Shh...'

He nodded and leaned against the bed, reaching down to his boots.

'Let me remove them,' she whispered.

While she pulled off his boots, he removed his coat and unbuttoned his waistcoat. A rational part of his mind listened for noises in the hallway, someone about to burst into the room, but mostly his thoughts were anything but reasoned.

Soon he was free of all clothing, and, like the night

in Paris, she gazed at him in frank admiration. Like that night, he murmured, 'Fleur.'

Her smile was mystical as she stepped away from him and slid her nightdress over her head, tossing it aside. She gazed at him, not moving, while he feasted on the vision of her, like Venus rising from the sea. Full lush breasts, narrow waist, curving hips, flowing hair.

He reached for her and she rushed into his arms, flesh against flesh at last. His hands stroked her smooth cool skin until she grew as feverish as he. She splayed her fingers on his chest, scraping against his nipples until he groaned aloud.

'Be quiet,' she cautioned, but tortured him none the less with her stroking hands.

He drew in a breath to keep silent and lifted her on to the bed, rising over her, filling his hands with her breasts, then leaning down to take a nipple in his mouth.

She made an urgent cry, and he slid his lips to the tender skin of her ear. 'Be quiet,' he murmured.

She laughed and seized his neck, bringing his lips against hers.

All thoughts of waiting, of stretching out the pleasure, building to a fever-pitch, were lost. He entered her, thrilled that her hips rose to meet him. He'd before coupled with women who enjoyed lovemaking, but Juliana's eagerness and delight felt special.

As if she were loving *him*.

He drove into her again and again, and she met him each time, urging him onwards, faster until all he knew was the sensation of joining his body to hers and the explosion of his seed spilling into her. He pressed her to him as he convulsed inside her. Feeling her release pulsate against him nearly aroused him all over again. He clamped his jaw tight to keep from crying out.

Juliana lost that measure of control, moaning as her pleasure overtook her, sighing audibly as Wolf relaxed, his body feeling like liquid.

A knock sounded at her door.

'Juliana? Juliana? Are you all right?' It was Lady Ashcourt's voice.

Both Wolf and Juliana froze. She covered his mouth with her hand as if it had been he who made the noise.

'What, Kitty?' she mumbled in a good imitation of a sleep-roused voice.

Wolf prepared to slip to the floor out of sight if Lady Ashcourt walked in.

'You cried out like you were hurt,' she said through the door.

'Hurt?' Juliana responded.

Wolf grinned and mouthed, 'Hurt?'

Juliana gave him a playful shove and answered Lady Ashcourt. 'I must have been dreaming. I can't think of what.'

'I can,' Wolf whispered.

She covered his mouth again and he held her hand there, tickling her palm with his tongue. She squirmed. 'Is—is anything amiss with you, Kitty? It must be late.'

'No,' came her voice. 'I thought I heard a noise outside.'

'Do you need me to get up?'

Wolf slid his lips to her wrist and was making his way up her arm.

'No,' Lady Ashcourt replied. 'I think I shall go back to sleep.'

'Goodnight, Kitty.'

'Goodnight.'

Wolf listened to her footsteps recede before daring to catch Juliana's eye. They both began to laugh. Trying to keep silent, the sound was like leaking bellows. Juliana buried her face in his chest.

'I should go,' he whispered when he had control of himself again.

'No,' she begged. 'Not yet.'

She climbed on top of him and he had no choice but to cede to her wishes. She rubbed her hands over his chest and ground herself against him, making him hard once more. She taunted him, making as if she would allow him entrance to her most secret place, but moving away again. His breath came fast and it was all he could do to keep the delight and frustration from becoming vocal. He loved her like this—erotic and playful—and knew he would never be content unless he could be with her like this again.

He played along with her, pretending to duel with her over the moment of penetration. Finally, he was there, and he pushed her on to him, more forcefully than he'd intended.

She gasped and panted, and he felt the ripple of her release inside her, intoxicating him more.

She leaned down to his ear, her moist lips touching his skin. 'Don't stop.'

He had no intention of stopping—indeed, doubted if anything could make him stop. No longer playful now, they moved together like wild creatures and again the exquisite torture built, stronger and stronger until he thought he would explode like canister from a cannon.

He did explode inside her, her pleasure coming at the

same moment, heightening the feeling of connection, of completing each other.

When they collapsed in satiated bliss, he held her against him. She felt warm and soft, and the thought of leaving her for his own empty bed seemed a cruelty.

'Is there anything I can do to help you care for yourself?' The risk in this act, after all, fell exclusively to her, though he took his part in it seriously.

She shook her head. 'I'll manage.'

They were quiet again until he whispered, 'A part of me warns that we ought not to be doing this, Fleur, but, I confess, I do not wish this to be the last time.'

She tensed. 'There is no harm in it, is there?'

He released a deep breath. 'I am not so certain of no harm.' The carnal pleasure was only part of it. Each moment he spent with her saw his heart more engaged. It would be excruciating to leave her. Would he cause her an equal pain?

She murmured against his chest, 'You know what I am, Wolf. I have never sold my favours, but you know I am not without experience. I chose to make love with you.'

He had not been referring to her experience, but suddenly jealousy surged inside him. Other men had touched her, had known her as he did.

He frowned. 'So tell me of these men who provided you with experience, Fleur.'

She did not answer right away. 'There were not so many, Wolf. Just one man, really.'

Somehow that information heightened rather than eased his jealousy. 'Tell me of him, then.'

She sat up and looked at him. 'Are you then going to tell me of the women you have been with?'

He grinned. 'I doubt we have that much time.'

Her smile seemed to have escaped unwillingly. 'Then tell me of your first time and I will tell you of mine.'

He paused, uncertain now that he could bear hearing of this man who'd possessed her the first time. 'Very well,' he finally agreed. 'But mine is a typical tale.'

She caressed his cheek. 'Tell it.'

He rolled over on his back. 'I was fifteen and travelling home for Christmas. Harris was with me—Lord Ashcourt's son. We spent a night in an inn and one of the tavern girls took a fancy to me.' He turned and grinned at her. 'Suffice to say, Harris was quite envious. I was the first of us.' He reached over and tweaked her chin. 'Shall I provide you with the details? I believe I remember every second of the experience.'

She grasped his hand. 'Spare me that.'

His smile fled. 'Your turn, Fleur.'

She paused, glancing away before speaking. 'I knew him my whole life.' Her voice was so low he had to strain to hear her. 'He was the son of a vicomte, only after the Revolution that meant nothing any more. His parents and his brother and sister went to the guillotine, but he escaped and fell into the company of my father's partner. They all fled to Naples, where I was born, and when the French came, we all ran to Jersey. When my mother died, I was left with my father, his partner and Lyon. That was his name. Lyon.'

He interrupted her. 'You had to flee Naples? How old were you?'

'Eight, then my mother died three years later. Her health was not good. Lyon was older than me. One day, when I was about seventeen, he looked at me…differently. It was not long after that I shared his bed.'

She related the story with little emotion, but Wolf felt

enough for them both. He ached with sadness for all she had endured and burned with jealousy at this Lyon fellow.

'So, what happened to *Lyon*?' He almost spat out the name and almost spoke too loudly, as well.

'Oh, he found some other girl, as men do. I tried being with other men. Only two, really, and very briefly for each of them. Until you in Paris, that is. And now.'

'Wait.' He searched her face. 'Was your father alive when this Lyon seduced you? I thought he died a good ten years before.'

She blinked rapidly. 'Oh. No. He died when Napoleon was exiled.'

He regarded her suspiciously. 'I am certain Harris told me he died much earlier than that.'

She laughed and waved a hand. 'I forgot. He made his family think he died. Had proof fabricated somehow. He really did despise them.'

'So, what year did he die?' If he was still alive when his brother died, he would have inherited the barony instead of Lady Ashcourt. And with his death, the title would go to Juliana.

Had she thought of that?

She glanced away, her expression sombre. '1814.'

Wolf released a relieved breath. This was one scheme he did not have to worry over.

He turned back to his original concern. 'So, your father was alive when this Lyon seduced you. And he did nothing?'

Her brow wrinkled. 'I do not understand.'

'Did he not protect you from this scoundrel?'

'Protect me?' She still looked puzzled. 'Protection was not necessary. I was quite willing. My father did send me to a woman who could teach me…how to take care of myself.'

'Your father sent you?' His voice rose.

'Shh!' she cautioned. She glanced away and then back to him. 'This was not the life of a *ton* lady, Wolf. I did not grow up in such an atmosphere.'

'But your father did,' he protested.

She averted her gaze and her eyelashes fluttered. 'My father—my father abandoned the ways of a gentleman.'

He rolled on to his back again and stared at the ceiling. She had grown up with standards so different from the people with whom she now surrounded herself.

He rose on one elbow. 'You have the manners of a lady. How did you contrive that?'

She gave a ghost of a smile. 'My father was able to send me to a fine school in Jersey. I learned there.' She knelt and looked down on him, her long auburn hair caressing his skin. 'Do you regret this now, Wolf? After what I have told you of me?'

He twirled a lock of her hair in his fingers. 'Never,' he murmured to her. 'Though I am consumed with jealousy towards this Lyon.'

She looked relieved and leaned down to kiss him. 'Do not waste such emotion on him,' she said against his lips. 'He is gone, and you are here. I am happy you are here.'

He captured her lips again, tasting her sweetness.

She made an urgent sound and deepened the kiss, sliding her hand down to that male part of him, stroking and caressing and squeezing until he hardened once more.

This time he was determined to set a languid pace, to draw out the experience and show her what pleasure he could give her. More pleasure than the dastardly Lyon, he vowed.

* * *

Never before had Juliana experienced such lovemaking. Wolf made her spirits soar.

She had once fancied herself in love with Lyon, but it had been a fleeting matter. A wounding of her pride more than anything else when he found another to fancy. She was reluctant to call herself in love with Wolf, either, for who knew how long it would last? She was the dalliance of the moment for him, a man destined for a diplomatic career, a man returning to Paris, a city to which she would never return. She at least had this moment, and she was determined to enjoy every bit of it.

He faced her, smiling into her eyes, connecting to her, she fancied, soul to soul. She wanted to sing, to dance, to cry out in joy in a way that would certainly rouse the household, if not all of Brighton west of the Steine.

This was the Wolf of her fantasies, all those lonely nights in Paris. Only he was real.

His smile turned regretful. 'I must go, Fleur, before the dawn gives me away.'

She clung to him. 'I do not wish you to leave me.'

He kissed her. 'I must go, but perhaps you wish me to return tonight?'

'I do.' She wrapped her arms around his neck, tasting him as if this would be her last time. 'You must return.'

'Then I will.' His glance was filled with warmth as well as passion. She drew her finger over his lips.

'Do not tempt me, Fleur.' He eased himself away from her touch and climbed off the bed, handing her the nightdress she'd left on the floor.

Juliana slipped it over her head and walked over to a chest in the corner of the room. She had slit the cloth lining inside the chest at the seam, creating a small hiding place for Lord Seabane's money and Lord Ruskin's watch fob, a simple gold chain.

Wolfdon pulled on his boots, watching her as she walked over to him.

She put the pouch in his hand.

He looked up at her, puzzled. 'What is this?'

She closed his hand over it. 'Part of the money I owe you.'

He scowled. 'This is Lord Seabane's money, isn't it?'

'N—no,' she responded. 'Of course it is not.'

His eyes flashed. 'You are lying, Fleur.'

She did not know how to do anything but lie. 'No. It is money I saved—'

'In two days? Do not play me for a fool, Fleur.' He spat out the sobriquet. 'You tried to make me believe I did not see you take it from Seabane, but now I know what I saw.' He threw the purse back to her. 'You stole Ruskin's watch fob, too, did you not?'

'No!' She made herself sound indignant. 'If I lied, it was about how much money I saved. I want to pay you back. This is part of it.'

'You are lying again,' he growled.

Her heart leapt into her throat, her lying throat. 'I am not lying. Just take it. I want you to have it.' She held it out to him, her hand shaking.

'I do not want this money, Fleur.' His tone was firm. 'Return it to Seabane.'

Her knees trembled. She'd badly erred in offering him the money. It was a terrible misstep. 'But I owe you—' she said weakly.

He raised a protesting hand. 'This is not Paris. You do not need to steal.'

She felt suddenly ashamed and trapped in the emotion with no way out. 'I did not steal—'

He merely shook his head and opened the sash. Without another word, he climbed out.

Juliana gasped for breath, her chest constricting painfully. After he disappeared, she ran to the window and peered out, catching sight of him dropping to the ground and hurrying into the shadows. She turned away and wrapped her arms around herself, breathing hard. She'd ruined the near perfect time they'd spent together.

But she could not dwell on that. Or on feeling ashamed of stealing and lying. Wolf was no longer the man of her fantasies.

He was her enemy again.

Chapter Nine

Wolf rose much later in the morning than was his custom. Much later. So late his parents were already out, hopefully not getting into any mischief, and all traces of breakfast in their dining room had been removed. He made himself some tea and walked out into the clear, brisk day.

High above him seagulls soared, as if dancing on the wind. Many other people promenaded on the Steine, enjoying the beautiful day. His mood matched none of this but would have been better suited to grey clouds and rain, or, more apt, a tempest.

He had no destination, no activity to occupy his restless, unsettled mind.

A street vendor cried, 'Muffins! Hot muffins!'

Wolf walked over to him and purchased one. He stood at the sea wall and watched the waves roll on to the beach as he ate. Several people strolled there or stood at the water's edge. Juliana's unmistakable figure was not among them, though. He did spy his mother on the arm of Lord Lymond. No doubt his father was somewhere with Lady Holback.

He turned his back on them and turned his mind back to Juliana instead.

He'd thought long and hard about her stealing Seabane's purse. Only two days ago Wolf had threatened to expose her. Perhaps he had driven her back to thieving, making her feel she must repay him or he'd expose her? In that first encounter, mere days ago, he had threatened her, but matters had changed, had they not? If only he could convince her to stop lying to him.

Why could she not simply tell him the truth? It was the lying that gave him the nagging fear that she was indeed merely a thief, plotting to steal from the Ashcourts. Was she waiting for an opportunity to make off with Lady Ashcourt's jewels? Or was there some other scheme she was brewing?

He shook his head.

No. He wanted to believe her to be what she appeared to be, the long-lost cousin forced to live a scandalous life in order to survive, now terrified that he threatened her new-found safety.

It was clear he needed to see her again. To sort this out. But how? Calling upon her might raise too many questions in the Ashcourts' minds. Or make them think he was courting her.

He must wait for the card party tonight. Find an opportunity to see her alone. He'd certainly contrived to see her alone at other entertainments.

In the meantime, he had a whole day to endure before then, and he could not bear to return to the hotel. What would occupy him there?

He detoured to the shops.

As he passed the doorway of the confectioner's shop, he almost collided with Lord Ashcourt and Gravier.

'Ah, Wolf.' Ashcourt's face lit with pleasure. 'Out and about, I see.'

'Good morning, sir,' Wolf returned the greeting with equal pleasure before turning to Ashcourt's companion. 'Gravier.'

'It is a morning *fantasique*, is it not?' Gravier responded jovially. 'We are here for the *pâtisseries*. You will appreciate them, I am certain. They rival any you can find in Paris.'

'Do they indeed,' Wolf responded without enthusiasm.

Lord Ashcourt piped up. 'We've just arranged for Gravier to receive invitations. I am happy to report he will be able attend the card party tonight. Everyone of consequence will be there.'

'I am so very grateful to you.' Gravier smiled. He turned to Wolf. 'Do you attend as well, *monsieur*?'

'I do,' Wolf responded.

'Then we shall see you there.' Gravier's smooth smile irritated Wolf.

Lady Ashcourt and Charlotte emerged from the shop and joined them. Gravier's smile changed to something almost wistful.

'Wolf!' Lady Ashcourt exclaimed. 'How lovely to see you!'

Wolf shook her hand. 'The pleasure is mine.' His gaze flitted to the doorway of the shop. Was Juliana there as well? 'How are you this day, my lady?'

Lady Ashcourt fluttered her lashes. 'Oh, splendid.' She peered at him. 'We shall see you at the card party tonight, will we not? I do hope you will play this time.'

Wolf could play. If he partnered Juliana he could keep an eye on her, stop her from any further stealing.

'I will be there and perhaps I will sit down at a table. Might as well play cards at a card party, you might say.'

To his disappointment, Juliana did not emerge from the confectioner's shop.

Charlotte turned on a smile to Gravier before facing Wolf. 'Papa says I may attend. So I will play cards, too, Wolf.'

'Splendid, Lottie,' he replied.

Gravier looked at Charlotte as though she was the confectioner's best creation. Wolf pressed his lips together.

Ashcourt pulled out his timepiece. 'We should go, my love. We'll be late.'

Lady Ashcourt took his arm.

Gravier spoke up. 'I must be on my way as well. May I accompany you? At least part of the way?'

'Indeed you may,' Ashcourt responded.

He and Lady Ashcourt led the way and did not notice that Charlotte flushed with pleasure as Gravier offered his arm to her.

Wolf watched them walk away, Charlotte clutching Gravier's arm.

'Damned scoundrel,' he muttered.

Guilt nagged at him for not leaving with them and escorting Charlotte himself. If he had, perhaps they would lead him to Juliana.

He walked on, trying to distract himself with displays in the shops. Many London shopkeepers brought their wares to Brighton during the busy summer season, only to disappear again when the fashionable—and moneyed—people departed. There were plenty of wares to look at. Napoleon had not been far off when he'd described England as a nation of shopkeepers.

He ambled by a flower stall where the blooms were arranged in colourful bouquets, easy to purchase for some pretty lady. He touched the petals of a pale pink flower, finding it as soft as Juliana's skin. Even the fragrance reminded him of her, fresh, intoxicating. The next shop was a perfumery, even more heady, the scents wafting into the street. Lovely bottles of porcelain, silver and Italian glass were displayed in the shop window. They, too, could be purchased and the scents decanted into them.

Next came a jewellery shop. Wolf began to see the logic in the shops' juxtaposition. One could purchase progressively more expensive gifts for a woman.

He paused in the open doorway of the jewellery shop, noticing the jeweller speaking with a woman. The jeweller raised a hand, displaying a heavy gold chain.

Wolf heard the woman say, 'You have been most generous, sir.'

Wolf froze. He knew the voice and knew the gold chain was Ruskin's watch fob. His anger flared anew. He'd caught her and, by God, he'd let her know it.

He waited in the doorway, hands on hips.

Juliana opened her reticule and dropped the coins into it. The jeweller had paid reasonably well for the gold chain. It had no distinctive characteristics, no one could possibly recognise it as Lord Ruskin's. It had been a safe item to sell.

She needed as much money as she could muster after Wolf's confrontation the night before. The sick feeling had returned, churning her insides. She must plan to run at any moment if he decided to expose her past. She did not know what else to do.

After Wolf's lovemaking, she'd been so happy, a giddy, rapturous, euphoric kind of happy unlike anything she'd ever experienced before. She'd believed the illusion, believed she was finally safe. With him.

How blind. How foolish. She'd been so enamoured of him, she'd impulsively decided to pay back part of what she'd taken from him.

A terrible mistake.

She'd confirmed the thefts, even though she denied them. He thought her a thief, nothing more. For all she knew, he might be speaking to Felix at this very moment, telling Felix all about her. Or worse, he might seek out the magistrate, although she doubted anyone could trace Lord Seabane's money to her and she no longer possessed Lord Ruskin's gold chain.

She might be safe from arrest at the moment, but not banishment.

She knew what her father would say. And Turstin. And Lyon. They'd say better to leave Brighton on her own terms, just to be safe. There was a coach departing near dawn and Juliana could be on it, although the thought of leaving depressed her even more than when she, her father and his partners had sailed away from the isle of Jersey. And then she'd have to find a way to make ends meet. Seabane's money and the money from the sale of Ruskin's watch fob would only go so far.

But perhaps she did not have to face that uncertain future now. It was all up to Wolf.

She extended her hand to the jeweller. 'Thank you so very much.'

'It is a fine piece, Miss,' he said, shaking her hand. 'Useful to any gentleman. I am delighted to have it.'

'I am delighted as well.' She turned to leave and felt the blood drain from her face.

Wolf stood in the doorway, a tall, powerful-looking

silhouette against the blue sky beyond the door. Her heart thumped fast, and she forced herself to walk directly towards him.

As she neared, he doffed his hat to her. 'Miss Walsh.'

With knees trembling, she managed a cordial smile. 'Mr Wolfdon. How nice to see you.'

The jeweller called to her. 'Good day to you, Miss. A pleasure to do business with you.'

She turned and nodded to the man, who looked at Wolf with curiosity.

'Do you wish an escort, Miss Walsh?' Wolf asked. 'I am at your service.'

'How kind,' she responded in a tight voice.

She took his arm and stepped out of the shop into the narrow, busy street.

'What business did you have with a jeweller, Fleur?' Wolf asked as soon as they were out of the jeweller's earshot. His voice was cordial, but she heard the edge in it.

She managed to put on a bland countenance. 'Oh, I had a gold chain I wished to sell.'

'A gold chain.'

She continued, averting her face. 'A chain of my father's. I decided to sell it.'

'You had a gold chain of your father's?' His tone turned sceptical.

'Yes. Of my father's.'

They walked several steps in silence.

He went on, his tone much less casual, 'Tell me, Fleur. If you had a gold chain of your father's, why did you need to steal my money in France?'

Her fingers flexed on his arm, but, unlike the previous night, her brain did not fail her. 'It was pawned,

Wolf,' she lied. 'I redeemed it after your money brought me enough winnings to buy it back.'

This story spilled from her lips without effort.

She felt the muscle of his arm stiffen under her fingers. They walked several paces in silence, until he suddenly pulled her into a small alleyway between the shops and led her into the shadows.

He placed his hands on her shoulders and made her face him. 'That is nonsense, Fleur. If it meant so much to you, you would not sell it now. That was Ruskin's gold chain.' He glared down at her. 'Admit it.'

She lifted her chin and gave him a direct, unwavering look even though she hated how easily she lied. 'It was my father's gold chain, Wolf. I sold it because I will need money to live on if you tell tales about me and turn my cousin against me.' She deflected the blame on to him, another trick her father taught her.

Wolf released her and stepped away, looking down at the hard-packed ground beneath their feet. He advanced on her again. 'Tell me the truth, Fleur. The truth.'

She forced her gaze to remain steady.

He placed his hands on her shoulders again, but this time with a gentler touch. 'Listen to me, Fleur. I will not betray your past, I promise you. I even forgive your debt. But do not lie to me. You must not steal. Do you hear me?' He gave her a tiny shake. 'Promise me you will not steal another thing. You risk a hanging.'

She held his gaze. Was he trying to fool her? Pretending that he cared? Why should she believe his promises when no man had ever kept a promise made to her?

She knew better than to be tricked into saying what could be used against her. 'I assure you, Wolf. I did not steal—'

He released her again and snapped, 'Stop lying to me!'

Pulling off his hat, he ran a hand through his hair and stared at her so long she feared he would notice that her legs were no more than quivering jelly.

Instead, he put his hat back on and cupped her face in both hands. 'No more lies. No more stealing. If I catch you stealing again, I will report you to the magistrate. That I promise you.'

She blinked. He was so near, his lips only inches away. Her senses came alive at his touch. Several hours ago she would have indulged in a desire to taste his lips and feel his arms around her, but no more.

She stiffened.

He broke away. 'Is Lady Ashcourt waiting for you?'

She shook her head. 'I told her I would shop this afternoon and convinced her to allow me to go alone.'

'Come with me.'

He led her through more alleys to a door that appeared nicer than the other alley doors.

'What is this place?' she asked.

'A place we can be private. Cover your face.'

He knocked on the door. A gaudily dressed woman answered. 'It is early, sir.'

'I merely wish the use of a room. Can you accommodate me?' He named the price he would pay.

The woman gave Juliana a knowing smile. 'A moment. Wait here.' She closed the door.

A brothel. Juliana held the hood of her cloak so that it continued to obscure her face, but her spirits sank. He meant to take her into a brothel.

'How do you know of this place?' she asked him.

'I was once young and foolish,' he responded.

'You hired a lady of easy virtue?' She spoke with thick sarcasm. 'I am shocked.'

'Cut line, Fleur,' he countered. 'You were once out in the world.'

She'd told him before. 'I never sold myself.'

'And I am to believe you?' He laughed. 'I suppose you would not believe me if I told you I never did hire a lady of the night.'

The Wolf of her fantasies would never have done so, she was certain. She did not know what to believe about this man. Did he think he could bring her to this awful place, and she would make love with him? Was that the price of his silence? She might be a liar and a thief, and she might be desperate, but she would never be that desperate.

The woman opened the door. 'Come in.'

Wolf put some coins into her hand and the woman led them to a small room containing no more than a narrow bed, two chairs upholstered in red brocade and a table upon which clean towels were folded next to a water pitcher and basin. At least it was clean. Juliana was glad of that for the poor girls' sakes.

The woman closed the door behind her. Juliana did not remove her cloak. She stood, waiting.

He blew out a breath. Noise from the street at the other side of the house could be heard, they were so quiet.

He broke the silence. 'I have truly lost my mind, Juliana. Forgive me. I was wrong to bring you here.'

She glanced at him, surprised.

He rubbed the back of his neck. 'All I thought was to find a private place to talk, but this is sordid, is it not?'

'You wanted to *talk*?' She could not believe him. Must not believe him.

He blinked. 'Did you think—?' He rubbed his face. 'Good God. Of course you did. You thought I would coerce you, treat you shabbily.' He gave a mirthless laugh. 'I dare say you have good reasons to think so, my bringing you to a place like this and after how I have behaved to you in the past.'

Her head spun in confusion. He was apologising? No. Impossible to believe.

His eyes looked pained. 'I threatened you with the magistrate. You must have thought I'd make you pay for my silence.' His voice turned low. 'I assure you, Fleur, I will not set the magistrate on you, and I will not force you to make love to me.'

What was she to say to that? Could she believe him?

He walked to the door. 'We leave immediately.'

She needed to pass by him to reach the door. When she did so he grasped her arm. 'Do not mistake me, Fleur. Until you stop lying to me and I can trust you, I will be watching you. Closely. Do not step out of line.'

A new threat, then. Nothing was changed. He still held power over her. He still could betray her in a trice.

Juliana held her head high and swept past him. She made her way back to the street but did not look back to see if he followed her.

Chapter Ten

That night when the clock struck nine Wolf walked with his parents through the Old Ship Hotel to the rooms set up for the card party. He'd overheard the row his parents had engaged in with the names of Lord Lymond and Lady Holback being bandied about. Wolf and his parents walked in a silence so tense they might as well have been shouting at each other.

Unfortunately, in the silence, all Wolf could think about was facing Juliana at the card party. It would be difficult. He was profoundly ashamed of his behaviour this afternoon. Taking her to a brothel? How disrespectful of him. What a risk to her reputation.

Of course, making love to her risked her reputation as well. Had doing so been akin to treating her as the Paris thief she'd once been? Or had she played on his desire for her so he would not reveal her past?

No. Their desire was mutual, the pleasure they'd shared, real. He had to believe that.

What he now saw clearly—or thought he saw clearly—was how he might have forced her into stealing again. He must watch her, make certain she did not steal again.

Make certain she was what he now wished to believe. A victim of her circumstance. If he cared about her—and he realised he most ardently cared about her—he must treat her as a respectable young lady, Lady Ashcourt's cousin, even if he still desired her with every muscle, nerve and sinew in his body. If she wished to marry respectably, he must do nothing to destroy her chances.

At the door of the card room, Wolf hung behind his parents who immediately separated. The card room was already filling with people, greeting each other, busy in conversation. Only a few had taken seats. Wolf scanned the room for Juliana. He did not see her. He went directly to the refreshment table for a glass of wine, gulping it down and taking another.

His mother appeared at his side. 'Hand me a glass, Wolf dear,' she asked.

He complied.

At that moment the Ashcourts entered, Charlotte with them. And Juliana.

Juliana searched the room as Wolf had done. Her gaze stopped when she saw him.

'That Juliana Walsh is a nobody, you know.' His mother inclined her head towards Juliana. 'You cannot know what her past has been. Her father was the very worst sort of man.'

Wolf turned to her. 'You knew her father?'

'I heard of him,' she responded. 'He had the reputation of being a conniving cheat only one step ahead of dun territory. He fled to the Continent and to a dishonest life, it was said. Apparently, it killed him.'

'A dishonest life?' he asked.

'Swindling, cheating, theft. Things like that.' She leaned towards him and spoke in a conspiratorial tone.

'The daughter looks the very picture of a well brought-up lady, but I wonder if one can trust her, having a father like that? The apple does not fall far from the tree, you know.'

Wolf glanced towards Juliana. How *had* it been for her to have such a father?

Lord Seabane approached Juliana, speaking in her ear. He escorted her over to Lord and Lady Vespond, a wealthy couple known for their love of cards and willingness to bet deep. They chose a table together. If Juliana wanted to win a tidy sum at cards, she had chosen her opponents well.

At least card playing was an honest business. Mostly.

Wolf's mother finished her wine and handed the empty glass to him. 'I need to find a partner, I suppose.' She smiled at her son. 'Not you, dear.'

Her skirts swished as she walked away.

Wolf felt suddenly like a ship without a rudder. He wandered the room a bit, then caught sight of his father sitting down to partner with Lady Holback.

And saw Gravier approach Charlotte. Lord and Lady Ashcourt led the two of them to a table and the four sat down.

At least Lady Ashcourt would be present to chaperon Charlotte, if she even noticed the looks that man gave the young girl. Wolf's mother pulled Lord Lymond over to a table, all the while glaring at his father with Lady Holback.

Wolf picked up another glass of wine.

Lady Allyse walked up to him. 'Do you play tonight, Wolfdon?'

He made himself smile at her. 'I usually do not,' he responded.

She gave him a kind expression. 'Be my partner. If we lose, it will be no great amount.'

He hesitated.

'Do accept,' she said quietly. 'It will be better for you. You look as if you need distraction.'

Perceptive of her, he thought.

Still, he chose a seat that had a good view of the room, the better for him to keep an eye on his mother, his father, Charlotte, Gravier—and Juliana.

Juliana and Seabane both played their cards with single-minded intensity. Wolf's father busily flattered the still-handsome Lady Holback and, in retaliation, his mother laughed gaily with Lord Lymond. Charlotte's colour was high with excitement as she practised her newly acquired feminine wiles on Gravier. Lord and Lady Ashcourt seemed oblivious of the flirtation that was as plain as a pikestaff to Wolf, even some distance away. Gravier, Wolf was forced to admit, behaved like a perfect gentleman.

At least Lady Allyse made no complaint when Wolf occasionally had to be reminded to play a card.

When the bell was finally rung for supper, Wolf lost sight of Juliana, but he caught Charlotte giving Gravier an exuberant hug. Gravier released her very quickly, but Wolf saw him stare longingly at her when she momentarily turned away.

Lord and Lady Ashcourt were detained by another couple and Gravier put his hand on Charlotte's back, guiding her towards the supper room. Wolf's parents were nowhere in sight.

'Lady Allyse,' Wolf said. 'I believe I must join Charlotte Ashcourt at supper. I promised Harris I would look out for her.'

She nodded. 'Shall I come with you?'

'Only if you wish it.'

When they entered the supper room, Wolf found Charlotte seated alone. Gravier was heading towards the buffet table.

Wolf hurriedly presented Charlotte to Lady Allyse and assisted Lady Allyse into a chair. He turned to Charlotte and tried to keep his voice low. 'Lottie, you must take care. You will create a scandal.'

Her bottom lip jutted out like it had done since she wore her hair in plaits. 'I fail to understand you.'

He leaned closer. 'Your brazen behaviour towards Mr Gravier.'

She lifted her chin. 'I have not been brazen.'

'You've been flirting with the man all evening and, if that were not enough, you embraced him.'

Her eyes pinched with pain. 'I was merely in high spirits over winning!'

Wolf met her gaze. 'Charlotte, take care. That is all I ask. You want an unblemished reputation when you have your come-out next spring. It does not take much for tongues to wag.'

'He is Papa's friend,' she protested. 'Nothing more.'

Her countenance betrayed her as she glanced in Gravier's direction. Wolf cringed. He glanced at Lady Allyse, who returned a look of sympathy and understanding.

He was grateful for it. 'Shall I fetch you a plate?' he asked her.

She smiled. 'That would be kind.'

When he stood, he saw Seabane and Juliana approach.

Juliana wore a very reluctant expression. She exchanged a pained glance with Wolf.

'May we join you?' Lord Seabane asked his daughter.

'It is for Lady Charlotte to say,' Allyse answered. 'We encroached on her.'

'Ah,' Allyse's father responded. 'May we join you, Lady Charlotte?'

'Of course,' Charlotte replied, tossing Wolf a scathing look. She turned to Juliana. 'Did you play, Juliana?'

Juliana's eyes went from Lady Allyse to Wolf to Charlotte. 'Yes. With Lord Seabane.'

Lord Seabane turned to Juliana. 'Let me present you to my daughter.' He made the introductions.

Lady Allyse gave Juliana a friendly smile as Juliana curtsied to her.

Wolf held a chair for Juliana and a lock of her hair brushed his hand as she sat.

Seabane stepped towards him. 'I'm going to fix a plate for Miss Walsh. Will you come as well, Wolfdon?'

Wolf nodded, reluctant to leave Juliana's side.

As Wolf stepped aside, Gravier returned, holding a plate of food. He froze, staring directly at Juliana.

Wolf swivelled around and caught the widening of Juliana's eyes, the paling of her complexion.

They knew each other. Wolf would wager on it.

Juliana recovered quickly, composing her features again.

Gravier set the plate on the table. 'Some delicacies for you, Lady Charlotte,' he said smoothly, then turned a smile on Wolf. 'Lord Wolfdon, good evening to you. May I have the honour of being presented to these beautiful ladies and to the gentleman?'

Wolf presented him, noting Gravier's brows shooting up when he introduced Juliana as Miss Walsh.

'Are you in Brighton for pleasure?' Lady Allyse asked him.

'Business, my lady,' he responded. 'But at the moment it is a great pleasure to be here.'

'Business,' Juliana repeated softly as Seabane shook the man's hand.

Tension crackled around the group like lightning in a summer storm. Wolf noticed Lady Allyse gazing at them all with curiosity.

'Shall we fetch the plates, Wolfdon?' Seabane asked.

Wolf reluctantly walked away with him.

Seabane strode ahead of him, and Wolf turned back to Juliana. Charlotte was filling her ears, probably with Wolf's highhandedness. Lady Allyse conversed with Gravier.

After Wolf and Seabane returned with plates of food, the supper did not become more tolerable. Although Juliana answered anyone who spoke directly to her, she seemed unusually quiet. Gravier never spoke to her, and she avoided even looking at him. Charlotte remained in a state of high pique. Seabane offered a comment or two when the opportunity arose, but he was akin to a fifth wheel.

Lady Allyse kept the conversation going and Gravier assisted her. If it had not been for Lady Allyse, the lack of cordiality at the table would have been quite obvious to any observer.

Wolf had difficulty tearing his gaze from Juliana, but his thoughts were not romantic. He wanted to know why she knew Gravier and why they both saw fit to disguise it. If he hoped to read the answers in her face, she gave away nothing.

* * *

When the call to return to the card tables came, Juliana rose quickly. 'If you will pardon me, Lord Seabane, I will meet you at the card table.'

Seabane nodded his agreement. Gravier's gaze followed Juliana's retreat.

Charlotte stood. '*Monsieur*, shall we return to the tables?'

Gravier rose, immediately turning his attention back to Charlotte. 'Of course, Lady Charlotte. It shall be as you wish.'

Following Gravier and Charlotte, Wolf escorted Lady Allyse back to their table in the card room. When he pulled out the chair for her, he saw Charlotte sitting alone with Lord and Lady Ashcourt. He glimpsed Gravier walking through the doorway.

'Forgive me,' he said to Lady Allyse. 'I shall return in a moment.'

He hurried after Gravier, finding him loitering near the ladies' retiring room. Wolf ducked out of sight. A moment later Juliana appeared and Gravier gestured for her to come with him. She hesitated, but followed him into the nearby corridor.

Wolf trailed them, keeping out of sight. He ducked behind a marble statue of Eros where he could see them, but not hear what they said. They spoke together very briefly before Gravier strode away again.

Juliana sighed, pausing before heading back.

Wolf stepped into her path. 'Explain this, Fleur.'

Juliana stared into Wolf's blazing eyes, as scorching as hot irons.

'I am waiting, Fleur.'

She pressed her lips together before speaking. 'Monsieur Gravier wished a word with me, that is all. What did you imagine, Wolf? That I stole his money at the supper table?'

She tried to move past him, but he seized her arm.

'Cut line, Fleur.' He backed her to the wall. 'You know Gravier. You *know* him.'

She'd not hidden her shock well enough, the shock of seeing one of her father's partners in Brighton, of finding him acquainted with Wolf. And Charlotte.

She more carefully disguised her emotions this time. 'I knew Gravier in Paris. He was someone who might have helped me after my father died, but he left me there alone.'

He pressed closer. 'Who was he to you?'

She drew a breath. 'He was someone my father knew.'

His eyes narrowed. 'If that is so, why not acknowledge your acquaintance? Why pretend to be strangers?'

She shrugged. 'He said nothing when he saw me. I merely followed his lead.'

He took her chin in his hand and forced her to look at him.

'Why would he say nothing?' he demanded.

Juliana wished he would not touch her so. It made her senses swirl. 'You must ask him, Wolf. How am I to know the answer?'

Juliana had several questions of her own to ask Gravier. Such as, what was his connection to Wolf? Why was he escorting Charlotte? Why of all the places in the world did he have to come to Brighton? Most of all, was Turstin with him? Would Turstin want to claim Kitty's title and fortune? Since he was not dead and was the rightful heir, would she have to give it up?

Juliana would find out the answers soon. She and Gravier had arranged a meeting for later that night.

Wolf's touch softened. He leaned down so close to her she felt the warmth of his breath on her face. 'There is much you are not telling me, Fleur.'

Her body melted under his fingers. How she wished she could lean on him, confide in him, trust him, share her worries about Gravier. It could not be good Gravier was here in Brighton. Undoubtedly, he had some scheme afoot.

Wolf stepped back. 'We cannot talk here, though. Put the candle in your window tonight. I will come to your room—'

'No!' she cried too loud. 'You cannot.'

He peered at her distrustfully. 'Why not?'

She bit her lip. 'Kitty is—Kitty is—suspicious. I dare not be so reckless again.'

His gaze sliced her like the blade of a guillotine. 'You are lying to me again, Fleur.'

He waited a moment, but she did not speak. She might wish she could trust him, but what man had ever cared about her enough to be relied upon?

With a look of disgust, Wolf spun on his heel and walked out of the corridor.

Away from her.

'One more glass of wine?' Felix smiled hopefully at his wife as he stood aside to let her enter their lodgings.

The card party had finally ended, and they were back at last.

'What do you say, Juliana?' Felix asked. 'Can you convince her?'

'I'll have another glass of wine, Papa,' Charlotte broke

in. 'Say you will, too, Juliana. I do not want this night to end.'

Juliana fervently wished the night was over, but it was not over for her. She released an impatient breath. If only they would all retire for the night!

Instead, she nodded agreeably. Perhaps more wine would make them sleep more soundly.

She followed Felix, Kitty and Charlotte into the drawing room and Felix walked over to a decanter of claret. 'Let me pour, my dear.'

Kitty giggled. 'You will make me tipsy, Felix!'

He grinned as he handed her the wineglass. He looked over at Juliana, lifting a glass and raising his eyebrows.

'Very well,' she said. 'Thank you.'

'And me, Papa!' Charlotte cried.

'And you, my beautiful daughter.' He poured a half-glass for Charlotte.

Felix settled on the sofa next to Kitty. Excitement lit his face. 'I think we found more investors this evening. Enough, I believe, to go forward.'

'How lovely, Felix.' Kitty shifted closer to him.

'What investors?' Juliana asked.

'A quite secret investment opportunity. It is strictly confidential so do not speak of it. We shall be investing in the salvaging of treasure.' Felix took a sip of wine. 'Antiquities.'

'You did not tell me it involved treasure, Felix,' Kitty chided. 'From where? Greece?'

'From Malta,' Felix said.

'Malta!' Kitty clapped her hands together. 'How thrilling!' Her brows knit. 'Is Malta a place where antiquities are found?'

Felix clasped her hand fondly. 'It is, dearest. It is said

that Napoleon's ships, the ones our Admiral Lord Nelson sunk in Egypt, were laden with coin and treasure from Malta, including Roman artifacts from that place. The ships have been discovered and investors are being sought to pay for the recovery of the treasure.'

'Oh, my goodness, that is exciting,' Kitty cried.

Juliana felt heavy with dread. 'Who offers this treasure?'

She knew the name even before it was spoken.

'Monsieur Gravier.' Charlotte sighed.

Chapter Eleven

Two hours had passed and still Juliana sat on the edge of her bed, waiting to hear Felix's snores. Thus far all was quiet, but she had to be certain they were all asleep.

She glanced to the wardrobe where her portmanteau was stored. Perhaps she should pack it now and flee on the dawn coach out of Brighton. It seemed the best course of action. Leave all this behind. Kitty. Felix. Charlotte. Wolf.

She would have much preferred to have put a candle in the window this night to signal Wolf to climb up to her room. Better to be with Wolf scolding her than spend even one moment in Gravier's company.

She hugged herself, remembering making love with him in this room. How glorious that was! Not only the lovemaking, but the banter and feeling as though she belonged with him, not alone.

'Ah!' she cried. It had all been illusion. She rose to her feet and paced the room.

There would be no more lovemaking with Wolf, no more shattering pleasure. He was her enemy, the one man who could ruin her.

Or one of two men. Gravier could ruin her as well.

Besides, Lord Seabane believed Wolf intended to court Lady Allyse. Juliana wanted to despise the woman, but Lady Allyse, she was forced to admit, was very likable. She was just what Wolf needed. Well bred, a woman of good character, able to converse comfortably even under stressful circumstances. A perfect diplomat's wife.

Not a low-born thief and imposter like herself.

A loud rumble broke the silence of the room. Felix was snoring at last, Juliana's signal that it was safe to leave. She grabbed her cloak, took a deep breath, and tiptoed to the door of her bedchamber. Quietly she made her way through the hallway to the front door and out to the street. Glancing around, she hurried across the Steine.

Juliana had instructed Gravier to meet her in the most private location that came to her mind, the base of the sea wall. Now she regretted the choice. Seeing Gravier there would for ever taint her memory of a place where she and Wolf had made love. She shut her eyes for a moment. Best not think of Wolf.

Streetlamps lit her way to the Steine and moonlight shone bright enough for her to see the rest of the way. She talked herself out of being frightened. She'd survived the desperate dark streets of Paris, after all. Brighton was trifling in comparison.

When she reached the stone stairs, she could see nothing but darkness below. Her heart pounded.

A figure stepped out of the shadows. *'Juliana, ma chérie. C'est moi.'*

Gravier.

She answered in English. 'I see you.'

He extended his hand to help her down the steps. She pushed it away and wasted no time, continuing in English, 'What is this hoax of yours, Gravier? This recovery of antiquities?'

His white teeth gleamed in the moonlight. 'Ah, you have heard of it?'

'Ashcourt said you seek investors in a scheme to recover antiquities.'

'Ah, but it was to be confidential.' He shrugged. '*C'est la vie*. Do you wish a share of the scheme, *chérie*?'

She shook her hand at him. 'Do not call me *chérie*.'

He laughed softly. '*Oui*, that is correct. You are Miss Walsh here, is it not so? *Cousine* to Lady Ashcourt. Very clever of you. I fear it will anger Turstin, however. He might wish to disown his family, but he would not like you pretending to be a part of it. You are pretending to be his daughter, *non*?'

Her heart pounded. 'Is Turstin here as well?'

Turstin posed the real danger. She shuddered to think what he would do if he discovered she was using his name.

'No. No. He is not here.' Gravier smiled, saying mournfully, 'I am alone, *chérie*. All alone.'

Relief washed through her, but she snapped, 'Do not expect my sympathy. Not after you left me alone in Paris.'

His forehead wrinkled. 'Alone in Paris? *Non, chérie*, you travelled to Jersey. Turstin said—'

'Turstin told you I went to Jersey?' She scoffed. 'Another of his lies.'

Gravier shook his head, reaching for her. 'I did not know this. I am sorry, Juliana.'

She backed away, not believing his protest or his apology. 'Do not act as if you care, Gravier.'

He lifted his arm again but dropped it. 'I do care. How could I not after all that has passed between us?'

This was too much. 'Enough nonsense. I want you to leave here, leave Brighton.'

He lifted his arms. 'I have just begun. I cannot leave.'

'If you have just begun,' she persisted, 'you will not have much to lose. Abandon your scheme now.'

He shook his head. 'A considerable investment has already been made.'

'You will lose it, then. I will expose you as a hoaxer.'

He did not miss a beat. 'If you expose me, I will expose you, *chérie*.' He crossed his arms over his chest. 'Besides, you have no proof that my scheme is not a real one. I have an impressive amount of evidence to prove my veracity.' He leaned towards her. 'You, on the other hand, are masquerading as someone you are not. A member of the aristocracy. I wonder what would happen to you if you were discovered to be an imposter.'

She knew.

She could not let him intimidate her, though. 'If you expose me, I expose you,' she repeated to him. 'I can raise suspicion about you. It will be enough.'

He smiled. 'We are at a stalemate, then. Surely there is a compromise, *chérie*.'

Her mind raced. Her only safe recourse was flight, but poor Felix was ready to fall for Gravier's ridiculous scheme. Well, gentlemen fell for poor investments all the time and Felix was much too trusting and gullible to protect himself from the likes of Gravier. After all, he'd trusted Gravier to play cards with Charlotte.

She crossed her arms over her chest, just as he had done. 'Tell me. Why were you with Lady Charlotte?'

He took a step back and did not answer her right away. 'How could I refuse? Lord Ashcourt is one of my targets. Lord Ashcourt. Sir John Wolfdon. A few others.'

Sir John. Wolf's father. Her heart pounded. Wolf's impoverished father. What would happen if Sir John invested his money? Surely Wolf would not allow his father to fall for such an idiotic plan?

Gravier's voice turned more casual. 'Why do you ask about the girl, *chérie*?'

Juliana made herself laugh. 'Do you take me for a fool, Gravier? She is seventeen, impetuous and very lovely.'

She expected him to make some witty retort, but he said only, 'It is the father who interests me. Not Lady Charlotte.'

She dropped her hands and glanced towards the water. The moonlight's reflection glistened on the waves. Their sound was rhythmic, soothing. She remembered standing in this spot with Wolf, gazing at the dark beauty of the night sea.

She turned back to Gravier. 'You asked for a compromise.'

He nodded.

'I will say nothing about you.' She used her strongest voice. 'In return, you must stay away from Lady Charlotte, and you must not include her father or Lord Ashcourt in your investment scheme.'

He took time to respond. 'I cannot do what you ask. Ashcourt will have too many questions if he is not included and Ashcourt is…' He paused. 'Ashcourt's participation is crucial to the plan.'

'Why?' she asked.

'Turstin wishes it.'

Her heart stopped. 'You said Turstin was not here.'

'*Oui,*' he said. 'But it is his scheme. I merely execute it for him.'

She gave Gravier a suspicious look. 'Turstin said he would never return to England.'

'I did not say he was in England,' Gravier responded.

Juliana's mind spun around this information. Even if Turstin was not in England, he was obviously targeting his niece's husband. Felix was 'crucial to the plan', Gravier had said.

Or maybe it was Kitty Turstin meant to injure. 'Does Turstin plan to claim his title?' she asked.

Gravier laughed. '*Mon Dieu, non.* He has another way in mind to make his displeasure known.'

Juliana could not see Kitty hurt, could she? Innocent, hapless Kitty.

She crossed her arms over her chest again. 'Very well, here is the compromise. You do whatever it is you plan to do, but do not disclose any knowledge of or connection to me. Do not spoil my scheme and I will not spoil yours.'

'What is your scheme, *chérie*?' he asked.

She ignored his question. 'Do you agree to my compromise?'

'I agree,' he replied.

She turned away from him and looked back at the sea. 'There, our agreement is made. You can have nothing more to say to me.'

'I will escort you to your lodgings, *chérie*.'

She shook her head. 'Leave me. And do not tell me you will worry about me, not after leaving me in Paris.'

'As you wish.' He walked to the stairs but paused on the first step and turned back to her. 'I shall keep your secret from Turstin as well.'

She felt a flash of fear. 'Yes. Thank you for that, Gravier.'

'*Adieu, chérie. À bientôt.*' Gravier climbed the stone steps, disappearing from her sight.

Juliana leaned her forehead against the cool stone of the wall. She thought of her portmanteau. She ought to return to Felix's rooms and pack and flee.

She twisted around and leaned against the wall, gazing out at the sea, its waves still shimmering, shining with memories.

If she stayed, she could look out for Kitty and Lady Charlotte. Make certain Gravier did not despoil another infatuated young girl and Turstin did not destroy Kitty. She must discover some way to foil the plan that had Kitty as its target, as well as Felix and Wolf's father.

She straightened and walked to the water, the breeze whipping her cloak. When she thought Gravier should be too far away to plague her more this night, she turned and walked to the stairway.

A silhouette appeared at the top of the sea wall.

She'd guessed wrong. He waited for her.

'I told you to be gone,' she spat out in French this time.

'Did you, *Fleur*?' The voice, not Gravier's, responded in English.

Wolf.

Juliana's pulse skittered wildly. Her senses were aroused at his presence. At the same time his arrival did not bode well for her.

He descended the stairs with that long-legged masculine stride that made her giddy inside. 'I had a fancy to discover why you would not meet with me tonight.'

Attack. Never defend, she told herself. 'Spying on me again, Wolf?'

The moon's light revealed a dangerous expression on his face. 'Yes, *chérie*.' He strode up to her and stood too close. 'I waited beneath your window, thinking a certain gentleman would arrive to scale the wall. Instead, I saw you crossing by the alley all in a rush.' His eyes looked black in the darkness. 'You met Gravier. Why?'

She lifted her chin in a show of bravado. 'Did you not eavesdrop on my conversation, Wolf? That is not good spying on your part.'

She heard his sharp intake of breath.

She decided to give him an answer. 'I merely wished to secure Gravier's silence.' She lifted one shoulder. 'He agreed.'

'Fustian!' He seized her by the arms. 'The truth for once. You could have had that conversation with him at the card party. Instead, you risk sneaking out at night alone.'

She made herself laugh. 'Do not tell me you worried for my safety, Wolf.'

He averted his eyes and when he gazed back at her, she thought for a moment perhaps he had worried about her. Even after her latest lies.

'Are you in some sort of trouble?' His voice was soft and low. 'I could hear enough to know this was not a romantic tryst—'

The change in his tone took her aback. 'No, it was not a romantic tryst. You are my only romantic tryst, Wolf.' She added in a whisper, 'Or were.'

'Why meet him in the night, then?' His touch turned gentle.

But she must not let down her guard with him, no matter how he sounded. Or how his touch sent shivers of delight through her.

She met his gaze. 'It was as I said before. To ask him not to reveal my life in Paris.'

He pulled her closer, so she could feel the heat of his body, inhale his scent mixing with the salty air. 'What was he to you, Fleur?' His voice rumbled now. 'Another gentleman who woke to find his purse gone?'

His words wounded.

She struck back. 'His name is Lyon Gravier. Does that answer your question more satisfactorily? *Lyon.*' Her first lover, who'd given her lessons in how not to trust.

Wolf's muscles stiffened and he released her. She staggered backwards, the distance between them growing wider and wider, even though she was only a pace away from him.

He put his fists at his waist. 'Do you know this *Lyon*, this former lover of yours, will be the ruin of Ashcourt if he takes too much money from the funds to invest? And my father is at risk, as well, if he contrives to borrow money or convinces my brother-in-law to release his money for this ridiculous investment scheme.'

Even Juliana knew no man should take money from the funds. Once that capital was gone, it was nearly impossible to recover it. Her father had always pined to put a fortune there and live off the interest, but, then, he'd never quite amassed that fortune.

'I know nothing of his scheme,' she lied. She knew what Felix had told her. Still, her stomach churned at how damaging Gravier's scheme would be to these people and their friends.

Wolf took a step towards her. 'Are you a part of it, Juliana?'

He called her Juliana. What did that mean?

She blinked before looking straight into his eyes. This time she told the truth. 'I am not. He is nothing to me.'

He tilted his head, as if thinking. 'If he is nothing to you, you will help me expose him.'

But exposing Gravier exposed her. Gravier would make her pay a harsh price if she broke their bargain.

She twisted her hands together. 'Expose him for what, Wolf? I know nothing of his business. The only thing I can say about him is I knew him in Paris. I fear that fact alone will cause speculation about my reputation.'

His eyes narrowed. 'You will not help me in this?'

She pleaded for his understanding, her voice ragged with emotion. 'I cannot. You must believe me.'

He stared at her, silent for what seemed to be an eternity. His arm rose and he touched her cheek. Emotions in a muddle, she leaned towards him.

For that moment she hoped he would enfold her in his arms and comfort her and reassure her that no harm would come to any of them, but he stepped back, shaking his head.

'Be warned, Juliana. I will do whatever I can to stop Gravier from ruining my family and the Ashcourts. If you are a part of his scheme, I will not be able to spare you, but I intend to stop him.'

'I am not—' she began to protest.

He held up a hand. 'Save your breath. I no longer believe what you say.' He turned and strode towards the stairway.

Juliana turned back towards the sea, her heart pounding. She hoped he would stop Gravier and spare the Ashcourts and his father and any of the other gentlemen Gravier had roped into the scheme, though it risked her ruin. When had she started caring for these people?

Make no attachments, her father had always said.

But she was attached. To Kitty and Felix and Charlotte. Even to Wolf's parents and others, like Seabane and his daughter. It scared her that she cared what happened to them, that she cared what they thought of her.

Especially her lovely Englishman. Her enemy. His justifiable anger felt like a shaft to her heart. She hated lying to him, but to trust him seemed incredibly dangerous.

Had he not threatened her again? Saying he would not be able to spare her?

There was no question but that she should flee Brighton and Gravier and Kitty and the home she'd found with her. And Wolf.

The wind picked up, and the waves grew wilder, mirroring the agitation inside her. She climbed the stairs resolutely and, wrapping her arms around herself for warmth, started back to the Ashcourts' town house.

A voice came from behind her. 'Juliana.'

She turned.

Wolf stood there. 'It is dangerous for you to walk back alone,' he said. 'I will accompany you to your lodgings.'

She opened her mouth to protest, but instead silently waited for him to catch up to her.

At least she would walk with him in the moonlight one last time.

Wolf trudged back to the Old Ship Hotel, his emotions as black as the night sky. On his 'diplomatic' missions during the war, he'd managed to remain clear-headed even when facing danger and discovery, but it took only one woman to do what Napoleon's spy network could not accomplish—cause him to throw good sense to the wind.

If he exposed her as the thief he knew her to be and reported Gravier to be her cohort, who in the *ton* would not believe him? Would the Ashcourts believe him? Perhaps not, but others would. Men like Seabane would.

Wolf could stop Gravier, but he'd have to ruin her, he had no doubt.

There was every reason to reveal what he knew about her. She'd stolen from him. Stolen from others. She'd lied. She still lied. She knew that villain Gravier.

But, then, into his mind flew an image of her young and untutored in the ways of men, Gravier seducing her, getting her in his bed.

Curse the man. Wolf wanted to plant Gravier a facer for deflowering her, leaving her, abandoning her to the dangerous streets of post-war Paris.

He paused on the pavement leading to the hotel. No matter what she had done, Wolf would not ruin her. He'd not hurt her as Gravier must have done.

Even now he longed to make love to her, to join with her as intimately as a man could join with a woman. When they joined together in that pleasure, he felt as if he held the real Juliana, the true Juliana, the woman she might have become if not for the likes of men such as her father and Gravier.

No, he would not ruin her.

Wolf walked by a tavern whose sign was the head of a Druid, a Celtic learned and priestly man. Sounds of a bawdy song drifted from its doors, a tune Wolf had often heard sung by men in their cups.

Some say women are like the seas.
Some the waves and some the rocks
Some the rose that soon decays...

Wolf walked on to the Old Ship Hotel and made his way to his room, but he was still too restless to think of sleep. He opened the door to his parents' sitting room and removed a decanter of brandy and a glass, taking them both back to his bedchamber. Wolf drank as he sat at a window overlooking the sea. The sea was restless too and no help in calming his emotions.

He had to think.

There must be some way to expose Gravier without harming Juliana.

If only he could think of one.

Dawn gradually lit the sky orange and the sea violet before Wolf rose from his chair by the window. He paced his room. Would the light of day render his nocturnal thoughts foolish? Or had he hit upon a scheme? An insane scheme, to be certain.

But it might work.

He searched the drawers of the bureau and table in his room for pen, ink and paper. Finding none, he looked in his parents' sitting room. No luck.

Still in the clothes he'd worn the night before, he walked down to the hotel clerk who directed him to a room where he might compose a letter.

He could not execute his scheme alone, but he might count upon one person. He did not know him well, but he might be the only one who could pull the strings necessary to make the proper arrangements.

Wolf sat at a desk in the hotel's drawing room. Dipped his pen in the inkpot in front of him and began to write.

To his brother-in-law. The Marquess of Hale.

Chapter Twelve

Later that morning Gravier crossed the Steine on his way to the Circulating Library. No missive had reached him regarding the next step in Turstin's elaborate swindle. The whole matter seemed a great folly. A great deal of expense and preparation for questionable profit, if not total failure. Turstin refused to listen to reason, though.

Gravier bowed his head as he walked. Now that Juliana was here, the scheme had become even more risky. She was playing a dangerous game, using Turstin's name.

He wondered who to believe about Paris. Had Turstin lied to him? Had they left her in Paris alone?

Gravier would have gone after her if he had known. He would never have left her, especially after her father—

Gravier heard the sound again, the zing of the guillotine blade as it fell, the thud of it hitting its mark, the cheers of the crowd as the victim's head rolled off the platform. He started to shake and his stomach twisted into knots.

What might his life have been like if his mother and father and sister and brother had not been sent to the guillotine? Might he have been worthy of a Lady Charlotte?

A chilling breeze threatened to lift the hat off Gravier's head. He held it on until he entered the Circulating Library, the most likely place for him to encounter the victims of this investment scheme.

He wandered around, greeting the people to whom he had already been presented. Only the select few knew him as anything but an expatriate of France seeking diversion in Brighton, not unlike the scores of Frenchmen who'd once fled to Brighton to escape the guillotine.

He shook again.

The melodious sounds of the pianoforte reached his ears. He walked to the displays of new sheets of music where also sat the instrument to play them.

He froze. Seated at the pianoforte was Lady Charlotte, her long graceful fingers moving over the keys. He struggled to catch his breath.

The girl was a vision. Dark hair with curls that begged to be wrapped around a man's finger. Pale translucent skin in contrast. Full kissable lips. And her figure?

She was not much younger than Juliana had been when he'd taken Juliana to his bed. Old enough for seduction.

Mon Dieu. Seduction would ruin everything. He must content himself with admiring her from afar.

Like a moth to a flame, however, Gravier walked directly to the pianoforte. 'You play divinely, Lady Charlotte.' He bowed.

Her finger hit a discordant note. 'Why, *Monsieur* Gravier, you startled me.' She smiled up at him and he was caught for a moment by the length and thickness of her eyelashes, fringing living sapphires.

'I did not mean to make a disturbance for you,' he murmured.

'Never.' She rose and came much too close to him. 'If you are looking for my father, my parents are not here. I came with my maid.' She glanced around, then leaned towards him as if sharing a secret. 'She is meeting her lover, you see, so I have an hour to wait for her.'

Her scent, like spring lilacs, filled Gravier's nostrils.

Lady Charlotte fluttered her eyelids at him. 'I wished to walk in the Regent's gardens, but I cannot do so alone.'

Mon Dieu. Mon Dieu. Mon Dieu.

Gravier took a breath, but it merely filled him with her essence. 'Shall I walk with you, Lady Charlotte?'

She smiled, showing her white even teeth. 'I should like nothing better, *monsieur.*'

He offered her his arm.

Juliana walked behind Felix and Kitty, feeling as restless as a cat in a cage, as wild as the breeze that tried to toss her hat and tangle her skirts as she walked.

The night before, after Wolf silently left her at the town house, she'd crept back to her bedchamber and pulled out her portmanteau. She could not make herself pack it, even though it went against everything her father had ever taught her.

She could not shake the sense of obligation to Felix and Kitty. And Charlotte. And Wolf's parents. And all the others Gravier planned to defraud.

And especially to Wolf for whom she wished she was a better person.

She put the portmanteau back in the wardrobe, changed into her nightclothes and finally fell into a fitful sleep. Her maid woke her at the usual time, and she'd joined Felix and Kitty for breakfast as if nothing concerned her but assemblies, card parties and bracing walks in the sea air.

Felix and Kitty turned towards the Circulating Library, chattering with each other in oblivious contentment. Juliana heard snatches of their conversation full of trivialities, totally unaware that Gravier—and Turstin—planned to trick them out of their money.

Juliana frowned. She, of course, was little better than Gravier and Turstin. She was deceiving them as well, wearing the pretty gowns Felix had paid for, accepting his food and residing in elegant rooms that cost him a bundle. How much money had she cost them already?

Kitty turned around. 'You are walking so slowly, Juliana. Are you certain you are not ill?'

'I am not ill, Kitty. I was merely wool gathering.' She quickened her pace, feeling a pang of conscience. While she took complete advantage of Felix and Kitty's generosity, Kitty unknowingly fussed over her like no one had done since Juliana's mother had been alive.

Kitty made Felix stop until Juliana caught up with them.

She took Juliana's arm. 'Let nothing trouble you, dearest. Felix says I have stressed finding you a husband much too strongly.' She sent a loving glance at him. 'It is only that I wish for your happiness.'

Felix leaned towards Juliana. 'You are welcome in our house until you have found the gentleman who deserves you.'

Tears stung Juliana's eyes. She deserved none of this kindness. 'Thank you, Felix,' she managed to say.

Kitty sent another adoring look to Felix and he patted her fondly on the hand. The two of them stood gazing into each other's eyes with such devotion Juliana had to turn away from them. And away from her own unworthiness.

She took a deep breath and glanced towards the Circulating Library. Her eyes widened, then narrowed. Walking out from behind the building were Gravier and Lady Charlotte.

She glanced back to see if Felix and Kitty had noticed them, but those two were still too consumed with each other to take heed of a scoundrel making way with their innocent daughter.

Juliana quickened her step. She reached the library a moment after Gravier and Lady Charlotte entered the building. As she hurried inside, she nearly collided with Gravier, who was on his way out again. She did not see Charlotte.

Juliana grabbed his arm. 'I would speak with you.' She spied a private corner shrouded by bookshelves. 'Come with me.'

She managed to get him behind the shelf before the door opened again, undoubtedly admitting Felix and Kitty.

She rounded on him. 'You were trifling with that child, Gravier. First you make eyes at her over cards, now you walk with her alone?'

He looked ashen. 'It was a mere stroll. On public paths.'

She grabbed the lapel of his coat. 'Leave that girl alone, do you hear me?'

His face contorted before he averted his gaze. When he turned back, his voice was low. 'She has nothing to fear from me.' He took Juliana's hand and forced it away. 'What else, Juliana? I am late for an appointment.'

'I do not care.' She glared at him. 'I do not care about our bargain either, Gravier, if you persist in trying to seduce that child. I vow I will tell the world what you are if you do.'

Would she really sacrifice herself? She feared she was bluffing. She feared Gravier could tell.

To her surprise he merely nodded. 'I will do nothing to harm her.'

And even more to her surprise, Juliana almost believed him.

Almost.

Juliana stepped aside and he strode resolutely to the door. She went to look for Lady Charlotte, concerned that Gravier might have upset her, even more concerned that Charlotte was falling for his seduction. Juliana spied Charlotte seated at the pianoforte, picking out what sounded like a funeral dirge.

Before she could approach the girl, Kitty bustled up to her. 'Juliana, my goodness! I have been looking everywhere for you.' She grasped Juliana's arm. 'Lord Seabane is here, and I thought I should tell you.' She gave a significant look. 'Just in case.'

Juliana glanced to where Lord Seabane stood chatting with Felix. 'Thank you, Kitty, but I was about to speak to Charlotte. I did not know she would be here.'

Kitty glanced over to her daughter and waved. 'Yes, she came ahead of us. Hello, Charlotte dear.'

Charlotte seemed to force a smile in return.

Kitty turned back to Juliana. 'If I have an opportunity, I will let Lord Seabane know you are here with us.' She paused. 'Just in case.'

Lord Seabane was the last thing on Juliana's mind, but she merely smiled.

Kitty hurried away and Juliana joined Charlotte at the pianoforte. 'I did not know you were out and about, Charlotte.'

Charlotte glanced up, giving a wan smile. 'Yes. With my maid who is here somewhere.'

Juliana sat next to her on the piano bench. 'What sad song is this you are playing?' She looked at the music.

Juliana's musical talents were modest, but she could read music and play a little. Her father had sent her to a school to learn all the talents of a proper lady so she would know how to act when he made his fortune. Or was it so she could pass herself off as a proper lady when he needed her to?

The title of the song on the music sheet was 'A Maid's Love Be True'. She looked back at Charlotte. 'This is not what you were playing.'

'I played from memory.' Charlotte sounded as sad as her music.

Juliana placed a hand on Charlotte's. 'I saw you walk in with Monsieur Gravier. Has he upset you?'

Charlotte bristled. 'Not at all. Why would you say such a thing?'

'Because it looked as if you were alone with him,' Juliana explained.

'I wished for some air, and he was kind enough to accompany me.' Lady Charlotte's voice was clipped.

Kindness, indeed, Juliana thought. 'Where was your maid?'

The girl's complexion turned a guilty red. 'She…she was near.'

Juliana recognised a lie when she heard one—another skill learned at her father's knee. The skill failed her, though, when spoken by a man who made promises to her.

'I shall presume to give you advice, Charlotte.'

Charlotte stared at her blandly.

Juliana continued, her voice stern. 'You must be very careful of men like Monsieur Gravier. He is the sort who is well schooled in the art of pleasing women, the sort who will ruin reputations.'

The girl's eyes flashed before she glanced away. 'But he is not like that. He is…sad.'

Juliana's brow furrowed. She had never thought of Gravier as sad. Selfish, perhaps, deceitful, certainly, but not sad.

She took a breath. 'Sad or not, he is a single gentleman, and you must be very mindful of your reputation.'

'I know that.' Charlotte's tone was petulant.

Juliana squeezed her hand.

Kitty broke in to their conversation, gesticulating without an ounce of discretion. 'Psst!'

Juliana acknowledged her. 'Kitty is wanting me.'

Charlotte straightened. 'Are you going to tell her?'

'That you were alone with Gravier?' Juliana responded.

Charlotte pleaded, 'Promise me you will not tell. Please, Juliana.'

'I promise,' she said. 'But you must not endanger yourself with him again. I mean it.'

Charlotte looked relieved and rebellious at the same time. Juliana feared for her.

She grasped Charlotte's hand in farewell, surprised at the surge of affection she felt for the girl.

She rose from the bench and took a fortifying breath before making her way to where Kitty stood with…not Seabane.

Wolf.

'Why, Juliana, there you are,' Kitty said. 'Look who is here.'

Kitty looked especially pleased. Wolf was, after all, Kitty's first choice of a husband for Juliana.

Wolf bowed. 'Miss Walsh.'

'Sir.' She curtsied.

Kitty edged away, tossing Juliana a knowing smile. They were alone.

The painful knot in Juliana's stomach remained.

'I know you could not wish to converse with me,' she said to him in a voice quiet enough that no one else could hear. 'Perhaps you could simply pretend to chat with me for a minute or two. Kitty would be happy with that.'

He looked puzzled. 'Kitty would be happy?'

Juliana shrugged. 'She still fancies you a potential suitor.'

She expected him to scoff at that, but instead he seemed to examine her more closely. 'You look distressed, Fleur. I am unused to seeing you so.'

She immediately erased all emotion from her face, a well-honed reflex. 'Distressed?' She intentionally turned sarcastic. 'Whatever would I be distressed about?'

Typically, this tone would precipitate a sparring match between them, but this time his expression turned earnest. 'Fleur. I do not intend to do you harm.'

His tone surprised her. Touched her. But she snapped back, 'Do not think you consume all my thoughts, Wolf.'

His brow furrowed. 'Is there trouble between you and Lady Ashcourt? Lord Ashcourt?'

She gaped at him. Was this genuine concern he was showing?

'Charlotte?' he persisted.

Charlotte.

Wolf would comprehend her worries about Charlotte. She longed to talk with somebody about this. She did not know what to do to ensure Charlotte was safe from Gravier.

She continued to stare into his eyes.

Wolf cared about Charlotte; she knew he did. And he certainly had no fondness for Gravier.

He waited patiently for her to say something, the look of concern in his eyes unwavering.

'It is just that…' she said, then faltered, then gathered courage again. 'It is just that I am worried about her. I fear she has developed an infatuation—'

He cut her off. 'With Gravier?'

'Yes,' she responded in surprise.

'I have noticed.' Wolf frowned.

Oh, dear. How many other people had noticed?

She went on. 'I have warned her about him and about the danger to her reputation. I have warned Gravier, too. I do not know what else to do.' She touched his arm and spoke impulsively. 'Will you help me, Wolf? Will you keep an eye on them? Perhaps a warning from you would do more than from me.'

'I have already spoken to her,' he said gruffly. 'At the card party. Perhaps I should speak to Gravier.'

'Could you?' Wolf was taller and stronger than Gravier. Juliana had no doubt he could be intimidating. 'But do not let on I asked you.'

His brows shot up. 'Why would that concern you?'

She glanced away. 'It will do you no good if Gravier thinks you are in my confidence.'

He stiffened. 'Or it will do *you* no good? Is that what you mean? Will it ruin your scheme?'

She met his glaring eyes. 'I meant it would do *you* no good, but, yes, Gravier could ruin me quite as effectively as you might do.'

She curtsied and walked away from him.

He still thought her a part of Gravier's investment scheme. Well, Wolf might not believe her denial of that, and Gravier might indeed make things worse for her, but at least Charlotte would be safe.

Chapter Thirteen

That evening Brighton's gentlemen and ladies strolled to the Theatre Royal on New Street for the play, *The Tragedy of Jane Shore*. Wolf's father begged off, citing fatigue, but assuring Wolf he was not unwell. Wolf's mother insisted Wolf escort her.

He was glad to do so. Gravier was sure to be there.

After his conversation—altercation?—with Juliana, Wolf had searched for Gravier, but he did not seem to be among the *ton*, as was typical of him. He'd thought about calling upon the man at the Black Lion but thought better of it. Gravier was not near Charlotte that afternoon, so there was no reason to be hasty.

As Wolf and his mother made their way to the theatre, he found himself searching the crowd for Juliana. They had been almost cordial to each other at the Circulating Library that morning. Until it became clear she would hide the truth about her and Gravier.

Was he threatening to expose her? That was what she implied.

Even though matters were inexorably altered between them, the essence of her still hovered inside him, waiting for a chance to flash a memory of her smile, her touch, her scent.

His mother spoke. 'I presume you have a seat, Wolf dear. I am to be a guest in Lord Lymond's box.'

He stopped. 'Lord Lymond's box? I thought you and Father had a box of your own.'

She laughed. 'Oh, my, no. Your sister would consider that an unnecessary extravagance. But you need not escort me home. Lymond will do so, I am sure.'

Wolf frowned. Charlotte was not the only one who needed a warning.

'I do not think it prudent you spend so much time with Lymond,' he told his mother. 'He has a terrible reputation. No good can come of it.' Besides, the man was a good fifteen years younger than she.

She pulled away from him. 'I do not need to be scolded by my son! Besides, Lymond's reputation is no worse than Lady Holback's, and I don't see your father worrying over that!'

Memories from childhood rushed back. The shouting. The tears. The accusations. The desire to run as far away from it all as he could get.

'Take care, Mother,' he retorted. 'You can still be hurt.'

She pushed his arm away and strode ahead of him without another word.

He watched to see her walk safely through the theatre door before turning back the way he'd come.

Neither of his parents would listen to reason. Had he not always known that? He could not wait to return to Paris—

But returning to Paris meant leaving Juliana.

A shaft of pain pierced his chest.

But leaving her was inevitable, was it not?

Wolf walked only a few steps before spying Lord and Lady Ashcourt in his path. Gravier was with them, like a leech attached to their skin. Although this time he walked next to Lord Ashcourt. Juliana walked with Charlotte.

Juliana looked like a beautiful painting, framed by the people around her. All the colours around her suddenly intensified.

Charlotte noticed him first, skipping ahead of her parents. 'Wolf, you are here!'

Gravier reached him. 'But surely you are walking the wrong way.'

Wolf responded to Gravier's ingratiating smile with a suppressed glare. 'I am not staying. I merely escorted my mother.'

Lord and Lady Ashcourt also gathered around him. Juliana held back, but still filled his vision.

Charlotte took his arm. 'But you must stay for the play! It will be wonderful!' She turned to her father. 'Wolf can sit with us, can he not, Papa? There is room in our box, surely.'

'Of course he can.' Lord Ashcourt clapped him on the shoulder. 'I insist upon it.'

Lady Ashcourt nodded her approval, her curls bobbing with the effort.

'Monsieur Gravier is to share our box. If you come, as well, our numbers will be even,' Charlotte added.

Gravier's smile stiffened and for once his eyes avoided Charlotte. 'Lord Ashcourt is so generous, is he not?'

Juliana frowned and averted her gaze.

Wolf supposed she, like him, was not as enthusiastic about this idea.

Although it might afford him the best possibility of confronting Gravier. 'I would be honoured to be your guest.'

'It is done, then!' cried Charlotte.

The bell sounded for the crowd to enter the theatre. To Wolf's surprise, Gravier offered his arm to Lady Ashcourt.

Gravier smiled ingratiatingly. 'May I have the honour of escorting you to your box, my lady?'

Lady Ashcourt flashed a disappointed expression to her husband before saying, 'You may, sir.'

Lord Ashcourt escorted his daughter.

That left Wolf with Juliana.

He offered his arm. 'Miss Walsh?'

She hesitated before resting her gloved fingers on his sleeve. To his surprise even this light touch reminded him of bedchambers rather than theatre boxes.

He glanced down at her, knowing his desire for her must be apparent. As if her thoughts were akin to his, her eyes darkened in response. They walked into the theatre, the crowd pushing them up against each other in bittersweet torture.

'You are forced into my company tonight,' Juliana murmured to him as they climbed the marble stairway to the boxes.

He wanted to tell her he desired nothing more than her company, but with no crowds, just the two of them alone, but without the barriers between them.

The barriers of her lies.

They were last to enter the box. Lady Ashcourt and Charlotte had taken the front chairs. Gravier sat behind Charlotte and was already in a deep discussion with Lord Ashcourt.

Two chairs remained, set back out of view of the other boxes. Juliana baulked.

'We are left to the shadows, Fleur.' Wolf stepped ahead of her and held her chair.

'We are indeed,' she responded as she sat down.

Charlotte turned around and waved happily to them, sliding her chair backwards as she did so, crowding Gravier's knees. At least Wolf had plenty of leg room.

Gravier glanced back at them, nodding cordially to Wolf before bending his head towards the Earl again in whispered conversation. Wolf sensed Juliana stiffen.

He leaned over to her. 'Your friend Gravier seems to be avoiding Charlotte.'

She frowned. 'I did not expect this. Perhaps he decided to heed me after all.'

'It would seem strange to warn him away from her when he's paying her so little attention.' What would Wolf even say to him?

'I agree,' Juliana responded. 'Let us merely observe them for a while, do you not think?'

Wolf nodded. 'If you see him act like a moon calf around her, send word to me.'

She smiled. 'I will.'

Wolf relaxed in his chair, glad to merely enjoy sitting next to Juliana. And to not have to browbeat Gravier into keeping his hands—and eyes—off Charlotte.

'The theatre seems quite full,' she commented.

'It does indeed.' Wolf suppressed a smile as he scanned the other boxes. Who would have guessed he and Juliana would be conversing as if they were a normal lady and gentleman attending a play?

Then his eye caught his mother leaning her head close to Lymond and laughing at whatever nonsense he spoke to her. The sight spoiled the moment.

He gazed past them and noticed Lord Seabane and

Lady Allyse in another box. When he returned to Paris, would Seabane offer for Juliana? He would be a kind husband.

Juliana stared at the playbill even though the light in the box was too dim to read it. What was she thinking? he wondered. Was she thinking of the passion they'd shared? Or the problems between them?

Or was she not thinking of him at all?

The small orchestra began to play, its sound not quite piercing the din of the audience's voices. With no other recourse Wolf settled back in his chair, all too aware of Juliana next to him, each rustle of her skirt, each turn of her head.

The curtain rose and the play commenced, the story of King Edward IV's mistress, a woman also pursued by Lord Hastings. In the end she was forced to wander the streets as an outcast as her punishment for bewitching men.

Wolf could hardly attend to the actors on the stage, the drama in his own life taking possession of him instead. His thoughts about Juliana swayed back and forth like a sapling in the wind. One thing was certain: it mattered to him what happened to her. He did not want to threaten her or ruin her.

He wanted her to be free of worry.

He doubted she was free of worry at the moment.

She turned her head to him, and they stared into each other's eyes, neither moving nor looking away. In the dim light of the box Wolf was reminded of holding her in his arms like one would do to comfort a child. A wave of sadness and regret washed over him.

Her expression softened. 'Wolf,' she mouthed, and he

had the illusion his emotions were again mirrored on her face.

Without thinking, he reached for her hand. Her gloved fingers wrapped around his, clasping tightly. Just as he lifted her hand to his lips, the curtain fell for intermission and applause filled the theatre.

He released her.

Juliana had quietly suffered at Wolfdon's side throughout the play. Jane Shore's story made her shiver. Juliana's own crimes seemed so much worse in comparison, as would be her punishment should she be discovered. Or betrayed.

After the play, several made their way to the Old Ship Hotel where a supper would be served. Before Kitty had known Wolf was to attend the play, she'd invited Lord Seabane and Lady Allyse to join their party.

The gentlemen left to fix plates for the ladies. Lady Allyse gave her a friendly smile, but Juliana could think of nothing to say to a woman who was, in her eyes, perfection.

She glanced away and saw Lady Wolfdon glare at her husband, seated in the corner with a lady he often was with. Lady Wolfdon was accompanied by Lymond and she seemed to make a grand show of enjoying the rake's attention.

The gentlemen returned to their table. Seabane sat next to Juliana and Wolf next to Lady Allyse. Felix, Kitty and Seabane were soon in Gravier's thrall as he talked of recovering a cask of jewels on a previous expedition.

Recovering? thought Juliana. Stealing was more like it. That was the theft that had cost her father his life.

Charlotte seemed to be avoiding Gravier and he certainly was avoiding her. Juliana would have rested easy on that score, except she caught the girl sending adoring glances Gravier's way when he wasn't looking.

It was too soon to relax about that concern, Juliana thought.

After the meal was mostly consumed, Gravier and Felix excused themselves and walked to the corner where Sir John sat. They all had their heads together in some intense discussion. After a few moments, Gravier walked off and Felix returned to Kitty.

Suddenly Charlotte stood. 'Pardon me, I shall be right back.' She left the table and walked swiftly to the door.

'Charlotte!' Kitty cried to the girl's retreating back.

Juliana stood as well. 'She has probably gone to the retiring room. I believe I shall accompany her.'

Juliana doubted very much that Charlotte had gone to refresh herself, and, indeed, she was not there. Nor was she in the private nooks where Juliana interrupted a few clandestine couples. She found the girl on the veranda.

With her arms around Gravier's neck.

'Charlotte!' she cried.

The girl jumped back.

She strode to Charlotte's side. 'Have you gone mad? If anyone sees you, your reputation is ruined. You know this.'

The girl looked both chagrined and defiant. 'No one would see.'

'I saw you!' Juliana countered. She seized Charlotte's arm. 'Go back now and say you have been to the retiring room if anyone should ask.'

Charlotte slanted a glance towards Gravier.

'Go now, or I inform your father of this.' Juliana gave

her a push towards the door, watching until she was out of sight.

Juliana rounded on Gravier. 'I told you to leave her alone.'

He made a helpless gesture. 'She followed me, *chérie*. It was not a situation of my making.'

'Well, you did nothing to resist, did you?' She glared at him.

His eyes pleaded. 'She threatened to make the commotion.'

Juliana put her hands on her hips. 'And you could not manage her? I do not believe a word you say. You leave her alone!'

His expression turned scornful, but still pained. 'Or what, Juliana? You will break our bargain? I am what I seem to be. An entrepreneur, offering a lucrative investment. You, on the other hand—that is a different matter, is it not? You are a deceiver of the first order. An imposter. So do not threaten me or I may lash back at you.'

She did not falter, even though she could not deny that he possessed the bigger club with which to clobber her. 'I need not prove anything. All I must do is arouse a little suspicion.' She glared at him. 'I can tell this is a deep game, whatever it is, Lyon. Have you spent a great deal of money preparing for it, coming to Brighton? Would Turstin wish to lose that money?'

'It would be a temporary setback, *chérie*.' He held her gaze. 'But for you? Tell me, are the English hanging people who impersonate nobility or merely transporting them?'

She lifted her chin, refusing to be intimidated. 'I will say something to Wolfdon. I am certain he would make swift work of a Frenchman trying to seduce his friend's sister.'

Gravier grabbed both her arms and shook her. 'You will tell him no such thing. Do you hear me? No one is to know any of this.'

A voice came from behind her. 'Know any of what?' Wolfdon walked steadily towards them. He held up a hand. 'Ignore the question. I withdraw it. I cannot expect the truth from either of you.' He stared pointedly at Gravier. 'Remove your hands from the lady.' His voice deepened. 'Now.'

Gravier did so immediately, but he directed a questioning gaze to Juliana.

She answered it. 'He knows all about me, Gravier. So beware.'

Wolf added, 'I do indeed know about her, and I am beginning to know about you, sir.' He looked daggers at the man. 'Do not plague this lady again.'

Gravier straightened. 'I assure you, *monsieur*, you misunderstand—'

Wolf clasped Gravier's arm. 'I understand you had your hands on her. Leave her. And do not touch her again.'

Juliana spoke up. 'I caught him embracing Charlotte.'

Wolf's hand clamped down harder on Gravier's arm. 'Good God, man. Lady Charlotte is a child.'

Gravier winced. 'I well comprehend her age, sir, but I fear she has the *passionné* for me. Foolish girl. I have been, you see, pleasant towards her. Her father is one of my potential investors. Of course, I would be pleasant to his daughter, but I believe she mistook my geniality for something more. She embraced me. I could not stop her.'

Wolf gave a derisive laugh. 'Do you expect me to believe you?' Wolf let go of his arm. 'I ought to tell Ashcourt you had your hands on his daughter. Do you suppose he would invest in your scheme then?'

Gravier's eyes flashed. 'Then Lord Ashcourt and your father will lose a fortune needlessly, because the only hands I had on Lady Charlotte were to pull her away. I am in earnest, sir.'

Juliana again pictured what she'd seen, Charlotte and Gravier in that embrace. It was entirely possible that Gravier *was* attempting to extricate himself from Charlotte.

She turned to Wolf. 'Perhaps he is telling the truth, Wolf. Her arms were around his neck. He was not holding her.'

Wolf paused a moment. 'Then perhaps we should speak with Ashcourt.'

Perhaps this was a way out for all of them, Juliana thought. If, through Felix, they accused Gravier of seducing Charlotte, then surely Felix would give up his investment and Gravier would be driven out of town.

But Charlotte would be tainted; the woman always was.

And what would stop Gravier from exposing her?

'Do not speak to Lord Ashcourt about this, I beg you.' Gravier pressed his palms together. 'It is the young lady who put me in this situation. It was something I could not help!'

'Very well. We'll not mention you,' Wolf said, then his voice turned stern. 'But stay away from Lady Charlotte. Make certain you are not in this position again.'

'You have my word,' Gravier said. 'May I leave now?'

Juliana had never heard Gravier give his word before. He had better mean it.

Wolf gestured for him to leave.

Gravier made a curt bow before turning and walking away without a backward glance.

Wolf faced Juliana again, and the two held each other's

gazes. Juliana's head felt light, and her blood raced with excitement.

'Thank you, Wolf,' she finally managed to say.

'Fleur,' he said in a low voice. 'Please tell me you are not connected with that man.'

She answered honestly. 'I once was, but no longer. I am not part of this scheme of his. I want nothing to do with him. I told you—he abandoned me in Paris.' And let her father die. 'He and his partner.'

Wolf moved closer to her. 'I believe you, Fleur,' he said softly.

He believed her? How pleasing those words were! He *believed* her.

Why did it suddenly mean so much to her, to be believed? She'd been taught to make people believe her lies. Why care that he believed her telling the truth?

She felt almost joyous about it. This certainly was a new way of feeling.

It *mattered* to her.

'I believe you,' he repeated, touching her lips with his finger. 'This time.'

That snatched the joy away.

Nothing was changed between them.

He stepped away from her. 'Go back to the supper room. I will wait here a few minutes.'

She slanted a look at him, again on edge with him. Vigilant. Wary. But she simply nodded and turned away.

Chapter Fourteen

When Juliana re-entered the supper room, several tables were empty, some guests having retired for the night. Kitty was still there, though, scanning the crowd with a worried expression.

Juliana hurried over to her. 'Here I am, Kitty. Were you looking for me?'

Kitty nearly melted with relief. 'Oh, yes! I was so worried, Juliana. I could not imagine what happened to you.'

She'd not been gone any longer than if she had used the retiring room.

Kitty went on. 'Charlotte came back, you see, and she was quite upset. Or ill. Or something. Dear Felix took her home immediately. I insisted. I waited for you, though. Otherwise, you would not have known what happened.'

Juliana, of course, knew precisely what had happened.

'Of course, I could have told someone to tell you,' Kitty continued. 'But would that have been discreet? Would people have talked? I couldn't bear it if Charlotte became the topic of gossip.' She waved a hand. 'In any event I did not think of telling anyone and neither did Felix. We thought only of Charlotte.' Kitty frowned. 'Besides, I could not leave you to walk home alone.'

Juliana put a comforting hand on Kitty's arm. 'I am so sorry to have caused you such distress, Kitty. I was looking for Charlotte. I didn't find her in the retiring room as I suspected I would. I must have missed her.'

'She would not tell us where she'd been,' Kitty said worriedly. 'I do hope she is not ill!'

Infatuation could be like an illness, Juliana thought.

Several more guests left, though a few continued to sit at their tables, talking and laughing.

Kitty glanced around. 'I thought perhaps we could ask Monsieur Gravier to escort us home, but he has not come back. Have you seen him?'

Juliana suspected that Gravier had fled as quickly as he could. 'I did see him briefly when I was looking for Charlotte.'

That was at least the truth. Or the least amount of truth she was willing to tell at the moment.

Was that like lying? She did not know.

'Oh, there is Wolf!' Kitty cried.

Juliana saw Wolf entering the supper room at a door further away from the one she'd used.

Kitty waved him over. 'Wolf will escort us home. We will be perfectly safe with him.'

Juliana could not feel perfectly safe with him, though.

He crossed the room to them. 'Yes, Lady Ashcourt? May I be of service to you?' He did not look at Juliana.

Kitty managed to repeat all that she'd said to Juliana. When she told of Charlotte's upset, Wolf glanced at Juliana then, and again when Kitty mentioned Gravier.

'I would be honoured to escort you home,' Wolf told her.

Kitty sighed in relief. 'I am so sorry to put you to the

trouble. You are staying in this hotel, so I am sending you far out of your way.'

'It is no trouble at all.' He smiled at her. 'The night air will do me good.'

The ladies collected their shawls and Wolf draped Juliana's over her shoulders. His hands lingered on her shoulders a few seconds longer than necessary.

Something had changed in him when he saw Gravier's hands upon her, something primitively protective. What's more, he'd believed what she told him about Charlotte, even believed that, as she'd said, Gravier had not enticed Charlotte. And that she was not his partner.

It rattled him, though, that he was believing in her and wanting to protect her and that he still craved that physical closeness that they'd previously so wildly explored.

So he offered Lady Ashcourt his arm and Juliana walked alone at her side. Lady Ashcourt kept up a rather constant conversation. Worried about Charlotte. Worried that her darling Felix was distressed. How beautiful the night was. How dark the sea. How kind it was for Wolf to escort them, and did not Juliana look lovely tonight?

Juliana indeed looked lovely that night, but she said so little that he might have forgotten she was there, except he was always aware of her presence.

Finally, they reached the street where the Ashcourts were staying. As they reached the town house, the door opened and Ashcourt burst out.

He skidded to a halt upon seeing them.

'Kitty, my love,' he cried, rushing directly to her. 'I was coming for you. I could not let you ladies walk alone.'

The two clasped hands as if they'd been apart for months and gazed adoringly into each other's eyes.

Only then did Ashcourt notice Wolf.

'My boy!' He left Lady Ashcourt and extended his hand to Wolf. 'I am so grateful to you for escorting my precious ladies.' He shook Wolf's hand rather too energetically, then pulled him towards the door. 'Come inside, my son. Have a brandy for your trouble.'

There was no refusing the man.

They all walked in to the town house together. Holmes, the butler, was there to take the ladies' shawls and Wolf's hat and gloves.

'How is Charlotte?' Lady Ashcourt asked her husband. 'Did she say what was troubling her? Is it illness?'

'She would not talk to me at all,' he responded, his brow furrowing. 'But she said she was not ill.'

'I will go up to speak to her.' She turned to the stairway directly in front of her.

'I will go with you,' Ashcourt said. After climbing two steps, he turned to Juliana. 'Juliana, dear, would you take Wolf up to the drawing room? I believe you know where the brandy is. We will be with you directly.'

That left Wolf alone with Juliana. He followed her up the stairs to the first floor and into the drawing room. In silence she walked over to a cabinet and removed two decanters and four glasses.

She poured one glass from one decanter and handed it to Wolf. 'Brandy,' she said, then shrugged. 'Forgive me. I need something stronger than claret.' She poured another glass for herself, downing it quickly.

Wolf could not help but smile. 'I presume you will switch to claret when the Ashcourts return.'

She frowned. 'Yes. I hide that part of my past as well, that I occasionally desire brandy.'

He'd not meant it as a rebuke, but a jest.

He took a sip of his brandy and thought better of addressing the many complications between them.

He changed the subject. 'I think we must say something about Charlotte. Lord and Lady Ashcourt need to know. They need to watch her more closely.'

To his surprise she said, 'I agree. I have felt constrained from speaking. I rather promised Charlotte I would not. This was not the only time she contrived to be with Gravier.'

'Then I will tell them.' He watched her face to see how she felt about this. 'I am a little like family to them, because of my long friendship with Harris. They may listen to me.' He wanted her approval, he realised. 'Do you trust me to find a way to address this?'

It was her turn to look surprised. 'You are asking me this?' She averted her gaze. 'It is a way out of Gravier's investment scheme, is it not? If you suggest he acted improperly towards her, Felix will turn against him.'

Wolf responded, 'Yes, I have thought of that.' He tried to catch her eye. 'But that would endanger you, would it not? Did he threaten to expose you? Is that what he holds over you?'

She did not answer him.

That was enough confirmation for Wolf.

He took another sip of brandy. 'And then there is the fact that I told Gravier I would not mention him.' He tapped on his glass absently. 'I think I must in some way, though.'

She flashed him a worried look.

The door opened and Lord and Lady Ashcourt entered.

'She will not speak with us,' Kitty said immediately. 'I am beside myself with concern about her.'

Lord Ashcourt immediately poured his wife a glass of claret and himself a brandy. He waved them all over to a seating area, one meant to foster conversation. Ashcourt and his wife settled on one sofa, leaving Wolf and Juliana to sit together on the sofa facing it. Lady Ashcourt released a disquieted sigh.

Wolf fortified himself with another sip of his drink. 'If you will permit me, I believe I know something of what might be upsetting Charlotte.'

Both Lord and Lady Ashcourt leaned forward in the seat.

'Tell us,' Lady Ashcourt cried.

Wolf was uncertain how to approach this, but he carried on. 'I believe Charlotte has developed an infatuation, an unrequited one, and she does not know how to handle it.'

'An infatuation?' responded Ashcourt. 'Whoever with? She has not been among that many young men.'

'Not a young man,' Wolf explained.

Ashcourt looked puzzled. 'Who? Who is this man?'

'Monsieur Gravier.' Wolf felt Juliana tense at the man's name.

'Gravier? No,' Lady Ashcourt protested. 'He is much too old for her.'

'Is he?' Wolf countered. 'I suspect there are not too many more years' difference between Charlotte and Gravier than between you and Lord Ashcourt.'

'Oh, no,' she protested. 'I was much older than Charlotte. I was almost twenty when I met Felix.'

'She is not far from twenty, ma'am,' he said.

She seemed to ponder that. 'And he is charming...'

Ashcourt sank back in his seat, looking like a wounded puppy. 'Not Gravier. We so placed our trust in him. I cannot believe a man I esteem so well would trifle with my daughter!'

Wolf held up a hand. 'I have no liking for the man, I admit, but I did not say he was trifling with your daughter. It was he who brought this infatuation to my attention.' Sort of. 'He asked for my assistance, not wanting Charlotte to do something rash.'

Lady Ashcourt cried, 'Charlotte would not do something rash! She is not the sort.'

Juliana spoke up. 'She would not be rash intentionally, I am sure, Kitty, but a young girl in the throes of romantic emotions for the first time might make a misstep. It does sound like this Gravier wishes to prevent that. Why else would he ask Mr Wolfdon to intervene? He knows you are great friends with Wolfdon, surely.'

Lord Ashcourt, his arms folded across his chest, peered out from a lowered head. 'Has Charlotte made a misstep?'

Wolf responded, 'At the first card party she attended, she hugged Gravier after winning.'

'That was nothing but high spirits!' Lady Ashcourt said. 'You cannot accuse her of infatuation based upon one hug!'

'I spoke to her about it,' Wolf said. 'She also called it high spirits, but, even so, such behaviour could make her the subject of gossip.'

Lady Ashcourt shuddered.

Her husband leaned forwards again. 'You have not convinced me of any of this! A hug is nothing. She is not infatuated with Gravier.'

Juliana spoke again. 'I am afraid she is. Have you seen how she looks at him? Like he's the last pastry in the shop.'

'What are we to do?' cried Lady Ashcourt.

'Watch her more closely,' Wolf said. 'Gravier said he will keep his distance so that should help.'

'Perhaps we should contrive to put her around young people her age,' Juliana suggested.

'Yes,' agreed Lady Ashcourt. 'But we have not been mixing with such young people.' An idea seemed to dawn on her face. 'I have it! Juliana, you must accompany her! You and Wolf! Would not that be ideal? She will much prefer it if you two are with her.'

Wolf glanced at Juliana and was almost amused at her chagrin. Was this not the ideal plan? Put two people together who've behaved most improperly and make them in charge of a young lady's virtue. Not to mention the conflict between them.

Still, Wolf did not mind spending more time with Juliana. Perhaps given enough time she might begin to trust him.

Lady Ashcourt went on. 'Tomorrow we will look for suitable entertainments for you all to attend. I am certain there are some that interest young people. This is a splendid idea.'

The next morning Charlotte refused to leave her bed no matter how much Kitty begged her to accompany her and Juliana to the Circulating Library. Kitty was determined to discover some entertainments that would appeal to young people and to arrange invitations for Charlotte, Juliana, and Wolf.

But it was just Juliana and Kitty who took the walk. Felix had gone out much earlier.

After Kitty had lamented Charlotte's absence sufficiently, she turned to a new subject.

'Do you not think it was a good thing that I suggested you and Wolf accompany Charlotte?' Kitty asked.

'I suppose,' Juliana responded.

Kitty grinned. 'It puts you and Wolf together! I am certain as he becomes more acquainted with you, he will recognise your virtues. Then perhaps he will come up to snuff.'

Goodness. Kitty was still thinking of Wolf as a potential suitor. Juliana doubted Wolf would recognise virtue in her, not when she lacked such a thing. He certainly knew in one way she was anything but virtuous.

No matter. Wolf already was too much acquainted with her to ever consider marrying her.

The thought saddened her, but only because she wished she could be the sort of person he would esteem. Someone like Lady Allyse, perhaps.

Certainly, he would dread being forced into her company, even if it was on Charlotte's behalf.

She had to admit that she and Wolf had worked together remarkably well the night before informing Kitty and Felix about Charlotte's calf love for Gravier. Juliana had admired Wolf's clever tact, never quite revealing how brazenly Charlotte had behaved or how despicable Gravier was, but making certain Kitty and Felix knew precisely how to watch out for her.

He'd told half-truths doing so, she realised. Was it acceptable for him to do so and not for her? Her father had always said the rules were different for the nobility and the wealthy than for others.

Kitty discovered there was to be a picnic in the gardens of the Prince Regent's Pavilion the next day. She decided that would be perfect. She'd have Felix send a message to Wolf to inform him.

After the library, Kitty wanted to visit the shops. All too often when Kitty shopped with her, Kitty would insist on buying her *cousin* something. Juliana hoped she would not today. She already felt guilty for how much she'd accepted from her.

The streets were crowded, and a man jostled her. Juliana tripped against him.

'Beg pardon, ma'am,' he said as he helped her regain her balance.

She felt the bulge of his purse in one of his pockets. One quick dart of her hand and she could make it hers.

She merely nodded. 'Sir.'

She'd had other chances while out and about in Brighton to nab a purse or snatch a small article left momentarily unattended in a shop. In fact, when she'd visited the jeweller to sell him Ruskin's watch chain, the jeweller had momentarily left a ring in easy grasp when he'd been distracted by other customers. Juliana had let that opportunity slip away as well. She supposed desperation would tempt her to steal again, but, even if desperate, she expected she would imagine the disapproving look in Wolf's green eyes if he caught her.

Juliana quickly checked to be certain the man had not pilfered her purse. She needed the few coins she carried in it.

As they passed the confectioner's shop, Felix popped out of the doorway.

'Kitty, my love!' he cried.

Kitty turned and greeted him happily.

He gestured to them. 'Come. Come in. I stopped in here to buy some special treat for Charlotte, to cheer her up, and we decided to stay for tea. Come join us!'

Kitty took his arm and entered the shop, never having checked if Juliana wished to stop for tea or not.

Juliana supposed she could accept a cup of tea and a biscuit or two from Felix without too much guilt.

She paused, though, when she saw it was Gravier who shared the table with Felix. There were no other customers in the shop.

Gravier stood. 'Lady Ashcourt. Miss Walsh. What a delight it is to see you.'

'Sir,' she said.

Felix helped Kitty into a chair and Gravier pulled another one out for Juliana.

As soon as Kitty and Juliana were seated, Gravier leaned towards Kitty. 'My lady. Your husband tells me you were told of my worries about your daughter. I want to assure you I have the highest respect for her and for you and I would never step out of my place with her. I assure you, at the entertainments, I will keep my distance. So as not to distress her, you see. I hope you will understand.'

He sounded completely earnest.

Kitty was easily persuaded. 'I do understand, sir.'

He grasped her hand and squeezed it. 'I am entirely in your debt.'

The waiter approached with tea and Felix ordered four cups of chilled custard.

'I'll purchase some chocolate drops, barley sugar candy and some pretty marzipan for Charlotte before we leave,' he said.

After the waiter brought the tea and custard, Kitty asked, 'Have you been discussing business?'

Felix looked apologetic. 'We were, my dear, but we will try not to bore you and Juliana with petty details.'

Gravier slanted a glance towards Juliana. 'But perhaps the ladies are interested.' He smiled ingratiatingly. 'Ladies do have minds. Some very fine ones, in fact.'

'I am interested,' Kitty said. 'I am always interested in what matters to Felix.'

Felix smiled at her. 'I confess Gravier and I have been discussing his project.'

So the fact that Gravier so upset his daughter that she would not leave her room did nothing to dampen Felix's enthusiasm for Gravier's swindle. Juliana half wished Felix had been bludgeoning Gravier for enticing his daughter.

Of course, the other half of her was relieved that she would be safe from Gravier's threat to expose her.

'The antiquities!' Kitty said enthusiastically.

Juliana slanted a sarcastic look at Gravier.

Felix leaned towards Gravier. 'Do you suppose we can tell Juliana how you plan to retrieve the antiquities? I kept that part confidential.'

Gravier opened his palms as if giving her a gift. 'By all means. Tell her.'

Felix leaned towards her conspiratorially. 'Do you not wonder how the salvage will take place?'

'I had not thought about it,' she confessed. Gravier had undoubtedly concocted some story of how he would salvage the antiquities. None of it was real, however.

Felix bubbled with excitement anyway. 'A submarine.'

She stared blankly.

Gravier gave her a patient look. 'A submarine is a vessel that goes below the water. We have acquired the original one, the very vessel that Napoleon commissioned from some American. Before L'Empereur abandoned warfare at sea, that is.'

Juliana almost laughed aloud. This was the story he'd made up of how to salvage the supposed treasure? A boat that went underwater? And Felix and Sir John and the others believed him? This was too nonsensical.

'What is so gratifying,' added Kitty, 'is the opportunity to rescue antiquities that would otherwise be lost for all time.' This very un-Kitty-like statement had undoubtedly originated in Felix's mouth.

'That does sound gratifying.' Juliana slid another glance to Gravier, whose mouth twitched ever so slightly.

Gravier scooped out the last of his custard. 'The treasure, you see, is what Napoleon plundered in Malta and loaded on the ships that Admiral Lord Nelson sunk in Egypt's waters.'

And he'd convinced the others that retrieving such treasure was possible? Could they not see how impossible such an expedition would be? A boat that went under water. Who would credit that?

'The submarine should arrive any day now,' Gravier said. 'Then we will have the demonstration.'

Felix sat up straighter. 'There will be no investment without the demonstration.'

Juliana was beginning to see what Gravier meant about already shelling out a great deal of money to set this up.

The shop's clock struck eleven.

Gravier stood. 'I fear I must take my leave.' He inclined his head towards the attendant behind the shop's counter. 'Allow me to pay for this, my lord. It will give me pleasure to do so.'

Felix looked a little embarrassed. 'As you wish, sir. Kind of you.'

Felix and Kitty stood as well. Juliana rose more slowly.

Gravier extended his hand to Felix. 'Your alliance is most welcome, my lord.'

Felix had fallen for the scheme completely, thought Juliana dismally.

'My lady…' Gravier took Kitty's hand and blew a kiss over it.

'Monsieur,' tittered Kitty.

Then he turned to Juliana, his expression more serious. 'Miss Walsh,' he said aloud, bowing.

With a tight smile, she curtsied.

After Gravier paid the bill and left, Felix gave an elated laugh. 'Let us celebrate, ladies. Some ices, perhaps?' He signalled to the waiter. 'Bring us some elderflower ices, my good fellow.'

Kitty giggled when the waiter placed the ice in front of her. 'I shall be big as a house after all these sweets.'

Felix perused her lovingly. 'Never,' he murmured. He lifted his teacup in the air. 'Let us have a toast.' He waited until Kitty and Juliana raised theirs. 'To history! We shall do our part to preserve it.'

'History!' Kitty cried happily.

Juliana waited until they placed the cups back in the saucers. She poured them more tea. 'How much does Gravier ask you to invest?'

It was perhaps not a proper question for an impoverished female relation to ask, but Felix only blinked twice before answering, 'Twenty thousand pounds.'

'Twenty thousand pounds!' Juliana cried. 'You cannot mean this!'

Felix looked a bit chagrined. 'Well, they must purchase a ship and hire the captain and crew. They cannot chance anyone who is not directly in their employ.

They have the submarine, but, still, it is not a simple proposition.'

'Not simple at all,' Kitty added, shaking her head.

Juliana's heart raced. 'What will become of your fortune if you lose such an amount?'

Felix faltered, looking as if he had not yet considered this. 'Oh, it will not fail. Gravier insists it will not.'

'But what would such a loss do to you?' Juliana persisted.

Felix grimaced. 'I cannot say it would break me entirely.' He turned defensive. 'But, recall, one must sacrifice to preserve the past. Regard Lord Elgin.'

Lord Elgin had rescued friezes and sculptures from the Parthenon in Greece. Of course, some said he'd stolen them. It was well known he'd hoped to earn a fortune from them, a fortune that never appeared.

Felix attempted a reassuring smile. 'We shall not lose the money, however. The profits will be tremendous.'

Mercy, could Felix be more taken in by Gravier?

Juliana shook her head. 'You cannot know if this scheme will work. A boat that goes under water. It is not to be credited.'

Her heart pounded. This was the perfect moment to tell Felix and Kitty all about Gravier, to save their fortune before these foolish people risked so much.

She opened her mouth to speak, but shut it again, turning away so they could not see her face. She could not breathe. She ought to tell them the truth, but she was too afraid.

'Sir John believes in the scheme,' Felix said somewhat defensively. 'In fact, he believes he has convinced his son-in-law to release the funds.'

'His son-in-law?' she asked.

'Lord Hale,' Felix replied. 'Lord Hale controls his funds.'

Because Sir John could not be trusted? Juliana wondered. She wished she could talk to Wolf about this.

'How much does Sir John invest?' she asked Felix instead.

'Eight thousand pounds.'

'Eight thousand!' Her stomach clenched. Had they all gone daft?

'Besides,' Felix went on, 'we will neither of us invest before we have seen the capability of the submarine. You heard Gravier say it will arrive soon.'

'Any day now, he said.' A tiny worry line creased Kitty's forehead, and the giddiness disappeared from her voice.

Juliana closed her eyes. She should run. Now. But, then, she really must stay to accompany Charlotte to the picnic. Perhaps she could see Charlotte abandon her tendre for Gravier before leaving.

And she would see Wolf tomorrow. Urge him to find a way to stop this.

That felt like the only other chance—unless she sacrificed herself.

Chapter Fifteen

Wolf had received Lord Ashcourt's message the previous day and sent an immediate reply that he would be happy to escort Charlotte and Juliana to the picnic. Truth was he would be happy to be in Juliana's company again. Openly. In daylight. Not sneaking into alleyways. Or taking her into brothels.

He still berated himself for doing that.

He set out for the Ashcourts' town house, glad that the sky was clear, the wind quiet and the day warm. It would be a fine day to spend with Juliana.

They'd found a common ground in protecting Charlotte. To be so in accord with Juliana was as novel as spending daylight with her. It heartened him.

When he sounded the knocker on the Ashcourts' door and was admitted by Holmes, he found two subdued companions. At least they were dressed to spend an afternoon outdoors, light filmy dresses, wide-brimmed hats to shade their faces. Charlotte looked as if she were a lamb facing slaughter, though, and Juliana looked wary and withdrawn.

Perhaps the day might not be so fine after all.

The gardens of the Regent's Pavilion were a short walk away. The Prince Regent was not in residence in his Brighton Pavilion, not with renovations to the building still not complete. The building was embellished with onion-shaped domes and nearly a dozen minarets. Wolf thought it odd and fanciful, but also exotic and classical with its gleaming white façade.

Its grounds included great expanses of lawn, many beds of flowers in bloom, their fragrance mixing with the salty brine odour of the sea.

When they reached the entrance to the garden it was already busy with other guests. Tables were set up laden with food and drink, blankets and pillows dotted the grass for guests to lounge upon.

'This looks dreadful,' Charlotte muttered as they walked around looking for an empty place to sit.

Lady Ashcourt had indeed selected an entertainment that appealed to the younger set of Brighton's visitors. The guests were mostly of an age with Charlotte. There were a few familiar faces, but Wolf had been out of the country for so long that he did not know most of the younger men and women there. Juliana did not know anyone, of course.

They found an unclaimed blanket and pillows and sat themselves on the ground.

'We will stay just a little while,' Charlotte said. 'Do not tell me we have to endure the whole afternoon.'

Wolf silently echoed her sentiments.

'Is it not too soon to tell?' Juliana said. 'Besides, you promised Kitty you would try to enjoy yourself.'

'I'll bring you something to drink,' Wolf said.

He did not have to go far. A servant was carrying drinks on a tray and offering them to the guests.

The picnic was hosted by the Castle Inn, parts of which had also been purchased by the Regent, which explained, perhaps, why they were able to use the Pavilion's gardens.

Wolf returned to their blanket and lowered himself down next to Juliana.

'A servant will come around momentarily,' he told her.

Charlotte turned to them both, a determined look on her face. 'What did you tell my parents? I know you talked to them.' She glared at Juliana. 'Did you tell?'

She did not spell out what she meant, but Juliana knew. It must have been about what Juliana promised not to tell.

'I did not,' Juliana said.

Wolf broke in. 'I talked to them, Lottie. I warned you about your behaviour, if you remember. You did not heed me, obviously. Your parents needed to know.'

She glared at him. 'What did you tell them?'

'Only enough for them to better supervise you,' he responded. Better to say as little as possible.

The servant brought them glasses of lemonade, which they took gratefully. The sunny day meant a hot day, as well, and the lemonade was welcome.

Wolf gulped his down.

Juliana took a sip. 'Your parents know that you are infatuated with Gravier. They do not know how indiscreetly you behaved towards him.' She gave Charlotte an understanding look. 'We know that infatuation makes us do foolish things.'

'Infatuation?' Charlotte glared at her scornfully. 'Why is it that if Wolf's mother looks upon Lord Lymond—or any man, for that matter—it is called having a *regard* for him? Or a *grand passion*? Be my age, however, and all is dismissed as mere infatuation!'

'Charlotte!' Juliana's voice turned sharp. 'That was unkind. You should not say such things about Wolf's mother.'

Even though it was true.

Wolf spoke up. 'Lottie, there is a difference. A married woman is permitted more licence than an unmarried one. My mother does not have to protect her reputation. You do.'

Charlotte huffed. 'Men do not have to protect their reputations. Married or not, they can have their liaisons and no one cares a whit.'

That was true enough.

Juliana caught Charlotte's eye and spoke solemnly, 'It is not fair. Nothing in life is fair, but I can tell you that you do not wish the life of one of those women with whom men have their liaisons.'

Charlotte lifted her chin. 'What do you know of it, Juliana?'

'I have been in the world, Charlotte.' She gave Charlotte a direct gaze. 'And I know that your feelings make you vulnerable. You must control them. If the man is worth your *regard*, your *passion*, he will not allow you to be compromised. He will court you properly.'

Wolf had not behaved properly to Juliana. He had never seen her as one to whom he must behave properly.

He felt mortally ashamed of himself.

Who in her life had behaved properly to her? Protected her? Respected her? Probably Lord and Lady Ashcourt had been the first. And Wolf had threatened to take even that away from her.

Good God. He despised himself even more.

A young man approached their blanket. He bowed to Charlotte. 'Lady Charlotte, do you remember me? I am Wevenly. We attended dance class together two years ago.'

'I remember you, Wevenly,' Charlotte said rather blandly.

He glanced at Wolf and Juliana and back at Charlotte, but she did not get the hint that he wished for introductions.

Wolf stood. 'Wevenly, I am Wolfdon. Sir John Wolfdon's son and a good friend of Lady Charlotte's brother.'

'The diplomat?' the young man commented. 'I have heard of him.'

'Yes. Harris and I are attached to the embassy in Paris. I am merely visiting from there.' Wolf turned to Juliana. 'But allow me to present you to Miss Walsh who is Lady Ashcourt's cousin.'

'They are both my chaperons,' Charlotte said scathingly.

Because you need chaperons, Wolf wanted to say.

'Please sit, Mr Wevenly,' Juliana said.

'It is Lord Wevenly, Juliana.' Charlotte spoke as if Juliana ought to have known this. 'His father is the Earl of Norwood.'

The girl was being hateful. It was all Wolf could do to keep from ringing a peal over her head.

Wevenly ignored that exchange. He turned to Charlotte. 'Have you been in Brighton long? We have just arrived.'

'A few weeks,' she replied.

'Have you dipped in the ocean yet?' he asked her.

'No,' was all she replied.

'I am keen to bathe in the sea,' he went on, then asked Wolf, 'Have you done any sea-bathing, sir?'

'Not yet,' Wolf said.

'You might wish to join us tomorrow. My friends and I are meeting at the men's beach at eleven o'clock.'

'I will consider it,' Wolf said.

Wevenly looked around, somewhat uncertainly. He turned to Charlotte again. 'I wonder, Lady Charlotte, if you would like to join me and my friends in a game of battledore and shuttlecock? I believe you are acquainted with one or two of our group.' He turned to Wolf and Juliana. 'With your permission, of course.'

'You may go if you like, Lottie,' Wolf said.

She rose and Wevenly gave her his arm. As they walked away, Wolf heard her say, 'I have not played the game in ages.'

'That is no problem,' Wevenly responded. 'None of us are very good at it.'

When they were out of earshot, Juliana said, 'I am beginning to think Kitty is a genius. This is precisely where Charlotte belongs.'

'I agree.' Wolf sat down on a pillow and perused her face. 'How do you fare today, Fleur?'

She shrugged. 'I am well.'

But he had the sense she was withdrawn, like in Paris. Hiding what was inside her.

They saw Charlotte join a group a little distance away. They walked to an open space of lawn and took turns batting a shuttlecock back and forth, laughing as they did so. Charlotte played, but she did not laugh with them.

Juliana spoke up suddenly. 'Did you know that Gravier is telling the investors that they will recover treasure by using an underwater boat?'

'A submarine,' he responded. 'Yes. I knew that.'

'He's found men who believe an underwater boat will retrieve treasure?' She shook her head, then sat up straighter on her pillow. 'Wolf, Gravier says this underwater boat will arrive here in a matter of days. There will be a demonstration.'

'Days?' He frowned.

That did not leave him much time. He'd received a letter from Lord Hale approving his plan and promising to make as many arrangements as possible. Hale had travelled to London to do so. Wolf had not known he'd have to go to London to meet with Hale so soon.

Juliana touched his arm. 'Do you know how much your father intends to invest with Gravier?' she asked.

'I have not heard the amount.' Wolf had not heard, because it would never happen. Hale knew the scheme was a fraud.

She waved an exasperated hand. 'Eight thousand pounds.'

Eight thousand pounds? Where did his father think he would get that kind of money?

Juliana stared at him. 'Why would your family invest so much? It will ruin them, will it not?'

He kept his expression composed. 'Did Gravier tell you this?'

She shook her head. 'Felix told me. He plans to invest twenty thousand, which will ruin him.'

'Twenty thousand.' Wolf shook his head. 'Is the man daft?'

'His motivation is not the money, but to rescue important pieces of antiquity. Maltese antiquity lost in the sea around Egypt.'

He laughed derisively. 'You jest.'

'They are all daft.'

He peered at her. 'Why would Ashcourt speak to you about money?'

'I asked him,' she said simply.

'And he told you just like that?'

'Yes, Wolf, he did.' Her eyes flashed.

He frowned. 'And he told you my father's business?'

'Yes.'

His brow furrowed.

'Ask them yourself, if you do not believe me.' She turned away from him.

He touched her arm. 'Juliana.'

Her gaze met his and he felt as connected to her as if they were joined together again in bed.

'Why do you tell me this?' he asked.

'I do not wish any harm to come to you or your family,' she said.

He inhaled sharply, wanting to reply that she could stop the harm if she exposed Gravier, but he knew she could not do that. He knew his idea must work to stop this insane plan.

'Juliana, I am leaving tomorrow for London,' he said, having decided in that moment.

'Leaving,' she whispered. 'Oh.'

She glanced away, looking as vulnerable as she had briefly appeared in Paris.

'Listen to me,' he said. 'Can you find out exactly when Gravier intends to have his demonstration?'

She blinked. 'Do you mean you will come back?'

She thought he would not return? That he would abandon her like Gravier and the other partner did?

He felt like holding her in his arms and assuring her she was not alone now.

But Charlotte and her new young man were playing battledore and shuttlecock, a violinist was tuning his violin, and countless guests were talking, eating, playing as if having no cares at all.

He lowered his voice. 'Of course I am coming back.'

She released a relieved breath.

'Find out whatever you can,' he said. 'I'll be back as soon as I am able.' He stopped short of telling her about his plan to thwart Gravier's scheme, although he was not sure why.

'I'll try,' she responded. 'I am certain Felix will tell me whatever he knows. I suspect Gravier will not be as frequent a visitor in the house, so I am not certain what I can learn directly from him.'

'Yes.' Wolf thought about it. 'Gravier will keep his distance because of Charlotte.'

He glanced over to Charlotte. She jumped to hit the shuttlecock and missed. Wevenly picked it up off the grass for her. Charlotte was not exactly smiling and laughing like the others with rackets in their hands, but it was a good start.

'I am sorry I will not be here to help you chaperon.'

She smiled and inclined her head towards Charlotte and Wevenly. 'I suspect you will not be needed as an escort, although I might still be required to chaperon.'

He smiled back.

This is what he liked best, even more than the love-making with her. He liked sitting comfortably next to her. Talking with ease. Working together instead of as enemies. He was leaving right when she was starting to trust him a little.

He would miss her terribly while he was in London.

The next morning Gravier made his way towards the sea wall as the sky showed glorious red, deepening to a purple that promised rain before the day was out. He hoped to see Lord Ashcourt or Sir John or Seabane or any of the investors. The need to stay away from Lady Charlotte meant not being as present as he thought he ought to be. These gentlemen often sought the morning sea air.

He'd much prefer sleeping late.

He glanced at the sky again, hoping the rain would hold off until his task was accomplished.

There were few people out this early, though. Perhaps they'd not wanted to risk being caught in the rain. He ought to have stayed abed himself, especially after another restless night.

Sleep proved difficult in Brighton.

He started back in the direction of his inn when footsteps sounded behind him. He turned.

It was Charlotte, her skirts fluttering in the morning breeze, hurrying towards him, like some colourful bird in flight.

'Gravier!' she cried. 'Wait a moment.'

Mon Dieu, he ought to run in the other direction.

'What are you doing, Lady Charlotte? You are not to be seen with me.'

She did not carry an umbrella and only had a paisley shawl to keep her warm.

She reached his side, complexion flushed and radiant. 'I heard gentlemen like to walk early in the morning, so I watched for you.'

Foolish girl.

'How else was I to be with you without Juliana and Wolf making my parents guard me every moment?' She pursed her lips—her rose-pink lips.

He glanced around. Luckily there was no one near. 'No. You must go home. You endanger my work.'

He seized her arm and propelled her in the direction of her lodgings. Fat raindrops splattered against his face, promising a downpour. He ought to walk her home, but he did not dare. He'd promised to stay away from her.

'Go. Now,' he ordered.

She turned to him. 'I—I am not mistaken, am I? You do want me?'

He stepped back as if struck. Because he did want her.

'Go!' he again ordered.

The wanting of her made him turn his back on her and stride away. And made him loathe the man he'd become, a man totally unworthy of her.

The rain fell in sheets by the time he reached his room in the inn. After brushing the wet from his coat, he opened the door.

'Who is the young beauty?' a voice asked.

His head snapped up.

Turstin was there, sitting in comfort in Gravier's room, feet up on a stool, his thin, still-blond hair slicked back against his scalp.

'What the devil are you doing here?' Gravier snapped.

Turstin's expression turned stormy. 'I came to witness my triumph.'

The destruction of Lady Ashcourt and her family, his revenge against a family that had disowned him and banished him. And likely saved his life by so doing.

Gravier did not want him here. 'You said you would never set foot in England again.'

Turstin stretched. 'Oh, this one time should make it worth it. The submarine is on its way. It should arrive in three or four days. Or sooner. I cannot resist seeing the face of my niece, knowing everything will be taken away from her like my family took it away from me.'

Gravier felt sick to his stomach. Turstin's mere presence made him ill.

'I've never seen this niece of mine. I want to set eyes on her. I want to let her know who has stolen her and her husband's money. I want her to spend every day wondering if I will come back to claim my title.'

'You are after the title as well?' Gravier asked. What else could he take away from his niece?

'No, of course I am not,' Turstin snapped. 'But she won't know that. We'll be enjoying ourselves in Rome or Venice.'

Gravier realised he was done. After this scheme, he was going to get as far from Turstin as he could.

Turstin leaned back in the chair again. 'So tell me. Who was the beauty?'

Chapter Sixteen

The day after Wolf left for London in the pouring rain, Juliana sat in the pew at Chapel Royal, holding her hymnal, mouthing the lyrics to the hymn:

> *Holy Lord God! I love thy truth,*
> *Nor dare Thy least commandment slight...*

She did not know the tune but appreciated the irony of her attending a Sunday church service. Truthfully, she thought the ceremony quietly soothing.

She glanced behind her.

Gravier was seated towards the back. Good. As far away from Charlotte as possible. Still, she needed to speak to him, to get any new information from him about his demonstration and the silly underwater boat. She needed to catch him when Charlotte was otherwise occupied. He would probably attend the afternoon's promenade and tea, but she preferred to catch him this morning.

For Wolf.

She closed her eyes, already missing him. Their afternoon together chaperoning Charlotte had been one of the most pleasant days she'd ever spent. Once Wevenly had taken Charlotte under his wing, Juliana and Wolf had been left alone together.

That was when she'd promised to find out as much as she could about Gravier's plans and she was determined to keep her promise.

Imagine. She'd made a promise she was determined to keep.

One of her father's favourite sayings was *promises are meant to be broken* and now she was determined to keep one.

Next to her in the pew, Kitty's clear soprano and Felix's baritone melded together as perfectly as their personalities. Unlike herself, Kitty and Felix certainly belonged in this lovely church. Goodness shone within them like the sun through the coloured glass of the church windows. If only Felix and Kitty would not be so easily taken in by Gravier.

And by herself, of course.

It had been folly for her to think she could marry into the *ton*. She glanced across the aisle to where Lady Allyse, elegantly dressed, hymnal in hand, stood with her father. Lady Allyse belonged in the *ton*.

Or as a diplomat's wife.

Her throat tightened and the words on the page of her hymnal blurred. She blinked and pretended she was finishing the hymn. As the organ faded, Kitty gave her a fond look and squeezed her hand.

Juliana dared compose a prayer before the service ended. Silently she prayed she could find a way to convince Gravier to leave the Ashcourts and the Wolfdons—and even Seabane and others—out of his swindle and to leave Brighton for ever.

She thought it might be acceptable from a woman

of her character as long as she did not ask for anything for herself.

As the people filed out of the pews to the outside of the church, they stood in clusters, greeting each other and speaking pleasantries. Sir John had joined Lords Seabane and Plackstone conversing with Gravier.

She'd promised Wolf...

Luckily Wevenly engaged Charlotte in conversation, so Felix and Kitty headed towards Gravier as well.

Someone called Juliana's name. 'Miss Walsh?'

It was Lady Allyse. Juliana had no choice but to approach her.

'How are you today?' Lady Allyse asked, a friendly look on her face, shaded by a beautiful wide-brimmed hat set on an angle and adorned with silk flowers.

'I am well,' Juliana responded, uncomfortable in the presence of all Lady Allyse's perfection.

Lady Allyse smiled. 'I heard Wolfdon rode to London in all that rain yesterday.'

What was she to say?

She'd worried about him on horseback, rain soaking through his clothing, chilling him, perhaps making him ill.

'He told you he went to London, did he not?' Lady Allyse asked.

'I knew of it.' Juliana spoke stiffly, unsure if she should admit to being in Wolf's confidence.

'We shall miss him.' Lady Allyse smiled again.

Juliana's brow furrowed at the word *we*. 'Indeed,' she managed to say.

'Do you go to the promenade today?' the woman continued.

'Yes.'

'I hope to see you there.' Lady Allyse curtsied.

Juliana curtsied back and the lady walked back to her father, who was still in the cluster of people around Gravier. Juliana continued to stare at her. For Lady Allyse to greet her was not so surprising, but so pointed an effort at conversing? And speaking about Wolf?

Lady Allyse glanced back at her and smiled. Juliana nodded and quickly averted her gaze.

Charlotte walked up to her. 'I cannot ask Mama or Papa.' She tossed a pointed glance towards them, still in conversation with Gravier. 'Wevenly has invited me to join him and his friends on a walk by the sea. Am I permitted to go?'

It seemed a good thing to Juliana. A group of carefree young people taking a walk together. 'Yes, I am sure your parents would agree. Go and enjoy yourself.'

Juliana would have felt better about it, except she caught Charlotte tossing one long, yearning gaze at Gravier before she left with Wevenly and his friends.

Kitty hurried over with Felix.

'I told Charlotte she could take a walk with her new friends,' Juliana told them. 'Do you approve?'

'Oh, yes!' Kitty said enthusiastically. 'I think them precisely what she needs. I do hope the young people will attend the promenade this afternoon. Monsieur Gravier told us he would be attending. Or I should say he rather *warned* us he was attending. Perhaps that is an entertainment Charlotte could miss.'

'That would be safest,' Juliana agreed.

Juliana watched Gravier's pale blue eyes turn to gaze at Charlotte walking off on Wevenly's arm. He appeared aching and melancholy. Like Charlotte had said. Sad.

Juliana watched the others claiming Gravier's company drift away and saw her chance to speak to him.

'I believe I shall attend to an errand at the shops,' she told Kitty. 'But I'll follow directly.'

Kitty added two other errands for her before she and Felix strolled away.

Gravier saw Juliana alone and approached her.

'Walk with me a little,' she asked.

He nodded. They headed in the direction of the Pavilion's gardens.

'Are you still planning your swindle?' He'd expect her to be direct.

Gravier turned a false smile upon her. 'Certainly I am. The submarine is on its way.'

Her insides twisted. She switched to French. 'You must know the amount Lord Ashcourt wagers on your scheme will completely impoverish the family. They will not be able to recover.'

A muscle in Gravier's cheek flexed, but his eyes flashed. 'If they are foolish enough to fall for this nonsense, they deserve the loss, do they not?'

This was the excuse her father always made for a swindle. 'Does Charlotte deserve it, Lyon? Surely she will be the innocent victim in this.'

He held her gaze almost too steadily, as if he were doing so with effort. 'Did your father not train us to avoid any attachments, *chérie*? Or are you merely afraid there will no longer be enough money to support you?'

She held steady, too. 'At one time I believed you were attached to me, Lyon. I know you have feelings for the girl.'

He swung away and started walking again. 'It is too late—'

She pursued him. 'You will ruin her life, Gravier.'

He stopped abruptly and rounded on her, his eyes flashing with more emotion than she'd ever seen him express. 'Leave it, Juliana. We are not supposed to have hearts, are we? Why do you wish to pretend I have one?'

He strode away without a backward glance.

In London that same morning Wolf woke to a bright sunny room. Disorientated for a moment, he realised he was in Lord Hale's London town house on Half Moon Street and that he'd slept a lot later than he'd intended.

The journey from Brighton had taken much longer than anticipated. The rain. The mud. The crowded inns. He'd finally reached Half Moon Street after eleven hours. Tired. Hungry. And soaked to the skin.

He'd been surprised to see his sister Elizabeth there—he'd assumed she'd stay at Hale's country house with the children. She'd quickly dispatched the servants to prepare a hot bath for Wolf and had forbidden her husband to discuss anything until the morning. Soon he was clean, warm, in dry borrowed clothes, fed and, most gratifyingly, given some excellent brandy.

Then sent to bed.

He'd forgotten how imperious an older sister could be.

How long had he slept? He could not see the clock on the mantel from his bed.

After a light knock on the door, a footman peeked in and, seeing Wolf awake, he asked, 'Are you wishing to rise, sir?'

Wolf nodded. He sat up and rubbed his face. 'What time is it?'

'Almost ten o'clock, sir.'

Ten o'clock? He never slept that late.

The footman carried folded clothes. He lifted them towards Wolf. 'Your clothing is still drying, sir. Lord Hale has provided you with some dry ones.'

Wolf was not used to being so thoroughly attended to. He and Harris shared a servant in Paris and cared mostly for themselves.

The clothes fit him reasonably well. Hale was broader in the chest and slightly taller, but the effect was merely as if Wolf had a poor tailor.

Once dressed, the footman told him, 'Breakfast is served in the dining room, sir.'

Odd. Wolf would have expected the smaller sitting room. He walked downstairs and entered the dining room but halted.

Seated around the table were, not only his sister Elizabeth and Hale, but also his other two sisters and their husbands and Lord Locksworth, his sister Susan's father-in-law.

'By God,' he exclaimed. 'This is a surprise.'

Hale grinned. 'I thought we could use some help.'

Susan and his other sister Joanna bounded out of their chairs and hurried over to hug him.

He laughed. 'You two are daft to be here.' London in the summer simply was not the thing to do.

'We couldn't resist being a part of this,' Susan said.

Joanna led him to his chair.

'But all of you?' Wolf had only written to Hale.

Hale spoke up. 'There was much to do and who better to help than family?' He sent a fond look towards his wife.

Before Wolf sat down, he reached over to shake Lord Locksworth's hand. 'My lord, you are especially a surprise. So good to see you.'

'I feel honoured to be included,' Lord Locksworth said.

'Please, Wolf,' Elizabeth said. 'Have yourself some breakfast.'

She signalled a footman who brought him selections from the sideboard. Joanna poured him some tea.

Wolf, suddenly too hungry to be self-conscious about the rest of them watching him eat, cut a piece of ham and put it in his mouth.

Hale said, 'It is all set.'

Wolf gaped at him. 'All set?'

'All set,' Hale repeated. 'We shall execute your plan. Set up a treasure-hunting scheme of our own to out-swindle the swindlers. We have arranged a diving bell and divers to demonstrate how treasure can be salvaged more effectively than with a submarine. Afterwards, of course, we'll tell them it was all a ruse and warn them that Gravier's plan must be a bigger ruse.'

'You have arranged it already?' Wolf had thought he must do most of the arranging.

'We're all in,' added Everly. 'I've already found a man—Mr Fisher—who used a diving bell to salvage a mass of rock lost in a shipwreck. He and his men are already on their way to Brighton with the diving bell. They will be ready to make the demonstration whenever we say.'

Bentham broke in. 'And I have a map-maker making us some false maps showing treasure right on the shores of England.'

Lord Locksworth added, 'I will come along, saying I've already invested, and I'll recommend they do as well. Do you think they will believe a Frenchman over the Marquess of Locksworth?' He spoke his title in an exaggerated voice.

Hale laughed. 'An English apparatus will be trusted more than a French one, especially a French apparatus invented by an American.'

Wolf's sisters had made good matches. Bentham was Joanna's husband and Viscount Winbray's eldest son. Everly, married to Susan, was Lord Locksworth's younger son and a rising star in the House of Commons. Elizabeth, of course had made the best match, marrying Hale, a marquess. Even more, these men all seemed decent fellows, devoted to their wives.

And they seemed to have embraced him, distant as he'd been to them.

Struck with emotion, he attacked his breakfast while the others talked.

For so many years, busy with diplomatic duties and the war, he'd hardly given his family a thought between the letters they wrote him on occasions of marriages and births. And deaths. He'd thought his sisters had escaped the chaos of their parents by marrying into other families, but never had he anticipated how it felt to have his own family suddenly grow to include everyone around the table.

The next day Juliana accompanied Felix, Kitty and Charlotte on their daily walk to the Circulating Library. They had just left the town house and were nearing the end of the street when Juliana saw Gravier approach accompanied by another man. Surely with Charlotte with them, Gravier would simply pass them by. As he came closer, however, the hairs on the back of Juliana's neck rose.

Turstin was with him.

Turstin!

No! He was not supposed to be here!

Her heart pounded. There was no escaping him.

'Good morning, Monsieur Gravier.' Kitty's greeting was wary as, of course, it would be with Charlotte at her side.

Juliana held back, just a little, dipping her head so that the brim of her hat shaded her face. Gravier would simply pass them by, knowing he needed to avoid Charlotte. Perhaps Turstin would not notice Juliana.

But Gravier seemed to head directly for them.

Felix nodded to him. 'Gravier.'

Gravier put on one of his smiles. 'How pleasant to see you this morning. I do hope you are all quite well.' He doffed his hat to Kitty.

'We are quite well, are we not, Felix?' Kitty responded.

'Quite well,' echoed Felix.

Juliana noticed Turstin eyeing Kitty directly. She was the surviving member of his family, although Kitty had told her that her black sheep uncle had been banished and all his portraits destroyed before she was born.

Felix made as if to pass them by, but Turstin did not move. Did he expect an introduction? Was he going to tell Kitty who he was?

Juliana's knees trembled.

Gravier cleared his throat. 'Allow me to present a colleague of mine. Lady Ashcourt, Lord Ashcourt, Lady Charlotte, please meet Mr Turstin.'

A tiny frown creased Kitty's brow. 'You seem familiar, sir.'

Turstin looked Lady Ashcourt directly in the eye, a tactic Juliana's father had taught her when she was a child. 'We have not met, my lady. I have been out of the country many years. Trade, you know. Besides, I would have remembered someone as lovely as you.'

Kitty coloured at the sort of compliment that usually gave her pleasure. Did she sense they were in the presence of malevolence? She turned to glance at Juliana, calling attention to her.

'And this other lady, Gravier?' Turstin asked.

'Gravier, you have not presented your friend to our cousin.' She stepped aside, putting Juliana in full view.

'Ah, yes,' Gravier said smoothly. 'Miss Walsh, may I present Mr Turstin.'

Juliana saw the change in Turstin, a stiffening of posture, tension crackling around him. She felt faint.

'Miss Walsh,' he said, drawing out the sound so that he reminded Juliana of a snake hissing.

'Mr Turstin.' Juliana feared her voice shook as she dropped into a curtsy.

A few more inanities were exchanged, and the characteristically garrulous Kitty and Felix had little to say.

When the others were not looking, Juliana mouthed to Gravier, 'You lied to me.'

'I will explain,' he mouthed in return.

'We must be on our way,' Felix said and finally they were free. Gravier and Turstin moved on and Juliana could breathe again.

'What an unpleasant man,' Kitty murmured.

Unpleasant, indeed. The sound of his boot heels tapping against the cobbles rang in the air like a death knell.

Chapter Seventeen

By the time they reached the Circulating Library, Juliana was hardly aware of putting one foot in front of the other.

Turstin was in Brighton and he'd seen her.

Charlotte parted from them immediately and Juliana hoped it was because of Gravier and not a fright caused by Turstin. Felix and Kitty made their way to the Master of Ceremonies book to see who had arrived since the day before when they'd checked.

Juliana could not move. Her heart pounded wildly in her chest, and she felt panic choking her. She wanted to run, to not even take time to pack a portmanteau or to wait for the next coach out of Brighton, to run as fast and as far as her legs could carry her, as far away as possible from Turstin.

Everything was suddenly more dangerous. He was capable of disposing of enemies without a backward thought, and she had no doubt she was now his enemy.

Turstin would be furious that she'd pretended to be a Walsh. He would see it as a personal affront to him that she'd used *his* name and pretended to be *his* daughter. He'd not blink twice at destroying her for it.

Juliana's vision turned black. She heard Kitty's voice speaking to someone. Kitty sounded far away. Juliana groped for something to lean on.

A man's arm crossed over her shoulders. 'Are you feeling ill, Miss Walsh?'

She blinked and her eyes focused. Lord Seabane held her steady.

She regained her balance and drew away. 'It is nothing, I assure you.' Touching her forehead, she hastily added, 'A bit of the headache, I fear. I am not at all certain I shall stay here very long.'

Reason had returned, as well. Her racing heart had slowed, and she felt as if she could breathe again. There was no doubt she must flee Brighton. Flee Turstin, before he enacted his revenge, but she would proceed as if this were an ordinary day, not the day Turstin arrived.

Lord Seabane looked upon her with kindness. 'I would be honoured to escort you back to your lodging, if need be.'

She gave a grateful smile. 'I am certain I will recover directly.'

Her attention was caught by a mournful tune being plucked out on the pianoforte. She turned in that direction and back to Lord Seabane. 'Do forgive me, sir. I promised Lady Charlotte I would listen to her play.'

It seemed even more urgent to keep Charlotte away from Gravier, now that Turstin was here.

Lord Seabane's brow creased in concern. 'Are you certain you are back to rights?'

She straightened. 'I am.'

'If you have need of me, Miss Walsh, I will be at your service.' He bowed.

She managed a curtsy. 'You are too kind.'

Juliana hurried over to the pianoforte.

Charlotte glanced up from the keys. 'Oh, Juliana,' she spoke without enthusiasm. 'Are you spying on me?'

'No,' Juliana replied, still unsteady enough to place a hand on the pianoforte for support. 'I was concerned about you, that's all.'

The young girl looked past Juliana and her face flushed with pleasure. Juliana did not need to turn around to know that Gravier had arrived.

Gravier bowed. 'Lady Charlotte.'

'Gravier,' the girl responded breathlessly.

He turned to Juliana. 'Miss Walsh, I desire to speak with you. Do you have a moment?'

Charlotte's face fell and her eyes shot sparks at Juliana.

'I have a moment, that is all.' Juliana's legs barely kept her upright as she followed Gravier to the bookshelves.

'He wants to see you,' Gravier said as soon as they were private. 'Meet me this afternoon.'

'I do not want to see him!' She turned away.

He seized her arm. 'Juliana, I must take you to him. He is determined. He will see you no matter what. He employs some thugs who will come after you and not care if you are injured in the taking.'

She pushed him off. 'Do not threaten me.'

He switched to French. 'I am warning you.' He swallowed. 'Heed me, I beg you. I did not betray you to Turstin. I did not lie to you. He was not supposed to be here. I fear if you do not come to see him willingly, he is going to suspect you of being against him and that makes him very dangerous to you.'

She stared at him, thinking she ought not to trust anything he said, but what choice did she have? She just needed to keep her wits about her until she could escape for good.

'Juliana? I am telling you the truth.'

She clenched her hands into fists and answered in French, 'Very well. I will tell Kitty I wish to go to the shops this afternoon. Meet me at the apothecary at two o'clock.'

He nodded and walked away. Juliana leaned against the bookshelf until she was steady enough to walk again. As she emerged from behind the books, out of the corner of her eye she spied a flash of colour and heard a swish of skirts. When she walked back to the pianoforte, Charlotte was gone.

Juliana arrived at the apothecary promptly at two o'clock. Gravier was already there, pacing to and fro in front of the shop.

He lifted his head at her approach. 'Come,' he said, his voice anxious. 'We must go to the harbour.'

He led her to streets where rough-looking sailors eyed her as she passed and brightly dressed women sauntered lazily.

She pulled him to a halt and glanced around her. 'Where are you taking me, Gravier?'

He urged her on. 'To a warehouse near the docks. *Pardon*, Juliana. This is not a nice place, but we will not stay long.'

'Do you expect me to just follow you to this place?' She pulled away from him.

He seized both her arms and leaned into her face. '*Mon Dieu*, Juliana! We must both be on our guard. I will protect you if I am able, but you must not further aggravate Turstin. He is not acting reasonably, do you comprehend?'

Juliana nodded, shocked that Gravier's typically smooth manners would so thoroughly abandon him.

They reached a row of warehouses and Juliana felt a frisson of anxiety travel up her spine. Gravier brought her to the door of a huge building made of weathered wood. He knocked on the door.

A man answered, greeting them in French. Turstin stood inside the doorway as if he had been waiting for her.

He clamped his thick fingers around her arm. 'Come with me.' Gesturing for Gravier to follow, he dragged her past a large cart with what must be the submarine upon it. Pulling her into a small room, he snapped at Gravier, 'Hurry up and close the door behind you.'

Gravier obeyed.

Turstin released her and sneered, 'It has been a long time, Juliana.'

She made herself look him in the eye. 'Long enough for my father to mount the guillotine, Turstin.'

His eyes flashed. 'Your father was a fool to get caught.'

His words enraged her, and she forgot her fear. 'You assured him there would be no guard on the jewels.'

He pursed his lips. 'He did not run fast enough.'

Juliana opened her mouth, but Gravier, standing behind Turstin, raised a quelling finger. She bit back more angry words and resolved to proceed with caution.

Turstin lumbered over to a desk and fussed with some papers. 'What are you doing in Brighton?' He swung back to her. 'I demand you tell me.'

She shrugged. 'I am merely surviving, Turstin.'

He strode towards her again. 'Surviving? You have some scheme, do you not? You are pretending to be a cousin of my niece? Pretending to be *my* daughter? You? The daughter of a nobody, an innkeeper's son—'

Juliana met his eye steadily. 'I had only myself to depend on, Turstin. If I wanted to survive, I had to pretend to be someone else. It was you who left your documents with my father's belongings. You gave me the tools. I crafted papers from them to make my story credible. You'd killed yourself years ago. I killed you off instead of my father and used your name. It was all I had.'

'You dared to use my name!' His eyes bulged.

She laughed. 'Do not claim familial outrage, sir! You rejected your family before I was even born. You cast away your family name long ago.'

'You have used me, girl.' Spittle flew from his mouth. 'No one uses me!'

Gravier stepped between them. 'Come now, Turstin. It was clever of her, you must admit. It does you no harm.'

Turstin wheeled on him. 'You kept her little secrets, Gravier. You betrayed me after all I have done for you—'

'We have neither of us betrayed you,' Gravier said in a mollifying voice. 'Indeed—' he shot a quick glance to Juliana, entreating her with his eyes '—Juliana has been instrumental in setting up Ashcourt. She has encouraged him to invest a huge amount.'

Juliana's eyes widened in understanding. Gravier was pretending she was an ally. If Turstin thought she was assisting him in his revenge, he might be cajoled into forgiving her.

'I'm pragmatic, Turstin,' she broke in, playing along. 'You stand to make a fortune here. I merely want my share. Then I will be pleased to become someone new again and never trouble you further.'

Turstin looked uncertain.

She put on a sly expression. 'Of course, I can use my influence with Lord Ashcourt to induce him to withdraw any offer of investment. He is an easily malleable man. Your niece, as well.'

Turstin's eyes narrowed. 'Or I can imprison you here where you can do no more mischief.'

She felt a flash of fear, but made herself laugh. 'Oh, I assure you that my disappearance will throw the Earl and Countess into a great tizzy. They are fond of me, you see. Unlike you, Lady Ashcourt has a strong sense of family loyalty. I am certain all thoughts of submarines and treasure will vanish from her husband's mind until I am safely found again.'

She held Turstin's gaze as he cogitated this. He swung away to snarl at Gravier, 'Why did you not tell me she was in Ashcourt's home? You knew of it.'

Gravier gave a Gallic rise of one shoulder. 'I considered Juliana's presence a trivial matter. I would not trouble you with it.'

Turstin slowly lost the wild, angry look in his eyes. His muscles relaxed.

Juliana seized this opportunity to change the subject of the conversation and solidify her new position as conspirator. 'Was that thing in the warehouse the submarine? How odd it looks.'

'Yes, it is the submarine.' Turstin's voice now sounded boastful.

'Might I look at it?' She made herself look eager, when all she really wished to do was leave the warehouse as quickly as possible. 'I have been madly curious about it. I confess, I could not believe it really existed. This will dazzle Lord Ashcourt, I assure you.'

He led her back to the warehouse where the strange-looking vessel sat on a huge cart.

Turstin gestured proudly. 'Here it is. The submarine.'

It was unlike anything Juliana had seen before, at least twenty feet long, rounded on both top and bottom, more resembling a fat cigar than a sea-going vessel. Its top contained a bulb, like a huge pustule on its surface. The pustule had a glass window from which the operators could look out. Also on top of the vessel was a complicated apparatus, the folded down mast and sails.

Juliana feigned interest in this ridiculous object, asking many questions about the safety of such a boat, about its construction, about the other men there and about the boat's security.

The boat, constructed of copper sheets over iron ribs, sounded impenetrable, but she still could not imagine sitting in it and letting it sink to the bottom of the sea surrounded on all sides by water. What if the water poured in?

She shivered at the thought.

But she tried to act every bit the willing conspirator.

'When is the demonstration?' she asked.

Turstin clapped his hands together in delight. 'Tomorrow. Half-past noon.'

Tomorrow? Her insides twisted in panic. Time had run out. Wolf was gone and she could not warn him.

It also meant she would not see him.

Before she escaped.

She must not arouse Kitty's suspicion. She would buy something from the shops to look as if she'd indeed been shopping. After the evening's Assembly, after the household slept, she would pack her portmanteau. When dawn came, this time she would really do it. She would run.

And Turstin would never find her.

* * *

Wolf arrived that afternoon from London. The diving bell and its crew had already arrived the day before. Lord Locksworth rode in his carriage along with all three sisters. Wolf and his brothers-in-law, Hale, Bentham and Everly, rode on horseback. Locksworth and Hale would act as the main backers of the diving bell, inviting others to invest. They all figured the *ton* could not resist a scheme backed by two wealthy marquesses.

While the others settled themselves in the hotel, Wolf quickly cleaned off the dust of the road and left to put down their names at the Circulating Library for the Master of Ceremonies to approve. No doubt they would be instantly approved. Lord Locksworth had procured a letter from the Prince Regent requesting it be so.

Wolf deliberately walked a long route, one that took him to the end of the street where the Ashcourts lived. He paused there.

To see if he could catch a glimpse of Juliana?

Instead, he saw Charlotte, very alone, running to her door.

'Charlotte!'

She stopped and wrapped her arms around herself as she waited for him to catch up to her. Tears stained her face. 'Do not scold me, Wolf. I know I am out without a chaperon!'

He held her shoulders. 'Look at me. What has happened? Tell me.'

Her lip trembled and she could not meet his eye. 'Nothing like what you might think.'

He reached in his pocket and handed her his handkerchief. 'What might I think, Lottie?' He made his voice gentle.

She wiped her eyes. 'That I have been meeting Gravier.' Her eyelids fluttered and tears formed again. 'That is what Juliana would think. But it is not the case.'

Meeting Gravier? Were Lord and Lady Ashcourt not watching her? 'Then what did happen?'

She took a shuddering breath. 'I heard them. Planning a meeting. I was so surprised because I did not expect it of her.' Her eyes became like slits. 'Now I know why she interfered. I went to their meeting place, and I followed them to the docks. They went in a big building…'

Wolf tried to calm himself. His friend's little sister had wandered out alone down to the docks. 'Who did you follow?' he asked.

'Juliana and Gravier.'

Wolf felt the blood drain from his face.

Charlotte sniffled. 'They are lovers, Wolf! I… I did not understand the rest of it, though.' She shivered. 'And to think I once loved her like a sister! Gravier…' Her voice trailed off again in a sigh.

He embraced her and she spent a few minutes sobbing against his coat.

'Come, Lottie,' he murmured. 'It will be all right. Better to know, is it not?' He was trying to convince himself as well as her. 'What did you mean about "the rest of it"?'

'I heard their voices at a window,' she said. 'Something about setting up Papa and Juliana wanting her share of the money. It made no sense to me.' She trembled. 'Then some scary man came near and I ran away.'

Wolf's muscles stiffened. Wanting her share? Juliana was a part of the scheme after all. He tasted bile in the back of his throat. Juliana had fooled him again, just as she'd fooled him in Paris.

'Do not fret over it, Lottie,' he consoled, squeezing

her tighter, wishing there were some consolation for the desolation he felt inside.

He released her and pulled a handkerchief from a pocket. He handed it to her. She wiped her eyes and blew her nose and balled up the handkerchief into her hand.

Wolf kept an arm around her as he walked her to her door. He sounded the knocker and gave her over to Holmes when he opened the door.

As she walked in, he said, 'I'll call later to see how you are. I—I have an errand first.'

He nodded to the butler, whose brows rose at seeing Wolf alone with his friend's sister and her being obviously distressed.

She gave a tiny wave goodbye, reminding him of the little girl who'd followed her brother and his friend everywhere. He altered his route once more, this time towards the docks. With luck he would catch Juliana and Gravier walking back to town. Wolf chose a lane through which most of the traffic to and from the docks seemed to pass. He waited.

Finally, he saw them, walking together, their heads bent together talking, their expressions intense. Although they walked side by side, Juliana did not even hold Gravier's arm. There was nothing lover-like between them, no longing glances, no light touches. Charlotte had been wrong about that part of it. They did, however, look like co-conspirators.

He followed them, expecting Gravier to walk her back to her lodgings. Instead, Gravier left her at a ribbon shop. Wolf waited for Gravier to continue on his way before entering the shop behind her.

The ribbons were hanging over lines strung across the store. Various widths and colours of silk strands fluttered gently in the breeze from the open door. Wolf spied Juliana through the slits between the ribbons. She made a quick choice, a sea-blue ribbon. When she pulled it off, her eyes widened. Wolf stood directly in her view.

'Wolf.' Her voice was low and husky, as if she whispered his name across a bed. 'You came back.'

'Fleur,' he said in a tone as black as his mood.

She dropped her gaze and made her way to the counter where the shop girl measured her ribbon, rolled it up and secured it with a pin.

He walked to Juliana's side as she handed the shop girl her coins and waited for change to be made. Juliana's hand shook as she stuffed her little package into the reticule hanging from her wrist.

He walked out of the shop with her. They had gone several steps before he spoke. 'I need to be private with you.'

She darted a glance at him. For an instant her expression shone with the intense desire that always flared between them, but a moment later it was replaced by resignation.

'Very well,' she murmured.

He spied the same alley he had taken her through before, the one leading to the brothel's door.

'In here,' he said.

She gazed at him, and he saw that she, too, remembered their visit to the brothel. This time he led her to a stack of crates that hid them from the street.

She faced him, looking resigned. 'We are private, Wolf.'

He waited no longer. 'Charlotte told me of your liaison with Gravier.'

Her eyes shot through with surprise. 'Charlotte?'

'She followed you.'

Juliana frowned at this. 'What did she tell you?'

'That you and Gravier are lovers meeting in secret and making a fool out of her.'

She gave him a distraught look. 'We are not lovers, Wolf. She is mistaken.'

He stared down at her. The shawl she wore had slipped off her shoulders and the neckline of her dress was low enough to reveal an expanse of creamy skin and a glimpse of cleavage. God help him, he remembered pressing his lips against that creamy skin. He started to turn away, ruthlessly wresting his emotions into some control.

He shook himself, forcing himself to remember she was a villain bent on ruining his family and his friends, nothing more.

He made his eyes bore into her. 'I saw you with him, Fleur—'

She interrupted him. 'That does not mean we are lovers.'

He heard a scuffling sound. They both jumped, but it was merely a cat chasing a fat rat.

'Do you think I care if you are lovers, Fleur? It will make no difference to me, knowing you are intent on ruining my family and the Ashcourts.'

He was taunting her with this talk of Gravier being her lover because he knew it was not true. That much he did know. It did not make him proud of himself that he taunted her, but she'd betrayed him. Lied to him. Over and over.

She shut her eyes and turned her cheek as if he'd struck her with his hand. Pain still shone in her gaze as she faced him again. 'You do not understand, Wolf. The demonstration is tomorrow. Tomorrow at half past noon. Time has run out. You must convince them not to invest!'

The demonstration was tomorrow? He believed her in this, but even if she lied, he could easily verify it.

He lifted his chin. 'I dare say I have time enough to alert my brother-in-law. One word from him and my family is protected. Ashcourt, though—he is too far gone to listen to me.' His muscles shook with anger. 'Tell Gravier to cancel the whole thing and take his hoax elsewhere.'

'He won't,' she cried.

'Then stop it yourself. You know how.' He glared at her. 'Or see these good people impoverished.'

Her face drained of colour and her expression turned to one of desperation. 'You must do something, Wolf. You must. Try to convince them. Believe me. I do not wish to see them in poverty.' Her pleas sounded as sincere as ever, but she'd never been what she seemed to be, not from the day he'd first set eyes upon her.

He would stop the hoax, all right, but he would not let on to her, especially now that she'd lied to him once again.

'Believe you?' He laughed, a sarcastic, wounding laugh. 'The truth is, you played me for a fool from the beginning, did you not? Who knows? Maybe your *Lyon* set up your little performance in Paris as well.'

She put her hand on his arm. 'No, Wolf.' Her eyes glistened with tears.

Her tears drew him in, weakening him. He pulled his arm away and closed his hands into fists to keep from reaching for her. 'Never again.'

He started to walk away, but spun on his heel to face

her again. 'You want to save the Ashcourts?' He leaned towards her. 'Then you stop this scheme.'

'I can't—' she said.

He lifted a silencing hand before striding away.

Not daring to look back.

Chapter Eighteen

That evening Wolf's nerves jangled as he walked
through the halls of the Old Ship Hotel to the Assembly
room for the night's entertainment. A ball. He pulled at
the cuffs of his coat and brushed off pieces of imagi-
nary lint. If it had not been for fact that he'd brought his
whole family to Brighton and this Assembly, he would
have happily avoided all of it.

Juliana would be there, of course. And Gravier. He
wanted nothing to do with them, but he needed to find
out for certain if the submarine demonstration was indeed tomorrow at twelve-thirty.

He'd already alerted his family, and Lord Locksworth
and his brothers-in-law all marshalled themselves to be
ready. Mr Fisher was certain they could discover the
exact location of the demonstration and have the diving
bell set up for the same time.

Arranging this kept his mind off Juliana.

Almost.

He still had moments of fury, of desire, of regret, of
heart-aching pain. The wounds only she could inflict
pounded with a dull ache. And now he would face her

again in the ballroom. Would the mere sight of her rend his wounds open and bleeding again?

He blew out a breath and spoke to his brothers-in-law. 'I cannot believe we've pulled this together.' This must have been his third time saying this, trying to convince himself that their counter scheme was all he cared about.

Everly responded, 'I consider it a good omen that we did.'

Hale leaned towards them. 'The important thing is we must act as if our interest is only in the submarine expedition. The surprise of learning about ours will work to our advantage.'

They neared the door to the Assembly room and all heads turned when the Marquess of Locksworth was announced, followed by the Marquess and Marchioness of Hale and the others.

Wolf was last. As he waited, he stared through the doorway.

Looking for Juliana.

Instead, he heard voices behind him. His mother and father. Bickering. They had insisted the others go ahead of them and now were each blaming the other for not being ready on time.

'If you would only walk faster,' he heard his mother say to his father.

His father was slowing down, Wolf had to admit. But at least the colour had returned to his face.

His parents had greeted the arrival of the whole clan with great pleasure as well as surprise, but obviously the distraction of their children and sons-in-law lasted only a brief period of time.

Wolf's mother's petulant tone changed when she saw Wolf. 'See, Wolf dear. I told you we'd be right behind you.'

Wolf extended his arm. 'But you and Papa go before me.'

By the time Wolf was announced the rest of the family had already begun to mingle with the other guests, and he was forgotten. He made his way through the crush of people in search of some wine. He saw Charlotte sitting alone and picked up a second glass of wine for her.

He walked over and handed it to her. 'You are alone.'

She raised a shoulder. 'Do not worry. Mama and Papa are enjoying themselves. And Juliana.' She spoke the name bitterly.

Wolf's senses came alive at her mention.

He lowered himself into the chair next to Charlotte. 'You ought to be enjoying yourself as well.'

She sighed. 'Impossible, but I shall make a good show of it in a moment. I've agreed to give Wevenly the first dance.'

'That is the spirit, Lottie.' He squeezed her hand.

She glared at him. 'Have you seen Juliana yet?'

He felt his face grow hot, but he answered in a casual voice, 'I have not looked for her.' Not much, anyway.

'Well, I suspect when you find Gravier, she will not be far away.' She sighed again.

Young Lord Wevenly approached, and Charlotte schooled her features into a more cordial expression.

He greeted Wolf, and looked upon Charlotte with earnest eyes. 'Lady Charlotte.' He bowed again. 'Come join our friends. We are all waiting together for the music to begin.' He gestured to the group of young people nearby.

She glanced at Wolf with sad eyes but turned on a perfect smile for Wevenly. 'That is so kind.'

Wolf watched her walk away on the young man's arm before taking a breath and making his way back into the crowd, wondering how so many family members could disappear so quickly. Wolf chatted with a few people who welcomed him back to Brighton, asking if he planned to stay in England or to return to Paris.

Paris. He'd not thought of Paris for days.

He caught sight of Gravier. As Charlotte predicted, Juliana was nearby, but it was with Lord and Lady Ashcourt that Gravier seemed engaged. Juliana stood alone, looking as forlorn as Charlotte had been. Wolf felt that familiar tug towards her, something more than sensual, something that made her treachery even more painful to him. Steeling himself, he walked over to the Ashcourts and greeted them all. Including Juliana. And Gravier.

'Why, how nice it is you have returned so soon, Wolf,' Lady Ashcourt said in her usual friendly manner. 'In time for the submarine demonstration.'

He played dumb. 'The demonstration is scheduled?'

Juliana turned her back and Wolf saw Gravier glance at her.

Lord Ashcourt responded though. 'Gravier tells us it is set for tomorrow, half-past noon.'

Just as Juliana had said.

Ashcourt went on, 'But we must keep that information close to our vests, because it is really intended only for the investors. Is that not right, Gravier?'

Several people within earshot turned towards him.

Gravier found his voice. 'Quite right, my lord.' He turned to Wolf. 'You, sir, of course, are welcome to attend.' He favoured Wolf with an ingratiating smile. 'You will wish to see the means of your family's great good fortune. I have met your *beau-frère* Lord Hale. He seems interested, so your father may reap the rewards after all.'

'So I gather,' Wolf responded in a tight voice.

'You will come?' Gravier persisted.

'I will be there,' Wolf responded.

The first dance was announced. Wolf slid a glance at Juliana and decided to be perverse and request the first dance with her. He knew it would make her uneasy.

He turned to her and bowed. 'May I have the honour of the first dance, Miss Walsh?' He spoke the word *honour* with sarcasm.

She stared at him a long time before nodding.

The orchestra sounded the first notes and Wolf led her on to the dance floor. The first dance was the old-fashion minuet in which the dancer more walked the dance patterns than danced them. It meant that Wolf and Juliana would sometimes join together holding hands, but then part again, mixing with the other dancers.

Not unlike his history with Fleur, Wolf thought.

They did not converse during this dance. True, there was little opportunity to do so, but, even so, what did Wolf have to say to her that he had not said already?

Eventually the music stopped, and Wolf led her back to Lady Ashcourt. He bowed and walked away.

Wolf found a place to stand across the room and saw Lord Seabane escort Juliana on to the dance floor for the second set. The line of dancers formed, and the orchestra played a quadrille. Wolf knew he ought to ask one of the young ladies present to dance, but he could not make himself do it.

Instead, his gaze returned to Juliana. She wore the same green gown she'd worn to his first Assembly in Brighton, when he'd first danced with her. A waltz that time.

He closed his eyes and bowed his head, remembering

that dance and the desire that had crackled between them as they twirled. Had she pretended that desire?

'Good evening, Wolfdon.'

He opened his eyes at the voice behind him. Lady Allyse joined him.

'It is good to see you back from London,' she said.

He forced a smile. 'I am delighted you think so. How do you fare, Lady Allyse?'

'I am well.' She gazed towards the dance floor. 'My father dances with Miss Walsh at every ball. Did you notice?'

Wolf watched Juliana execute a lively step. 'I was not keeping track.' Although he knew precisely what dances she'd shared with Seabane and others.

'He is considering a courtship with her,' she added. 'I thought you should know.'

Why did those words pierce him like being run through with a sword?

'Why should I know?' he protested. 'I have no attachment to her.'

Her brows rose in clear scepticism. 'Oh?'

She sauntered away before he could protest more.

Wolf spied his sisters and their husbands at last. Susan and Joanna had pulled their husbands to the dance floor, but his eldest sister was beckoning him from across the room.

He walked over to her. 'What is it, Lizzie?'

She inclined her head towards the dance floor where Lady Holback was dancing with Lord Lymond.

'Lymond has been monopolising all Lady Holback's attention and she seems pleased as punch about it.' Lizzie turned her gaze to a corner of the room where their parents sat looking bereft. 'Poor Mother and Father.'

The two of them suddenly looked very old.

'What should I do?' Wolf asked, feeling guilty he'd not given his parents a thought this night.

Lizzie smiled. 'What can you do? Hale and I will walk over in a minute and distract them. You just enjoy yourself. You've not danced yet, have you?'

'I danced the first dance,' he responded.

'Find a partner for the next set,' Lizzie said as she led Hale over to their parents.

He made no effort to do so, merely feeling guilty that Lizzie and Hale felt forced to do what Wolf thought was his responsibility.

He looked around for Charlotte. She was still in Wevenly's company, trying to look as if she was enjoying herself. Gravier was on the other side of the room, talking to Ashcourt. Juliana was on the dance floor, moving as gracefully as a swan gliding on a pond.

Wolf was suddenly miserable. When the next set began, he simply escaped. He walked through the hotel and out its front door, stepping on to the pavement.

The sky had darkened, and he tilted his head to gaze at the stars shining over the water. They looked as if someone had spilled diamonds on an expanse of black velvet. He tried to empty his mind, letting his senses fill with the coolness of the air, the scent of the sea, the muffled sound of the music from the orchestra inside. He remained that way, standing still as a statue, until it registered to him that the music had ended. He turned to go back inside.

Juliana stood in his path.

'Fleur,' he murmured, seduced by the night and the abiding need for her that even her betrayal had not entirely destroyed.

She walked closer to him, too close. 'Do you believe me now about the demonstration?'

'Yes.' He tried to step past her.

She blocked his way, searching his face with distressed eyes. 'Will you stop it?'

He stared at her, wanting to believe she truly wished the scheme thwarted, but he knew better than to trust in how she appeared.

'You stop it, Fleur,' he said, putting his hands on her soft shoulders and moving her out of his way. 'You stop it.'

That night when the Ashcourt household became quiet except for Felix's snores, Juliana packed her portmanteau, carefully folding and placing into it one of the ball gowns and two of the day dresses that Kitty had bought for her. She filled one hatbox with three hats, stacking them one atop the other. With her other necessary things, this was as much as she could carry herself. By the light of a candle, she counted her money. Her funds had grown a little, thanks to the evening card parties, but only a very little. She would be hard-pressed to start over somewhere else.

She tucked the money in the lining of the portmanteau and placed it back in her wardrobe with the hatbox, then she sat on the bed to wait for the first slivers of dawn.

Juliana struggled to think only of the future, to plan where she might go and how she might survive, but memories kept intruding. Memories of her mother, playing a game with her and telling her grand stories of how it would be when her father became rich. Memories of Paris, of news of her father's arrest, seeing him in shackles, hearing the sound of the guillotine. Memories of

Brighton. Of Kitty, being so kind to her, and Felix, so generous.

Most painful of all, memories of Wolf, of his smile, his touch, the exquisite pleasure of making love with him, the warm comfort of his arms around her.

She closed her eyes and saw him again, heard his last words to her, words about the swindle that would ruin Felix and Kitty and Wolf's family.

'You stop it, Fleur,' he'd said. *'You stop it.'*

At this point, she was willing to have him expose her, tell of her life in Paris, make her out to be a whore as well as a thief, tell of her thieving even here in Brighton, of her connection with Gravier. Discredit her and Gravier, too. She would be gone, a passenger on a coach to wherever, out of his life for ever. Her very disappearance would lend credence to his story.

Had Wolf allowed her to speak she would have told him to expose her. It was the only way she could think of that he could stop Turstin's wicked plan.

Instead, he'd said, *'You stop it, Fleur.'*

She'd realised then that he would never betray her. She'd always felt it in her heart but had been so reluctant to believe that a man could be so trusted. Just as he had always given her the free choice to make love to him or not, he gave *her* the choice to expose herself, tell of all her lies and deceptions, of pretending to be a Walsh, a member of a titled family instead of a nobody. To tell of the life she'd led in the past with her father and Gravier and Turstin. It was the only way to stop them.

She shook with fear. To do so risked prison or transportation or hanging. Or Turstin's revenge on her for foiling his scheme.

Better to run. Better to disappear from everyone. From

Felix and Kitty. From Wolf. Leave them to a fate they did not deserve.

She curled herself into a ball, her mind still whirling, her heart still shattering into tiny bits, Wolf's words still ringing in her ears: *'You stop it, Fleur.'*

But she could not. She could not.

Then like the glow of the moon lighting the night, an idea came to her, a plan so elegantly simple it could very well work. It meant Juliana must remain in Brighton a few more hours, but only until the submarine demonstration.

After that she could leave in peace.

The next morning Wolf took an early morning walk with his father and Lord Hale. Their pace was slow, but his father did not lose breath, although he did seem downcast. Because of Lady Holback? Wolf surmised.

His father roused a little when Hale talked business with him, the business of his father's property. Hale obviously controlled the purse strings, but Wolf was impressed that Hale treated his father more like a partner than a gambling fool and womaniser who must be kept from ruining his family.

Hale was impressive. He had several estates of his own to manage, as well as his duties in the House of Lords. And, of course, he had orchestrated and financed Wolf's plan to stop Gravier. It was not fair that Hale must assume the responsibility for Wolf's father's estate, as well. And to keep his parents out of trouble.

These were matters Wolf should attend to. The estate would be his one day, after all. Should he not be working to preserve it himself? Or did he really not care what happened to the ancestral home and all the people who depended upon it for their livelihoods?

He pushed such thoughts away and gazed over the sea wall out upon the rocky beach. Not far from where they walked was where he and Juliana had made frantic love beneath the sea wall.

And a little further still they'd perform a rival demonstration to prove just how easily it was to fabricate an investment opportunity.

Chapter Nineteen

By noon there were few clouds in the sky and only a mild breeze to stir the waves. Wolf could not have asked for more perfect weather. Wolf stood with his brothers-in-law on the pier where the boat carrying the diving bell was tethered. Fisher assured them all was ready, and their excitement was high.

Gravier had selected an excellent location. No other vessels were docked there, but the pier extended out over the water at least eighty feet and was a good twenty feet wide. The spectators would be able to see the demonstrations very well. There was both a stairway from the road to the pier carved from the rock and a narrow ramp where small wagons could be rolled down to it. The diving bell had come by sea. Wolf supposed the submarine would come by sea as well.

'Time to shove off,' said Fisher, the diving bell captain, jumping into the boat.

Wolf leaned on one of the piles and watched the men row out to the buoy they had placed there the day before. Some people had already gathered, shading their eyes from the sun, watching curiously as the oars swished rhythmically in the water and the boat made its way towards the buoy. Lady Allyse and Lord Seabane were early arrivals. They stood with Lord Locksworth as Wolf greeted them.

They had come to see the submarine, but would instead witness a duel. A duel of hoaxes, one that Wolf must win. It was noon and Gravier had not yet arrived, nor had Wolf's parents.

Nor Juliana.

Wolf wondered if she would avoid the submarine demonstration. He wanted her to come. He wanted to see her, see her reaction when he and his family succeeded in thwarting Gravier's scheme.

'Here comes Gravier,' Everly cried.

Bentham clapped his hands together in high spirits. 'The fun begins!'

Only Hale appeared as subdued as Wolf felt.

Gravier walked quickly to the pier. A man with greying hair walked a pace behind him.

Gravier put on his ingratiating smile. 'Have you all come to see our demonstration, m'lord?'

'And for a demonstration of our own.' Hale smiled back.

Although Gravier had met Wolf's family at the Assembly, their purpose for being in Brighton had remained a secret from everyone. Wolf had wanted Gravier to assume they had come so Hale could approve Wolf's father's investment, not for a demonstration of their own.

Gravier shot a glance towards Wolf, who returned it without expression.

The grey-haired man stepped up from behind Gravier. 'Demonstration? See here, you are intruding. This is our demonstration!' He glanced out at the boat, still slicing its way towards the buoy. 'Take your boat with whatever that is inside it and go elsewhere.'

Lord Locksworth approached the man. 'Forgive me, sir, but you are?'

'I am Turstin. Gravier's partner,' the man snapped.

Wolf's brows rose. Another partner? Was Juliana involved with both of these men? He instantly disliked this older one even more than he disliked Gravier.

'Who are you, sir?' Turstin demanded.

'Lord Locksworth, if you must know.' He peered at Turstin. 'Have we met before, sir?'

'I think not!' snapped Turstin, but he averted his face.

Locksworth looked puzzled for a moment, then gestured to Everly. 'May I present my son, Lord Jeffrey Everly, a Member of Parliament.' He continued. 'Hale, of course. The Marquess of Hale. Mr Bentham, Viscount Winbray's son, and Mr Wolfdon, Sir John Wolfdon's son.'

If this Turstin was impressed by all these aristocrats, he did not let on. 'Then move your boat, sirs.'

Hale swept his arm towards the water. 'The sea has room for us both, Mr Turstin, but if you insist we take our demonstration elsewhere, we will invite your spectators to join us. These people know us, sir, better than they can know you. I wonder how many will stay to watch your submarine?'

Bentham and Everly grinned from behind him. Others arrived, including Wolf's sisters and his mother and father. Unfortunately, Lady Holback and Lymond also stepped on to the pier, capturing his parents' attention more effectively than the events on the water.

Gravier paced anxiously, looking at his partner, the unknown Mr Turstin. 'We can still show the submarine,'

Gravier assured his partner. 'Their demonstration, whatever it is, will not diminish what the submarine can do.'

'Shall we make a competition of it?' Hale spoke loud enough for many of the spectators to hear. 'Your submarine against our diving bell?'

'Diving bell.' Turstin spat out the words. 'What the deuce are you about?'

Hale smiled. 'Treasure hunting, same as you.'

Turstin looked as if he might explode. 'Where is Ashcourt? And his wife?' He glared at Gravier. 'They must not miss this!'

Gravier looked up at the road leading to the pier. 'Perhaps they come now.'

Another group of people approached, Lord and Lady Ashcourt and Charlotte among them. A short distance behind them was Juliana. Even at this distance Wolf recognised her graceful figure. In spite of himself, his heart gladdened at the sight of her.

Wolf's sisters had remained at the pier's entrance, greeting the new arrivals as if they were the hostesses of this party. Lord and Lady Ashcourt and Charlotte hurried over to where Wolf stood.

'This is the day!' Lord Ashcourt spoke like a youth about to try out a racing phaeton.

'Indeed, sir,' Wolf responded.

Lady Ashcourt looked more worried than excited. Charlotte, behind her, was in exceptionally fine looks for a pierside demonstration at the sea's edge. She wore a pale pink dress, with matching pelisse and bonnet, and stood out like a lone flower among underbrush.

Wolf gave her a quick smile. 'You look pretty, Lottie.'

She darted a glance towards Gravier. 'Good.'

Ashcourt nearly skipped over to where Gravier stood

with Turstin. He pointed to the boat. 'Is that the submarine out there?'

Gravier's smile was smooth. 'No, but Lord Hale has brought an extra treat for you. A diving bell. We shall see which gives the better showing, no?'

'What is Lord Hale doing?' Charlotte asked Wolf.

'He and Lord Locksworth have brought a diving bell to demonstrate,' Wolf explained. 'They have an entirely different proposition for salvaging treasure.'

Her usually unlined brow furrowed. 'Do they mean to spoil Gravier's plans?'

'To present an alternative, Lottie,' he told her.

Charlotte glanced towards Gravier again, biting her lip.

'There it is!' someone shouted and the crowd, now risen to about twenty, hurried on to the pier, leaning eagerly over its railings.

All except Juliana who had not moved from the pier's entrance. She stood alone as a vessel under sail came into view. The submarine, no doubt.

Gravier held up his arms. 'Ladies and gentlemen, your *attention*!' He pointed to the sailing vessel. 'The submarine approaches!'

Hale moved to his side. 'Friends!' Hale, a former captain in the army, projected his voice as he must have done when on the battlefield, so his men could hear every word of command. 'You came to see Gravier's submarine, but I have brought you an even better treat. Another way to pull treasure from the sea. A tried and true way. A diving bell!'

Gravier was forced to wait for a turn to speak as Hale gestured like a showman to the diving bell. The spectators all turned away from the quite impressive sight of the submarine under sail while Hale explained the diving bell's workings. How it would be lowered into the sea with men inside. How it had been used successfully in Plymouth to retrieve heavy rock.

'You are all interested in treasure,' continued Hale. 'We intend to prove the diving bell the perfect means to recover it, not in distant lands where any mishap might occur, but here on the shores of England—' He fed the crowd's excitement with tales of treasure maps showing where ships had been lost on the shores of the great isles of Britain. 'After the demonstration we will show you these maps. Come to the Old Ship Hotel directly after we are finished here and enjoy some refreshment that we have arranged for you while you discover where English treasure will be found.'

That would be when they revealed their hoax, suggesting Gravier's scheme was easily a hoax as well. Did they wish to risk their money on mere words and props? Wolf wagered Gravier and his Mr Turstin would be long gone from Brighton by then.

Wolf glanced back at Juliana. Would she be leaving with them? Would this be his last glimpse of her?

Juliana remained as still as she had been before, the brim of her hat shading her face and hiding its expression, but even her stance, so steady and defiant, filled him with regret for what they could never have together.

The submarine sailed to a point parallel to the diving bell. It waited in the water, odd-looking, as if it were a boat that had capsized and now floated with its sail on its bottom side.

Gravier moved to stand in front of Hale. Wolf felt Charlotte tense at his side.

'We welcome Lord Hale and his considerable family,' Gravier said, his smile as charming as ever. 'But you will all, I am certain, be dazzled by the submarine, a vessel that can sail under the water and view what is at the ocean's depths, a vessel which shall retrieve riches beyond belief, riches Englishmen deserve to possess—'

Hale interrupted him. 'Our diving bell will retrieve treasure this very day. Earlier this morning, we dropped a bag of coin into the water. The buoy that you see out there marks the spot. When the diving bell is brought back to the surface, the bag of coin will be back in our hands.'

Gravier looked chagrined for a moment, but he seemed to rouse himself again. 'Excellent plan, Lord Hale! Clever of you. Let me ask you, once under the water, can your men move the diving bell?'

'It is moved by the crew in the boat,' Hale replied.

Gravier turned to the crowd. 'The submarine can move on its own under the water.'

Gravier spoke in a tone of good humour towards his unexpected adversaries, as if he were delighted by the surprise. Wolf thought this precisely the best way for Gravier to manage the situation. Had he treated the Marquess with hostility, as Mr Turstin—still glaring—had done, the members of the *ton* who came to watch this performance would have turned their backs on him. Instead, Gravier had renewed their interest in the exotic-looking submarine.

This was not yet a duel won.

'May I suggest, Lord Hale,' Gravier went on, speaking more to the spectators than to Hale, 'that you demonstrate your diving bell first. How much time will your crew need to recover your *treasure*?' He smiled at the word treasure.

Hale immediately said, 'One half-hour.' It was the amount of time Fisher had suggested.

'*Très bien,*' Gravier said, as if this were welcome news. 'Our submarine will wait for you. When you finish, we will begin.'

Hale darted a glance to Wolf.

'What the devil are you doing, Gravier?' Turstin snapped, but Gravier merely put up a quelling hand.

It was a puzzling choice for Gravier to make, Wolf thought. They had envisioned a simultaneous demonstration, a race with the diving bell rising quickly with the bag of coin in hand.

Hale turned to their audience. 'As Monsieur Gravier wishes!' He signalled the diving bell to descend with its two men inside carrying a lantern to illuminate the sea's floor.

'Why did Gravier let the diving bell go first?' Charlotte asked Wolf as everyone watched the bell be lowered.

'I do not know, Lottie,' he answered. He glanced towards Juliana, but she had not moved.

Once the diving bell disappeared, Gravier turned back to the crowd to point out features of the submarine. Its folding sail, the window underneath, the pincers that would grasp items to bring to the surface. He told them how the American inventor tried to sell his vessel to both Napoleon and the English, and he exploited their fascination with Napoleon and their greed, by relating tales of Napoleon plundering Malta of its riches, all of which were thought to have been on those Egypt-bound ships sunk by Admiral Lord Nelson.

Bentham and Everly walked over to Wolf. 'They seem to have forgotten about the diving bell,' Everly said.

Wolf rubbed his face. 'I noticed. I have a bad feeling about this.'

Bentham had an equally worried look. He took a watch from his pocket. 'Our half-hour is gone.'

They stared out at the water, but only the submarine was in sight, its mast and sail now dramatically being folded on its top.

Wolf glanced at Juliana again, but she still stood like a statue, separated from the enthralled crowd.

'How much time has passed?' Gravier very loudly asked.

'Forty-five minutes,' Bentham was forced to admit.

'Forty-five minutes,' Gravier said in a pensive tone. 'I do hope nothing is amiss.'

So did Wolf.

Several more minutes ticked by. The crowd murmured among themselves, getting restless. The crew in the diving bell's boat stared down into the water. Turstin paced back and forth, but now wore a sneer on his face. Hale shot a glance to Wolf.

Juliana, Wolf noticed, pressed her hand against her chest.

'Where the devil is the diving bell?' Bentham muttered.

Suddenly a man in the boat waved his arms, and moments later the diving bell reached the surface. Wolf's heart pounded in his chest.

One of the men cupped his hands around his mouth and shouted, 'Not there!' The other man shook his head and showed that his hands were empty.

'Blast,' growled Everly.

Hale shot them a worried look.

The spectators grew louder.

Gravier walked over to Hale. '*Mon Dieu*, you have not found your coin.'

Hale called to the boat, 'Move the bell and look again.'

One of the men shook his head and waved his hands for emphasis. A very animated discussion commenced among Fisher and the divers.

Gravier strode forward. 'It is the submarine's turn. Let them find your bag of coins.' He walked to the furthest end of the pier and shouted to two men standing on the submarine, awaiting their instructions. 'Treasure below!' he yelled, pointing to the buoy. 'Find it!'

They nodded and jumped down the hatch, closed it behind them. At the same time Fisher and another man on the diving bell boat were shouting and waving, 'No!' while the others began rowing back to the pier.

Bentham muttered to Wolf and Everly, 'This is a blasted defeat.'

Everly looked daggers at Gravier and Turstin. 'I'll be damned if I let those fellows get our bag of coin.'

Turstin strode over to Gravier and clapped him on the shoulder, laughing aloud. Gravier, oddly enough, did not look as joyful.

'I fear they will have the coin and the fortunes of these good people as well.' Wolf felt near despair. He'd failed. The Ashcourts faced impoverishment.

'We need a miracle,' murmured Bentham.

The crowd's excitement crackled around them, like flames ready to burn. Wolf shut his eyes; his breath came fast. He had been so certain this plan would work, but it merely succeeded in enhancing the submarine's show. Worse, if he talked against Gravier now, he would be like Aesop's fox, calling grapes sour because of his own failure to win them.

He frowned, blinking rapidly. He could still make Juliana reveal the truth about Gravier. All it would cost was her home with Ashcourt and her future with anyone else.

His despair deepened.

He glanced at her to see if she'd gained some joy over this impending victory. She looked as if she was holding her breath.

Suddenly someone shouted, 'The submarine!'

Wolf turned. The shadow of the submarine could be seen coming quickly towards the pier. It boded even worse if it had been able to grasp the bag of coin so quickly. As it approached it rose in the water, becoming more visible with each second.

Still some distance from the pier, its hatch broke the surface of the water and was flung open. The crew of two burst out in a rush.

'It is leaking,' one said in French. 'Full of holes. It is leaking everywhere!'

The vessel sank again beneath them and they swam for the pier. Some of the gentlemen gave them a hand out of the cold water. Turstin marched over to them, swearing in French. Gravier, stone-faced, backed away.

Panting, one of the submarine's crew looked up at Turstin. *'Sabotage,'* he cried.

Wolf spun around to Juliana.

She remained as she had been a moment before, the only person on the pier who was not suddenly talking or in motion. She lifted her head enough for Wolf to glimpse her face. The corners of her mouth turned up in a smile that disappeared as quickly as it had shown itself.

'She did it,' Wolf murmured, though no one was paying him the least mind. 'By God, *she* did it.'

Sabotage, he thought. Somehow Juliana had sabotaged the submarine.

The whole show was finished. The people who a moment before had been enthralled were now shaking their heads and laughing. Lord Ashcourt stood gaping into the water where the submarine disappeared, his wife now clinging to his arm. Wolf's father shook his head, but Lord Locksworth was speaking calmly to him. Everly and Bentham simply looked relieved, Hale puzzled.

Lord Locksworth stepped away from the crowd. 'Come!' he shouted. 'There are still refreshments at the Old Ship Hotel. Come and enjoy. We have much to tell you!'

Turstin brushed past Wolf, knocking into him. 'Where is Gravier?' the man growled to no one in particular. He barrelled his way through the departing crowd.

Wolf also looked for Gravier, but instead of finding Gravier, saw Charlotte rushing over to him.

Tears stained her cheeks. 'He is ruined, is he not, Wolf? Gravier is ruined.'

He reached for her. 'It appears so, Lottie, but—'

She pushed him away. 'You did it to him, Wolf. I know you did.' She swung around to where Juliana stood. 'You did it because of *her*, didn't you? Because of what I told you about her and Gravier. Oh, I shall never forgive myself!' She lifted her head to glare at him. 'I'll never forgive you either, Wolf, for ruining him. You sabotaged his submarine for *her*.'

Charlotte had it wrong.

Juliana had sabotaged the submarine for *him*.

Wolf took hold of Charlotte. 'Listen, Lottie. I did not sabotage his submarine, I promise you. Now, calm yourself.'

'But what is to happen to him?' she cried. 'His fortune is lost.'

'Gravier is not someone you should concern yourself over, Lottie,' Wolf told her.

'I cannot bear it!' She strode away, pushing her way through the crowd.

Wevenly, the young man who had befriended her at the Assembly, stepped up to Wolf. 'I will see she gets safely to the hotel or to her home, as she wishes.'

Wolf nodded.

He watched the young man catch up to her and offer his arm.

The crowd on the pier dwindled. Wolf's sisters walked their parents back. Only Wolf, his brothers-in-law and the Ashcourts were left.

Apparently still trying to make sense of what happened, Lord Ashcourt asked Wolf, 'Do you suppose this means they will not retrieve the antiquities from Malta?'

'That is a safe assumption,' Wolf told him.

Lady Ashcourt gazed around. 'Oh, dear! Where is Charlotte?'

'Wevenly is escorting her back,' Wolf told her.

'We should go, too, Felix.' She pulled on her husband's arm.

'Go to the Old Ship Hotel,' Wolf told them. 'You need to hear what Lord Locksworth has to say.'

Ashcourt nodded and the couple walked away as one might walk away from a graveside. Wolf vowed to find them later and help them with the disappointment that was in their every step.

The crew on the boat shouted a halloo. They had reached the pier.

'Lord Hale!' Fisher shouted.

Hale hurried over. Everly and Bentham joined him. They threw a rope and Everly tied the boat to the pier. Fisher scrambled out.

Wolf walked to the end of the pier and searched for Juliana among the departing spectators. He could not see her. A sinking feeling that he might lose her for ever came over him.

'Wolf!' Bentham waved Wolf over to where Hale, Everly, Fisher and the diving crew stood talking. 'The divers said they did find something—'

Wolf cared only about finding Juliana. Had he forced her back into the hands of Gravier and Gravier's unsavoury partner?

'I need to leave now, Bentham.' Wolf needed to find her, bring her back to him.

'Why?' Bentham asked.

'I need to find Juliana.'

'Juliana?' Bentham sounded puzzled.

Wolf backed away. 'Juliana. Miss Walsh. You do not understand. We have her to thank for this. She is our miracle.'

Wolf did not wait to hear any further protest. He hurried to the road and made his way through the others walking back at a leisurely pace.

'Have you seen Juliana?' he asked the Ashcourts.

'No,' Lady Ashcourt responded. 'Oh, dear. I forgot about Juliana.'

Wolf was frantic to find her, to tell her he was wrong about her, to beg her forgiveness for never believing in her. To hold her in his arms once more.

Chapter Twenty

Juliana calculated she had only a short space of time to make her escape. She walked as quickly as she could along the sea wall back into the part of town where the Ashcourt lodgings were. She guessed that Felix and Kitty would go straight to the Old Ship Hotel where Wolf's friend, the Marquess, said the maps would be shown and refreshments served.

She felt confident she could elude Felix and Kitty. She more feared Turstin. If Turstin guessed it had been she who'd sneaked into the warehouse and poked holes in his submarine, there would be no limit to his anger.

Sabotaging the submarine had been astonishingly easy. In the dark of the night, she'd donned dark britches and a coat she'd taken from a peg in the servants' hall. She'd slipped out of the town house and made her way to the warehouse that held the submarine. She'd broken in through a loose board that allowed a gap large enough for her to slip through, although she'd brought hairpins to pick the lock, if necessary.

With a penknife she'd also borrowed from Felix's desk and long pointed scissors she'd lifted from the maid's mending basket, she'd loosened as many rivets in the submarine as she could. Then, using her hatpin, she'd poked holes in the seals on the top hatch. She'd hoped her handiwork would only show itself when the vessel went under water. It was not until the crewmen scrambled out of that hatch that she'd known her efforts had succeeded.

Now she could leave Brighton knowing she'd done very little harm. Felix and Kitty would console each other about her running away and would find some other unfortunate soul to help. Wolf would return to his diplomatic work in Paris. Perhaps he would marry someone like the perfect Lady Allyse and soon forget all about the thief and imposter he'd met in that city.

She turned on to Felix and Kitty's street. As she reached the door, she caught a glimpse of Lady Charlotte darting across the end of the street. The girl was alone and hurrying in the wrong direction to be returning to her rooms.

Juliana ran after her. 'Charlotte!'

Charlotte turned her head, but continued on her way.

Juliana quickened her pace and reached the girl's side. 'Where are you going?' she asked, trying to catch her breath.

'To find Lyon,' the girl said.

'No, Charlotte, you must not.' Juliana seized her arm.

Charlotte jerked away. 'Why, Juliana? So you can have him?' She walked faster. 'You cannot want him now. He is ruined. His submarine is lost! I must find him.' She turned into one of the narrow streets leading to the docks, a different way than any of the submarine's spectators would be walking. It was the way Juliana had gone to the warehouse.

'Where are you going, Charlotte?' she asked again.

'To that place,' Charlotte said.

They entered the part of town where slimy-looking sailors leaned against buildings, leering and making cat-calls at them.

'This is not safe. He would not come here.' Juliana hoped she could convince Charlotte to turn around.

'He will come here,' Charlotte insisted. 'I shall wait for him. I cannot wait for him at his inn.'

'You do not know where to look for him!'

Charlotte slowed enough to glare at her. 'I know the building, Juliana. I followed you when you met Lyon in secret. I saw the building you went to with him. I heard you talking. I told Wolf all about it.'

Charlotte had followed them? And heard Juliana pretending to be in league with Gravier and Turstin? Wolf must have believed it was true. He must have thought she had betrayed him once more.

She suddenly wished she'd told him she'd been the one to poke holes in the submarine, then he would know she had not betrayed him again. On the contrary, she'd done what he'd asked her to do. He'd told her to stop Gravier and stop him she had.

Charlotte led Juliana around a corner close to the warehouse, smack into the path of Turstin. Turstin was flanked by two burly men and he barred their way.

'Well, well, Juliana. You've come back to me.' Turstin looked Charlotte up and down. 'And you have brought a gift as well.'

'Where is Gravier?' Charlotte demanded.

'I was about to ask Miss Parsons that very thing,' Turstin replied, his gaze sliding back to Juliana.

Charlotte blinked in confusion. 'Miss Parsons?'

Juliana stepped forward. 'Do not let us detain you,

Turstin. If Gravier appears, we shall surely tell him you are looking for him.'

Turstin grasped her arm. 'Not so fast, Juliana.'

He pushed Juliana towards one of the men, who closed his beefy fingers around her arms. Turstin clicked his fingers to the other man, who then grabbed Charlotte. Juliana glanced around frantically for help, but the few unsavoury men who had witnessed their abduction slunk away.

'I believe we may have discovered the means to recoup some of our money, perhaps even make a modest profit.' Turstin smiled malevolently. 'And to enact my revenge. Bring them to the warehouse.'

Wolf was breathing hard when he reached the door of the Ashcourts' lodgings. He sounded the knocker and Holmes immediately answered.

'I must see Miss Walsh,' he gasped, chest heaving.

The butler's brow wrinkled. 'Miss Walsh went with Lord and Lady Ashcourt to the demonstration.'

'She has not returned here?' Wolf asked.

'She has not and I have been attending the door the whole morning, sir,' the man responded.

Wolf did not wait another second. He rushed out of the residence to the end of the street, spinning around with indecision of where to next look for her.

Gravier's inn, he decided.

He turned in the direction of the inn where Gravier was staying.

'Mr Wolfdon!' a voice cried behind him.

He turned. It was Wevenly.

The young man rushed up to him. 'Fortunate to find you, sir,' he gasped. 'I am on my way to the Ashcourts. It is Lady Charlotte—'

Wolf seized his arm. 'What of Lady Charlotte?'

Wevenly's face contorted. 'I—I tried to see her home, but as soon as we left the others, she told me to leave her, but I would not, and she tried to walk away, but I would not let her. She said she had somewhere important to go, and I said I would escort her, but she became very cross and she ran off.' He swallowed. 'I—I tried to follow her, but she ran through an alley and I lost her.' He made a helpless gesture. 'I decided I must alert her parents.'

Wolf nodded. Could Charlotte be headed to Gravier's, as well? 'You did well, Wevenly. Come with me. I know where to find her.'

Wolf reached the Black Lion Inn and bribed the inn-keeper to direct them straight to Gravier's room. Wolf swore he would kick the door in if Gravier refused to open it, but first he lifted the latch. It was unlocked.

Wolf pushed the door with such force it slammed against the wall with a loud report. Gravier, a valise in hand, jumped in surprise.

'Where are they?' Wolf stood in the doorway.

Gravier bowed his head and headed towards the door. 'I do not know who you mean.'

'Charlotte,' Wolf told him. 'And Juliana.'

Gravier blanched. 'Charlotte?'

'I presumed they would come to you.'

Gravier dropped his valise. 'Lady Charlotte would not be so foolish.'

Wolf glared at him. 'Yes, she would. Where is Juliana? They both are missing.'

'I—I know nothing of either of them.' Gravier rubbed his brow. '*Mon Dieu*, if they fell into Turstin's hands…'

Wolf marched up to him and grabbed him by his coat. 'What then? Who is this damned Turstin of yours?'

Gravier's expression was pained. 'This submarine foolishness. I thought your diving bell would be the more impressive. *Mon Dieu*, I wanted—' He cut himself off and shook his head. 'You asked about Turstin. He conceived the idea. It has unhinged him, I fear. He was always ruthless, but now...' Gravier stared directly into Wolf's eyes. 'We must find them!'

Wolf released him. 'Tell me where to look.'

Gravier nodded. 'Yes, yes, but I must show you. I will lead you to where they might be, but we must take care. If Turstin discovers us...' His voice trailed off.

Wolf shoved him out the door. 'We go now.'

Juliana strained at the strips of cloth tying her hands behind the back of the wooden chair. The burly man Turstin called Briggs had started to tie them up with ropes, but Turstin insisted on strips of cloth. 'They will not leave marks,' Turstin said.

He'd brought them to the same room in the warehouse where she and Gravier had met with him before. Turstin sat at a desk, dipping pen in ink and writing. His henchmen had left. Charlotte, also tied up in a chair, was still nearly insensible with fright. Juliana worried about the girl but struggled to keep her own wits about her. She wriggled her hands, trying to free herself of her bindings.

'What is this grand plan of yours, Turstin?' she asked, using a mocking tone, while her hands were busy trying to loosen the tight cloth.

He looked up from his writing with the same calm expression he used to wear when planning the next grand scheme with her father, the scheme that would finally reap them all the riches they could desire.

'Not as lucrative as offering a chance at Napoleon's

riches,' he said. 'Such greed vastly exceeds your worth, but I suspect that Lord Ashcourt will pay a tidy sum for his daughter's release.' He laughed. 'Perhaps he will even pay for you. Unless you have lied about *Baroness Walsingham's* attachment to her lovely…cousin.'

He put particular emphasis on Kitty's title—a title he'd always disdained.

'I have not lied.' Still playing the role Gravier had assigned her, she added, 'And I want my share. It was my scheme that set up the Ashcourts, after all.'

She glanced over to Charlotte, but the girl did not seem to be listening. She was still breathing fast, still in the throes of panic, and near to fainting if she did not calm herself.

'You'll receive no share, Juliana, my dear.' Turstin rose and sauntered over to Charlotte, taking her chin between his finger and thumb and lifting her face up.

The girl stilled, but her eyes were wide with fear.

'We'll collect the ransom, of course, but I believe I am still able to make my family pay for what they did to me.' Turstin smirked at Juliana.

Turstin's family had banished him because he'd exploited, thieved and debauched so thoroughly as to be one step from the gallows. Still, they'd enabled him to escape, to live.

Turstin examined Charlotte's face. 'In the meantime, she will make a good reward for Briggs and Vachon, since I am now unable to pay them. Perhaps other seamen might also be willing to pay.' He caressed the girl's smooth cheek. 'For ever to be damaged goods, not fit for the *ton*. That is what they did to me, after all.'

Juliana fought a wave of panic. Poor innocent Charlotte did not deserve such a fate. Juliana made herself laugh at Turstin. 'You are such a fool! If you damage her, Ashcourt will see you hanged. They'll run you down even to the ends of the earth for it.' She gave a casual lift of her shoulder. 'Better to collect the ransom and release her unharmed.'

Turstin crossed over to her, his eyes blazing. 'I am not a fool, Juliana. I will have my revenge on all who have crossed me, including that Wolfdon fellow who was so intent on spoiling our plans. I am certain he sabotaged the submarine. Let him deliver the ransom money and walk into my trap.'

Juliana turned cold. 'Do not be absurd. He'll come in force. All his family members.' She struggled harder to loosen her bindings. 'Besides, why would Wolfdon sabotage the submarine? They thought their diving bell would spoil your plans.'

'That is enough reason for revenge, I admit, but he did the sabotage. I am certain of it.' Turstin snarled. 'Gravier told me Wolfdon has been suspicious from the start.'

Juliana forced herself to laugh again. 'You really are a fool, Turstin. I made the submarine leak.'

He gave her a patient look and patted her on top of her head. 'Amusing, Juliana.' He took her chin in his hand and forced her head up like he'd done with Charlotte. 'Do not tell me lies.' He glared down at her. 'I will begin to think you have a fondness for these people. Perhaps, after I've sold you to any willing buyer, I'll cut that pretty face.'

She'd worked her hand halfway through the cloth binding. With one painful effort, she forced her hand the rest of the way and the bindings fell to the floor. She kept her hands together as if still bound and, when Turstin walked back to the desk, she wriggled her feet from her shoes and twisted her feet, trying to work them free, hiding what she was doing beneath her skirts.

'Briggs!' called Turstin.

The man opened the door.

'Take this note and find some lad to deliver it to Wolf-don at the Old Ship Hotel.' He pressed a seal to the folded paper and handed it to Briggs. 'Give the boy a penny for it.'

The cloth securing Juliana's ankles loosened and she pulled her feet free, kicking the bindings and her shoes under the chair. When Briggs walked out, Juliana snapped her ankles together again.

'What I should like to know is where Gravier has gone off to.' Turstin rose from the desk and sauntered to the window.

'Gravier?' murmured Charlotte.

Turstin cocked his head towards the girl, giving Juliana a leering smile. 'Perhaps I ought to give her to Gravier if he ever shows up. I should never have let him out of my sight."

'Where is Gravier?' Charlotte demanded.

Turstin laughed at her. 'That, my dear, is an excellent question.'

A crashing sound came from inside of the warehouse.

'Now what?' Turstin huffed. 'Vachon!' he yelled and another crash came. He walked to the door, putting his hand on the latch. 'Vachon!'

It was Juliana's chance. She jumped to her feet. Quickly grabbing the wooden chair, she brought it down on Turstin's head with such force it broke into pieces. Turstin staggered backwards and fell with a thump as loud as a felled oak tree.

'Juliana!' Charlotte gasped.

Juliana froze for a moment, her heart pounding. She listened for Vachon, fearing he would rush in. She grabbed one of the chair's legs as the door burst open.

Wevenly, not Vachon, charged through the doorway.

'Wevenly!' Charlotte cried.

The young man glanced quickly around him at Turstin's prone figure, at Juliana. He rushed over to Charlotte. 'Charlotte,' he murmured as he untied her hands.

Another crash sounded from inside the warehouse. Juliana ran to the open door and saw Vachon punching Wolf, his fist thudding against Wolf's stomach. Wolf stumbled backwards and fell. Vachon lunged after him.

'No!' Juliana cried. She still had the chair leg in her hand. She ran towards Vachon, ready to strike.

Vachon swirled around and caught the chair leg in his hand, trying to wrest it from her grasp. She held fast. Wolf pulled Vachon's legs out from under him and sprang to his own feet again. Vachon rose and charged Wolf, grabbing him around his chest. The two men struggled together, spinning in a violent dance. Juliana stood with her weapon ready, but she could not strike Vachon without risking a blow to Wolf.

'Get back,' Wolf yelled at her.

She did not move.

Vachon lifted Wolf and heaved him away. As Wolf scrambled to stand, Juliana swung the chair leg as hard as she could into the small of Vachon's back. The man shrieked in pain and fell to his knees. Wolf rose over him and brought both hands down on the back of his neck, a forceful chop that knocked Vachon to the floor face first. He lay still.

'Wolf!' Juliana ran to him and he wrapped his arms around her.

He released her and ran his hands up and down her arms. 'Did he hurt you?'

'No.' She pressed herself against his chest. 'Nor Charlotte.'

'Charlotte.' He took her hand and rushed into the room where Juliana and Charlotte had been imprisoned.

Wevenly held Charlotte in his arms. Turstin still lay on the floor, as unmoving as Vachon.

'Juliana hit him,' Wevenly explained.

'Good God, Juliana,' Wolf said in an awed voice.

She glanced down at what she had done.

Wolf seized her arm. 'We must get out of here.'

'Wait.' Juliana pulled away and ran over to get her shoes. She hurriedly slipped them on her feet.

'Do we leave him like this?' Wevenly asked.

Wolf glanced at the prone figure. 'We can alert the magistrate later. I do not want the ladies connected with this.'

'Yes, yes. Of course.' Wevenly gazed at Charlotte.

They left the warehouse but detoured along the less-travelled road that paralleled the shoreline. As they hurried along, Wolf said, 'You nearly drove me insane with worry, Juliana. I had no idea where you had gone.'

She looked at him in surprise. 'I thought it was Charlotte you came to rescue.'

He squeezed her tighter. 'No, Fleur. I came to rescue you.'

Chapter Twenty-One

Wolf's blood still burned. His rage had been kindled by the glimpse through a window of Juliana bound to a chair.

He glanced at her. She made no complaint about their quick pace despite her ordeal.

Brave girl, he thought. *Brave, foolish girl.*

He would not have been surprised if she had succeeded in entirely freeing herself and Charlotte without his and Wevenly's assistance.

After showing them the warehouse Gravier turned and ran, and Wolf made no attempt to stop him. Good riddance to the man. Wolf and Wevenly watched one of Turstin's henchmen walk out the door and made their move.

They'd entered the warehouse quietly, creeping along the wall, staying in the shadows until close enough for Wolf to lunge at the huge man who sat near the inside door. While Wolf grappled with the man, Wevenly charged into the room where Turstin held Juliana and Charlotte.

But Juliana had already seen to Turstin.

'You hit Turstin?' Wolf asked her as they hurried along, Wevenly and Charlotte not far behind.

'With a chair,' she replied, short of breath. 'Do you think I killed him?'

He slowed their pace. 'If you did kill him, he deserved it.'

'He was going to ransom us,' she said between breaths. 'He blamed you for the submarine leaks. He was going to ambush you and revenge himself on you.'

He squeezed her tighter. 'So you freed yourself and hit him over the head. I am beginning to think there is nothing you cannot do, Fleur.'

'Wolf.' She clutched his coat and her voice became urgent. 'I—I was never partners with Turstin. You must believe me. I did not want Felix and Kitty to be ruined, or your family.'

He flashed a quick smile at her. 'So, you somehow managed to poke holes in a submarine.'

She stared at him in surprise. 'You knew?'

He glanced down at her. 'How did you accomplish that trick, Juliana?'

She averted her gaze. 'With a hatpin.'

He laughed out loud and cupped her face with his hands. 'That was dangerous, Fleur. Much too dangerous. What if Turstin caught you?'

She grasped one of his hands in hers and started walking again. 'It was all I could think of to do.'

They reached the sea road and slowed so Wevenly and Charlotte could catch up. The road took them by the pier where the demonstration had taken place. The submarine and its men were gone, but Hale, Everly, Bentham and the diving bell crew were still gathered there.

'What the devil?' Wolf waited for Wevenly to come close enough to hear. 'I want to see why they are still here. It should take only a moment.'

Wevenly piped up, 'I am taking Lady Charlotte to her parents.'

'Excellent idea, Wevenly.' Wolf closed the distance between them to shake the young man's hand. 'Thank you, Wevenly. You did well.'

Wevenly beamed.

As Wevenly and Charlotte continued on, Wolf and Juliana made their way down to the pier. The others looked up only when their footsteps sounded on the wood.

Hale strode forwards to meet them. He cast a questioning glance at Juliana.

'Hale, did you meet Miss Walsh? She is Lady Ashcourt's cousin. Turstin kidnapped her and Lady Charlotte. Young Wevenly and I rescued them.' He grinned at Juliana. 'Or half rescued them.'

'Kidnapped?' Hale glanced at her with concern. 'Miss Walsh, were you harmed?'

Wolf responded, 'They escaped in time.'

Juliana remained near the entrance to the pier, seating herself on one of the piles low enough to be comfortable.

'I'll explain later,' Wolf assured him.

He followed Hale to where the diving bell crew crouched with Everly near the end of the pier.

Everly waved him over. 'Come here, Wolf.'

They were gathered around a big chest half covered with wet seaweed, but otherwise looking like something they might have found in an old hacienda in Spain. One of the diving bell crew hammered at the huge old lock, the sound ringing loud in Wolf's ears.

Hale pointed to it. 'They found the chest on their first dive when they were searching for the bag of coin.' The din nearly drowned out his voice. 'They did not want to bring it up then, because of all the people watching.

When we finally rid ourselves of the submarine and its crew, they went under the sea again.'

'A real treasure chest?' Wolf shook his head.

It looked old enough. And the real treasure maps they'd been shown in London had marked several shipwrecks off the coast of the old town of Brighthelmston, now Brighton.

The lock broke, and the man made quick work of removing it. He tried the lid, but it stuck. He grabbed an iron bar and pried the lid open. It creaked with the rust of countless years under the sea. When it fell back with a bang, the group went silent.

Gold.

A whole chest of it, coins glittering in the afternoon sun. They all stared at it.

'By god,' whispered Mr Fisher. 'I believe we are rich.' He reached down and picked up one coin.

A scream rent the air.

Turstin and one of his henchmen, the one who had left the warehouse, had approached unnoticed down the stone stairway. Turstin, blood staining his face, held a blade against Juliana's throat. He and the henchman walked on to the pier.

Wolf ran to her.

'Stay away!' shouted Turstin. 'Or I'll cut her throat.' He dragged Juliana past Wolf. 'I want the boat.' He inclined his head to one of the diving bell crew. 'Get that contraption out of it. I just want the boat. Be quick about it.' As if to emphasise, he scraped the knife point against Juliana's skin, drawing a trickle of blood.

Wolf clenched his fists, burning with helpless rage. Two crewmen jumped into the boat.

'Be quick!' Turstin demanded, backing towards the end of the pier where the boat was tethered.

Wolf followed him.

'Keep your distance,' warned Turstin. He pushed the blade against Juliana's throat again. As he passed by the chest, his eyes grew wide. 'Gold!' he laughed. 'It seems we have treasure after all. Put the chest in the boat.'

Hale and Everly picked up the chest.

Juliana met Wolf's eye, steady and calm.

By God, he'd free her or die trying. He followed Turstin as closely as he dared until Turstin reached the end of the pier where the boat was tethered. The henchman at his side was eyeing the gold in disbelief.

Hale and Everly put the chest down at the end of the pier. Turstin glared at Wolf while they all tensely waited for the diving bell to be taken out of the boat.

'No heroics. I'll slice her head off,' Turstin growled.

Wolf took a step back.

Suddenly there was the splash of the diving bell going over the side. At that same moment, Hale threw a fist-ful of glittering gold coins at Turstin and his henchman.

Turstin's hand dropped in surprise and Wolf charged him. He, Turstin and Juliana flew off the edge of the pier and plunged into the cold sea. As they sank, two more bodies hit the water above them. His brothers-in-law, Wolf suspected.

Turstin lost his hold on Juliana but grabbed for her again. Wolf pulled her away just in time. She was strug-gling to swim, but her skirts were dragging her deeper. Turstin attacked Wolf before he could reach her, the knife swishing in the water. Wolf seized Turstin's wrist and they thrashed together, creating a swirl of white foam around them. As Turstin wrenched free from Wolf's grasp, Wolf glimpsed someone pulling Juliana to the surface.

Turstin tried to kick to the surface too, but Wolf grabbed his legs and yanked him downwards. Turstin slashed at him again, slicing into his coat sleeve. Wolf grabbed Turstin around the waist and the underwater struggle continued.

Wolf's lungs burned for air, but if he released Turstin, the man would swim to the surface and Wolf was not yet sure Juliana was safe. Wolf held on to Turstin while his body screamed to take a breath and he held on longer. Turstin thrashed even more wildly, kicking, flailing, pulling at Wolf's clothes and hair.

Suddenly Turstin went limp. Wolf yanked him deeper so he could make his escape. As Turstin floated down, Wolf saw that his eyes stared blankly. His hand went slack and the knife drifted away. Wolf kicked towards the sunlight, gulping for air as soon as he broke the surface of the water. Hale was next to him then, dragging him to the boat. He clung to the boat's side until the men hoisted him inside into Juliana's waiting arms.

Chapter Twenty-Two

Juliana rose carefully from Wolfdon's bed, staring down at him in the light cast by the moon shining in the window. The sight of him, so handsome, so strong, so caring, had always taken her breath away and did this time as well.

This last time.

She moved quietly, gathering her clothing and walking into his sitting room to dress.

After landing the boat near the Steine, Wolf and his brothers-in-law made arrangements to meet the crewmen later. Everly and Bentham carried the treasure chest to the hotel, while Hale ran ahead to alert the wives. Juliana walked in the shelter of Wolf's arm, her teeth chattering noisily as he spirited her into his room, stripping her of her clothes and wrapping her in warm blankets before he removed his own wet clothing. Once dressed again, he left her, promising to ensure Charlotte was safe and to bring her dry clothes. He said he'd return as quickly as he could.

She was not certain how long he'd been gone, because she'd fallen asleep in the warmth of bed linens still smelling of him. When he'd woken her, the moon was high in the sky. He'd made love to her and their passion was all the more precious after the danger they had endured.

She had almost lost him to the sea and Turstin's treachery. Her own lungs had ached for air while he'd been under water and she'd only breathed again when he rose out of the water, alive and unharmed.

She shivered, remembering.

Wandering back to the bedchamber door, Juliana peeked through the crack, again watching his chest rise and fall in his sleep. It was so good to see him breathe.

He'd told her Lord Hale volunteered to tell Kitty and Felix a version of what had happened. They knew she would be with Wolf all night. Wolf also told her they'd decided to make no report to the magistrate. When Turstin's body was found, he would be merely one more drowned man. There would be no one to raise a cry about his death, and he would soon be forgotten.

That seemed fitting.

When Hale returned from seeing Kitty and Felix, he'd brought Juliana's packed portmanteau and hatbox. Juliana's maid probably handed the baggage to Hale as the quickest and easiest way to send Juliana dry clothing.

It was like a sign to Juliana of what she must do. The portmanteau and hatbox contained everything she needed to make her escape, including her money.

She stayed with Wolf through the night, making sweet love with him for the last time. It no longer mattered if anyone knew of it.

By dawn none of it would matter.

Dressed now, she quickly put her hair in a braid and tiptoed back to the bedchamber for one last, silent goodbye.

I love you, Wolf, she mouthed. *I always shall love you.*

Before she lost her courage, she gathered her things and

walked resolutely to the door. She put them down again and turned the latch, opening the door slowly and quietly.

'Fleur?'

She jumped.

Wolf stood in the doorway of the bedchamber. 'Close the door, Fleur.'

She closed the door. 'I must leave, Wolf,' she pleaded. It would have been so much easier to steal away in the night as she had done once before.

He walked over to her, his naked, muscular body gleaming in the light from the fireplace.

He placed his hands on the door. 'An explanation this time, Fleur. That is all I ask.'

Having him naked so close to her made her ache again to be touching him, feeling his strength under her fingertips, making love to him one more time.

'Is it not self-evident, Wolf?' Her voice rasped with unspent tears. 'I have deceived everyone.'

He did not look convinced.

She tried again, lying this time. 'I was part of the plot, the swindle.'

He caged her in his arms as he'd done before. 'Cut line, Fleur. You were not part of the plot. Gravier admitted as much. No more lies. No more falsehood between us. If you must leave me, let it be with me knowing the truth about you.'

The truth. She was ashamed of the truth now. After that last awful day, she was ashamed to ever have known Turstin, to ever have been her father's daughter, to ever have made love with any other man but Wolf.

She averted her face and pushed against the bare skin of his chest. 'I will tell you the truth, Wolf. Please, just wrap a blanket around yourself.'

He seized her wrist. 'And have you run out the door while I do? I think not. Come with me.'

He led her back into the bedchamber where she gazed upon the tangled bed linens they'd shared. He kept hold of her wrist while he picked up his clothes.

'Sit,' he commanded, placing her on the bed while he stood between her and the door to don his trousers and shirt. He leaned against the door. 'Now talk.'

She took a breath. 'I will tell you all,' she said. 'And you will know why I must leave.' She glanced away before facing him again. 'I am not who I pretend to be. I am not Lady Ashcourt's cousin. I am not related to her at all.' She paused, looking for his response.

He merely nodded.

She took another breath. 'The man floating on the water, however, is Kitty's uncle.'

His eyes widened.

She began talking faster. 'He is William *Turstin* Walsh, but he never used his family name, just Turstin. My father was his partner, you see. And Gravier. Gravier had been with him since he was a boy. My father knew them both as long. My father was—well, I am not certain who he really was, but he called himself Edgar Parsons and said he was the son of an innkeeper—'

Wolf crossed his arms over his chest while he listened. Juliana chronicled her life, this time telling him the truth. Tears stung her eyes when she recounted her mother's illness and death, and her throat felt raw by the time she told of her father dying on the guillotine and Gravier and Turstin leaving her to fend for herself in post-war Paris.

'I devised a way to escape Paris,' she went on. 'I forged papers to make it seem like I was Turstin's daughter, and I used your money to play at cards until I had enough to get me to England. Then I went to Kitty and Felix with my false story, and they took me in…'

She swallowed again. 'You know the rest. I was prepared to take the ruse as far as I could. Perhaps I would even have married Lord Seabane or some other gentleman had not Turstin come for his revenge on poor Kitty.' She gave a tiny laugh. 'Fortunate. Think how awful Lord Seabane's life would have been with me.'

Wolf did not change his expression.

'So you see,' she concluded, 'I have impersonated nobility. I've committed the crimes of deception and forgery. Theft, too, in receiving all the lovely dresses Kitty had made for me and in taking Felix's pin money, and in stealing from you—'

'And from others,' he added.

'From only two others,' she said, although it hardly mattered. 'I stopped when you told me to.'

He lifted his brows.

She continued, 'I would very much prefer to disappear rather than be charged with these offences, so perhaps you will let me make the coach on time.'

He just stared at her.

The spectre of a hanging rope dangled before her. She squeezed her eyes shut. 'The best I can hope for is transportation.'

She heard him move and opened her eyes. He walked towards her. 'Not if no one knows of your crimes. Turstin is dead. He is the only one who would tell.'

She shook her head. 'Gravier knows.'

He inclined his head. 'Gravier is gone, but, even so, I believe he has proven he can be trusted. Besides, you have your forged papers as proof. People believe what is written down.'

Her mouth dropped open. 'I cannot continue this ruse.'

He stood above her. 'Why not, if there is no one to tell the truth of it?'

Her nostrils filled with his scent. 'Oh, Wolf. *You* know the truth.'

He took a tendril of hair that had escaped from her braid and tucked it gently behind her ear. 'I would not betray you, Fleur.'

She turned her face away, so he could not see the tears she could no longer control. 'I cannot go back to Kitty and Felix and accept their kindness. Not after all that I have done.'

He traced a finger along her jaw. 'I agree with you on that point.'

She looked back at him. 'Then you see why I must leave.'

He lowered himself to sit beside her, his hand stroking her shoulder. He swept her braid aside and planted a warm kiss on the back of her neck. 'There is an alternative.'

She sighed, feeling her body melting under his lips. 'I cannot see one—'

'Marry me.' He put his arm around her and leaned her head against his chest. 'Marry me.'

She pulled away to gape at him.

He smiled. 'You must admit I have thoroughly compromised you by bringing you into my bed. Shocking behaviour. I suspect Felix will charge in this morning and demand I marry you.'

Her hopes rose but plummeted just as quickly. 'Oh, Wolf. I cannot go back to Paris! I will not go back there!'

He reached out to stroke her cheek. 'We need not go to Paris.'

She took his hand and squeezed it. 'No. I will not be the cause of you giving up your desires.'

He pulled her hand to his lips. 'I am not returning to Paris.' He smiled at her. 'Ironically, I've discovered I now desire that from which I tried so hard to flee. I want to stay. Be a part of a rather remarkable family. Accept my responsibility to my parents and the family estate.'

She could not believe it. 'Oh, Wolf. Are you certain?'

His smile widened to a grin. 'Even if I had not just become rich from my share of treasure, I would stay. You might consider, Fleur, that I now am a man of fortune.'

She pulled her hand away. 'That means nothing to me!'

He made her face him again, made her look into his eyes. 'I know that, Fleur. You must know, though, that I am staying in England no matter what you decide. But I want you to marry me. Be a part of my family.' He smiled again. 'No thieving, I insist upon that. And only truth between us from now on.'

To be his wife? What could be more wonderful?

She pursed her lips and averted her gaze. If only she were deserving. Better he marry someone good, like Lady Allyse.

She faced him again. 'It is impossible. You want truth, but everything about me is a lie. If I marry you, I will be forever lying about who I really am.'

'You will not be lying about being Juliana Wolfdon,' he countered. 'That is who you will be. That will be the truth.' His expression turned achingly tender. 'Besides, who would it make unhappy? You know it makes the Ashcourts happy to have you as their cousin. Lady Ashcourt is very attached to you, is she not?'

Dear Kitty, she thought. She would miss Kitty greatly. 'Yes, but Charlotte. She will resent me—'

'Charlotte knows you saved her. How can she resent that?' He kissed her again. 'No more protests. I want to marry you, Fleur. I want to marry you because I do not want to live without you. I never knew this more than when I thought Turstin would kill you before my eyes.'

She put her hands to his lips to silence him. 'You saved me, Wolf.'

He crushed his lips against hers, wrapping his arms around her. She made a whimpering sound beneath his kiss, but kissed him back, her hands reaching beneath his shirt to slide up his chest.

'Fleur,' he murmured, loosening the laces of her dress and pulling it over her head. In another swift moment he removed his trousers and she, her corset and shift. They tumbled back on to the bed linens where he most thoroughly compromised her once again.

The sun was high in the sky when they finally lay quietly in each other's arms. Juliana drew one long satisfying breath, feeling sated and complete.

'Have you missed your coach?' Wolf asked.

'I have.' She snuggled against him, feeling she was where she would belong for ever. 'I suppose I must stay now.'

He chuckled, the sound rumbling in his chest. 'I suppose you must.'

A knock sounded at Wolf's hotel room door. He groaned and rose from the bed to walk to the sitting room. Juliana quickly donned her shift and padded after him.

'Yes?' he said through the closed door, gesturing for her to be quiet.

'It is the attendant, sir,' a voice came through. 'Forgive me for disturbing you, but there is a gentleman to see you. He waits in one of the private drawing rooms.' The man cleared his throat. 'A Lord Ashcourt, sir, and I am afraid he insists on speaking to you immediately. He said *immediately*, sir.'

Juliana covered her mouth.

'Tell the gentleman I shall be there directly.' Wolf grinned. 'See? We have to marry now. Felix will insist. I have compromised you.'

Wolf gathered Juliana in his arms, swung her around and gave her one more very compromising kiss.

Epilogue

Hale House, Surrey—December 1822

It was unclear who first suggested a family Christmas house party, but everyone agreed that the only place large enough to house them all was Hale House, the principal estate of the Marquess of Hale. Though the party originally was planned to include only members of the Wolfdon family, it very quickly expanded to include families of the spouses. If in-laws were included, Wolf insisted they invite the Ashcourts, as well. They were family to him and Juliana, after all. That spurred on more ideas of who must be included—the men who'd assisted in retrieving the treasure, for example. And neighbours. Hale said he could not host a ball and not invite his neighbours.

The ball was to take place this night.

Juliana had just finished nursing her son, dear little Marcus, and she put the baby to bed herself. Marcus and the dozen or more other children and infants should all be abed now, freeing the parents to dress for the ball.

Juliana hurried back to her bedchamber where Sally waited to help her dress.

Sally was still her lady's maid and still managed to arrange her hair in the most flattering styles and keep her clothes clean and mended. Juliana's ball gown this night was the same shade of green she'd worn so long ago in Brighton, but this gown was adorned with flowers made from the same fabric and the jewels she wore around her neck and on her ears were emeralds.

Wolf came into the room while Sally was putting the finishing touches to her hair. Juliana's heart leapt at the sight of him, dressed formally, even more handsome than that unexpected sight of him in Brighton.

Wolf. Her husband.

'There you are, ma'am,' Sally said, giving Juliana's puffed sleeves a final tug.

'Thank you, Sally.' Juliana stood and turned to face her husband. 'I'm ready.'

His eyes glowed with appreciation. 'You look beautiful, Fleur.' He turned to the maid. 'Would you leave us a moment, Sally? I need to speak to Mrs Wolfdon.'

Mrs Wolfdon. Juliana loved the sound of her married name.

Sally left and Wolf pulled Juliana into an embrace. He nuzzled her neck. 'Perhaps we could remove these clothes of ours…'

She touched his face. 'Do not tempt me.'

Was it possible? Their lovemaking had only become more exciting, more loving, more like coming home to where one always belonged. Juliana still marvelled at it.

'Now what is it you needed to speak to me about?' she asked.

He released her and took a folded paper from a pocket. 'I received this letter today. I want you to read it and tell me if I should share it with Charlotte.'

Charlotte was recently betrothed to Wevenly. The young man had patiently courted her for two years before she said yes, though they'd been nearly inseparable since he'd rescued her from Turstin.

Juliana took the letter in hand and unfolded it. She first glanced at the signature.

Her gaze flew up. 'From Gravier.'

'Read it,' Wolf said. 'It travelled far to reach me here.'

All the way from Belgium?

Gravier wrote to Wolf, leaving it to Wolf's discretion whether to share it with anyone. He went on to write that he'd seen a London newspaper with the announcement of Charlotte's betrothal to Wevenly and wanted to offer her his best wishes for a happy life. He wanted Charlotte to know that he was happily settled in Brussels, running a jewellery shop, and married to the daughter of the shop's owner.

Juliana laughed and read that part out loud to Wolf.

He smiled. 'I know. The irony.'

The rest of the letter make Juliana want to weep.

Gravier gave credit to Charlotte for making him want to be a good man and he wanted to thank her for it.

It was a lovely letter.

'What do you think we should do?' Wolf asked. 'Tell Charlotte?'

Juliana thought about it. 'Yes,' she decided. 'She should know.'

Juliana was certain it would not put even a scratch on Charlotte's love for her darling Wevenly, a young man who'd proven his devotion to her in countless ways, but she deserved to know she had mattered to Gravier.

Wolf put it back in his pocket. 'And how is it for you to hear from him?'

She could not answer that. 'I do not know.'

She ought to feel safer. Gravier was the only man besides Wolf who knew the truth about her. If Gravier was happy, he'd have no reason to hold that club over her head. She ought to feel safer, but reading his name and his words was like opening a door to her past, one she tried so carefully to keep closed. Locked. With bars across it.

She looked up at her husband. 'It brings it all back.'

He embraced her again and in his arms she did feel secure.

She sighed. 'We should go.'

They left the bedchamber and entered the hallway leading to the stairs. Hale's country house had numerous bedchambers, enough to house all these guests and their children and their servants.

'Wolf!' a voice sounded behind them.

It was Harris. Wolf's friend. Felix's son.

And… Lady Allyse's husband.

Harris had returned from Paris shortly after Wolf wrote to resign his position, that summer in Brighton. The following Season Harris become reacquainted with Lady Allyse, who had always had a tendre for him and their marriage had followed soon after.

Harris, with Lady Allyse at his side, caught up to them.

'Shall we walk down together?' Lady Allyse asked.

'Of course!' Wolf responded.

Harris made some inane jest. Wolf and Lady Allyse ribbed him for it.

Juliana trailed behind, her past pulling at her. Her father. Turstin. Gravier. The danger. The running. Always running.

Wolf had given her something she'd never had before.

A home. A family. She could not be more content—except for those nagging moments when she remembered her life was one endless masquerade and at a masquerade one could always be unmasked.

At the foot of the stairs, Wolf waited for her, putting his arm around her when she reached him.

'How are you faring?' he asked.

'I'm just a little shaken,' she replied truthfully.

Well, maybe more than a little shaken. She was trying to break the habit of lying and she succeeded most of the time, but it was not easy.

When the past flooded back to her, she had difficulty shaking the feeling—not feeling—the *certainty* that she was an imposter.

But her kind and loving husband offered his arm and they walked to the ballroom behind his lifelong friend. They waited their turn to be announced. Wolf's sisters Joanna and Susan and their husbands were ahead of them and inside the ballroom Juliana could see Elizabeth and Hale and a dozen others with whom she now had a connection.

Finally, it was their turn.

'Mr and Mrs Marcus Wolfdon,' the butler announced.

Wolf smiled down at her. 'Shall we go in, Mrs Wolfdon?'

Juliana hesitated, momentarily stunned.

Yes, she was Mrs Wolfdon. No need for a costume or mask. She was Mrs Wolfdon and belonged for ever right at his side.

* * * * *

If you enjoyed this story,
be sure to read the first book in
Diane Gaston's
A Family of Scandals miniseries

Secretly Bound to the Marquess

And why not read her
Captains of Waterloo miniseries?

Her Gallant Captain at Waterloo
Lord Grantwell's Christmas Wish

COMING NEXT MONTH FROM

HARLEQUIN
HISTORICAL

All available in print and ebook via Reader Service and online

THE WALLFLOWER'S LAST CHANCE SEASON (Regency)
Least Likely to Wed • by Julia Justiss
When impoverished Eliza helps an older viscount after he falls at a ball, his son Giles is suspicious she's out to wed his widowed father! But it's Giles who *actually* sets her heart racing...

BETROTHED IN HASTE TO THE EARL (Regency)
by Liz Tyner
Following two troubled courtships, Marianna has sworn off romance. Until Adam, the handsome Earl of Rockwell, is misdirected to her bedchamber after a soiree, and she's compromised into a hasty betrothal!

MISS FAIRFAX'S NOTORIOUS DUKE (Victorian)
Rebellious Young Ladies • by Eva Shepherd
Irene's latest life drawing is going well until her naked subject reveals he's *not* the man she thinks he is. He is, in fact, the notorious Duke of Redcliff!

DEBUTANTE WITH A DANGEROUS PAST (Regency)
by Samantha Hastings
Nancy's chance at a new life comes with the condition that she stay out of trouble! Easier said than done when she starts to fall for rebellious Lord Matthew Stringham...

THE WARRIOR'S RELUCTANT WIFE (Medieval)
The Warriors of Wales • by Lissa Morgan
Widow Rhianon had hoped to never be bound to a man again. But to seal an alliance, she's forced to marry Peredur. Only ruling with her new husband is revealing some unexpected desires...

A VIKING HEIR TO BIND THEM (Viking)
by Michelle Styles
Viking Tylir's life is upended when Melkorka reveals he has a secret heir! Tylir has no idea how to be a father. But the captivating Mel is the perfect person to teach him...

YOU CAN FIND MORE INFORMATION ON UPCOMING HARLEQUIN TITLES, FREE EXCERPTS AND MORE AT HARLEQUIN.COM.

HHCNM0723

Get 3 FREE REWARDS!

We'll send you 2 FREE Books plus a FREE Mystery Gift.

FREE
Value Over
$20

Both the **Harlequin® Historical** and **Harlequin® Romance** series feature compelling novels filled with emotion and simmering romance.

YES! Please send me 2 FREE novels from the Harlequin Historical or Harlequin Romance series and my FREE Mystery Gift (gift is worth about $10 retail). After receiving them, if I don't wish to receive any more books, I can return the shipping statement marked "cancel." If I don't cancel, I will receive 6 brand-new Harlequin Historical books every month and be billed just $6.19 each in the U.S. or $6.74 each in Canada, a savings of at least 11% off the cover price, or 4 brand-new Harlequin Romance Larger-Print books every month and be billed just $6.09 each in the U.S. or $6.24 each in Canada, a savings of at least 13% off the cover price. It's quite a bargain! Shipping and handling is just 50¢ per book in the U.S. and $1.25 per book in Canada.* I understand that accepting the 2 free books and gift places me under no obligation to buy anything. I can always return a shipment and cancel at any time by calling the number below. The free books and gift are mine to keep no matter what I decide.

Choose one: ☐ **Harlequin Historical** (246/349 BPA GRNX)   ☐ **Harlequin Romance Larger-Print** (119/319 BPA GRNX)   ☐ **Or Try Both!** (246/349 & 119/319 BPA GRRD)

Name (please print)

Address   Apt. #

City   State/Province   Zip/Postal Code

Email: Please check this box ☐ if you would like to receive newsletters and promotional emails from Harlequin Enterprises ULC and its affiliates. You can unsubscribe anytime.

Mail to the Harlequin Reader Service:
IN U.S.A.: P.O. Box 1341, Buffalo, NY 14240-8531
IN CANADA: P.O. Box 603, Fort Erie, Ontario L2A 5X3

Want to try 2 free books from another series? Call 1-800-873-8635 or visit www.ReaderService.com.

*Terms and prices subject to change without notice. Prices do not include sales taxes, which will be charged (if applicable) based on your state or country of residence. Canadian residents will be charged applicable taxes. Offer not valid in Quebec. This offer is limited to one order per household. Books received may not be as shown. Not valid for current subscribers to the Harlequin Historical or Harlequin Romance series. All orders subject to approval. Credit or debit balances in a customer's account(s) may be offset by any other outstanding balance owed by or to the customer. Please allow 4 to 6 weeks for delivery. Offer available while quantities last.

Your Privacy—Your information is being collected by Harlequin Enterprises ULC, operating as Harlequin Reader Service. For a complete summary of the information we collect, how we use this information and to whom it is disclosed, please visit our privacy notice located at corporate.harlequin.com/privacy-notice. From time to time we may also exchange your personal information with reputable third parties. If you wish to opt out of this sharing of your personal information, please visit readerservice.com/consumerschoice or call 1-800-873-8635. **Notice to California Residents**—Under California law, you have specific rights to control and access your data. For more information on these rights and how to exercise them, visit corporate.harlequin.com/california-privacy.

HHHRLP23

HARLEQUIN
PLUS

Try the best multimedia subscription service for romance readers like you!

Read, Watch and Play.

Experience the easiest way to get the romance content you crave.

Start your **FREE TRIAL** at
www.harlequinplus.com/freetrial.